GW01071893

Anger's Violin

David M Thomas

Published in 1998 by
Mount Eagle Publications Ltd.
Dingle, Co. Kerry, Ireland

Copyright © David M Thomas 1998

The author has asserted his moral rights

ISBN 1 902011 04 X
(original paperback)

10 9 8 7 6 5 4 3 2 1

Published with the assistance of the
Arts Council/An Chomhairle Ealaíonn

This book is sold subject to the condition that it shall not, by way of trade or otherwise, be lent, resold, hired out or otherwise circulated without the publisher's prior consent in any form of binding or cover other than that in which it is published and without a similar condition being imposed on the subsequent purchaser.

Cover design: Public Communications Centre, Dublin
Typesetting: Red Barn Publishing, Skeagh, Skibbereen
Printed by ColourBooks Ltd, Dublin

For Peter Bird,
and to the memory of Laura Martin
who died too soon

Thanks to:
Kenneth Maguire, Pepe Fernandez, Niav O'Higgins, Philippa Hayward, Mary Catherine Lucy, Paul Statham, Inge Stokking, Kees van Kersbergen, Andy Taylor, Carmen Ramón, Bernard Ryan, Brad Sherman, Lionel Bentley, Rachel Woodward, Susan Bisset, Peter Malone

1

"I am not what I am," the image in the mirror mouths back at me. "Roll on Paris," I sigh aloud, knowing that I shan't be able to be myself again until Paris, a quivering mirage on a horizon fourteen days distant, a minor eternity when you're travelling with people you've not chosen to be with. Fourteen more days on the road, a prospect as mouthwatering as colonic irrigation. I take a deep breath and continue with the habitual morning task of constructing my alter ego, the penguin man. On with the clean white shirt, the thin black tie, the black trousers with creases, the white socks and black Docs. And clean-shaven, too, impeccably clean, apart from the odd pinhead of dried blood. Smart black summer jacket. This is what my charges want to see, all the external credentials of such a nice young man. I am what they want to see. One last touch, the customised money belt, wind the strap twice round the belt of my trousers, tuck it in, and there it is, unseen, invisible, dangling down the inside of my trouser leg. Contents: Swiss cheques, a wad of cash, and two passports, one of them genuine. Excellent! Owen Morgan Parry is ready to do battle with the world outside.

Day Two: Brussels. Monday, if yesterday was Sunday. And on the second day God created tourists and He saw that it was a way of making Money. Brussels is where we start today and Amsterdam where we finish. Arriving from London yesterday, I did the standard city tour and told my passengers the usual load of Mannekin Pis you'd find in any brochure or guide book. That, after all, is my official job. Ah but! While the passengers were scuttling to the toilets, comparing exchange rates or taking photos, I was with a man in the upstairs room of a bar on the Grote Markt. But this they must never know. They would not even suspect in any case. I am above suspicion, thank God, diolch i Dduw, the nice Welsh boy from a place they can't pronounce. The penguin man in black and white from Porthiago in the North, there's lovely for you.

Still, at least Gilles is happy with my being Welsh, though, I suspect, only because he's a Breton. If truth be told, I couldn't really give a fiddler's fuck if he's happy or not with it, as long as he does his job alright and doesn't behave like the sulky little boys most coach drivers turn out to be. It's only the second time I've worked with him and the last time was grand but you never know. Everything's got to go as smooth as clockwork, at least as far as Heidelberg, where I shall pass on what the man in the bar on the Grote Markt gave me. After Heidelberg, I don't care too much what happens.

The door groans to as I stand my rucksack against the wall of the deserted corridor. I tap the mystery parcel in the inside pocket of my jacket and, briefcase in hand, head for the lift. That is the last I shall ever see of a hotel room in Brussels. After this tour I'm retiring. Stepping inside the lift, I press the button for the ground floor and wait until the doors have shut before I take a look in the mirror. I do not like the person I see.

It gets to you being on the road, constantly thinking about timings, money, numbers, appearances, constantly not being yourself. Organising everything, juggling forty-five balls in the air at the same time, trying to forsee problems like some ancient diviner, working on the solution to the problems, taking all the shit you'd never swallow in a million years from people not happy with their lives. If you met the same people at a party you'd end up either ripping the piss out of them or chinning them. And then there's all the people hanging round you, treating you like royalty and falling all over you just because of the business you can fix them up with or the size of the tip you'll press into their palm. A whole world in itself of sycophantry and false appearances. Still, one last tour and one last mission. For the Cause.

Young waitresses in sensible navy-blue skirts and white blouses busy themselves over clients in the breakfast lounge. And how much shit do they have to take in the course of a day? Same with the receptionists – the female ones anyway – who for all their professionalism get treated like strumpets by the bloated arseholes in suits who talk of sales figures, break-even points and "dolly birds". What do these waitresses say about them behind their backs? Do they ever imagine that, the ones with the expense accounts? Like that English businessman I saw in Llanberis chatting up the barmaid, thought he was doing ever so well, never once saw her winking at me on the blindside, never once suspected that she was calling him all the names under the sun in Welsh. Chewing on a beermat to stop myself laughing. Perfect theatre of farce it was.

Here comes Gilles with a big smile on his face. Thick forearms, shortish build, square shoulders, athletic, young. Was it five years younger than me I calculated? Which would make him twenty-eight. Build of a scrum half, or outside half maybe, with straight dark hair falling down to the shoulders. Friendly. One of the passengers yesterday said we could pass for brothers. Can't really see it myself. "Ça va?" he asks chirpily, "T'as bien dormi?" "Oui, impeccable," I answer. He sits himself down, saying he's loaded the bags and breakfasted already but he'll just have another cup of coffee before the off. And would I know where he could get an Ajax shirt in Amsterdam? He promised to buy one for his nephew, eight years old and already mad about football. I suggest trying the shops along the Nieuwendijk. He pulls a face. Drivers never relate to names. They refer to places only in relation to bridges, crossroads, rivers, motorway exits. If you give the name of a street you might as well say here be dragons. I sketch a map of Amsterdam on the tablecloth with my fingernail and put a little tub of blackcurrant marmalade on Nieuwendijk. Fine, says Gilles, now he knows where I mean. He drains his coffee and leaves for the coach.

On the way to reception I adopt a smile for all seasons in case I bump into one of my passengers without recognising them. With forty-five of them how can I be expected to remember all their faces after just one day together? Yet this feat of memory is expected of me. And since people get upset if you don't remember them I have to present this inane smile to everyone milling around the foyer, just to be on the safe side. I write out a hotel voucher on the desk and hand it to the receptionist whose badge identifies her as Esther. I ask if my passengers have handed in all their keys yet. She tells me that all outstanding bills have been paid but there are still a few keys missing. Ach well, I say, we'll sort that out later, once I've got everyone on board. It will be the same routine all the way through Holland, Germany, Switzerland, Italy, and France, all the way to Paris. Bog standard tour, really, clockwise round Europe. I go where the punters have paid to go. Done it millions of times before but each time you have to present it as though you're fresh as a daisy. The brochure tour, the set itinerary, written in tablets of stone, with no hesitation or deviation, just repetition. Suits their needs and suits mine, my hidden agenda, because it goes through Heidelberg.

Outside the air is cold, yet it's gladdening to see an almost unbroken line of heads already on the coach. A few determined smokers linger on the pavement. The on-board count reveals seven short, with three smokers at the ready, so in effect we're four down. "Time to go, Owen?" asks a guy with an Antipodean lilt, looking up at me as I hop down again. The last inch of a tightly rolled cigarette in his mouth. Green-brown cap on his head, fifty going on sixty but looking lively enough even at this hour. I shall call him Andy Capp. "Aye," I tell him, "sooner everyone's on, sooner we can get away." Instead of getting on board he asks me what language I count in. Welsh, I reply, and we're still pedwar short of a full load. He throws his cigarette to the ground and gets on. The others take their cue from him, giving me a few G'days as they climb up the steps. Australians. Gilles gets into the cab around the other side and starts putting in a new tacho. I try to picture an eight-year-old Breton in an Ajax jersey and see myself saying did you know Ajax was a Greek man really? No answer, maybe a slight disappointment on the kid's face. Oh aye, and he committed suicide and all because they wouldn't give him Achilles' armour. The things grown-ups get worked up about, eh? I don't know how to talk to kids.

A shiver comes upon me: Brussels in August, dear God! Summer, in the year of our Lord 1991. "Are we the last, Owen?" A woman's voice behind me. South African? The last four. "I think that's all of us now," I say, eager not to sound reproachful. I watch them board, the faithful collie herding the last of the stragglers in. Quick look at the watch: five minutes late already. They're going to have to do better than this if I'm to have the time I need for the other business. After a quick dash back to reception to check the key count, I hop on and give Gilles the all-clear.

Cold metal mike in hand, I face the assembled travellers to wish them a cheerful good-morning as we trundle through the traffic, following the paperchase signs that point either to Anvers or Antwerpen or both. Silently I pay my last respects to Brussels, this city of two identities where language is identity, where half the town calls the main square the Grote Markt and the other half the Grand' Place. Brussels must be the only place where I'm prepared to bow to English as the universal language. Address a Walloon in Flemish or a Flem in French and you're just asking for trouble. But there wasn't any problem of protocol with the man in the bar on the Grote Markt, the man with the ponytail and clipped Oxbridge accent. He gave me a rather limp handshake and we got straight down to business. I tucked the parcel he handed me into my jacket pocket and then he asked me

-How was the last job?

-Went like a dream.

-No problems, then?

-No, none. Did he make it alright?

-Yes. You'll be pleased to know that "Kane" is now safe and sound in New York. No more porridge for him. It'll be all bagels and hotdogs now.

-They don't really do porridge in German jails, do they?

-A figure of speech . . . Still, he's a very valuable Volunteer to have back in circulation. So, no problems, then? It all went seamlessly?

-No, no problems. I just told my punters he was another Austerlitz tourist just like them who'd been left behind by his tour guide in Cologne and we were helping him to catch back up with his group. Had a beneficial effect on my lot as well. After they heard his story they weren't late for anything. Once we were in Switzerland, all he was worried about was the flight. Well, there was one other thing.

-Tell me.

-He wasn't happy about having to use a British passport either. Or the name "Kane".

-No, I can imagine. Did you see Nolan in Cologne?

-Only from a distance. I saw him on the bridge, you know, the footbridge overlooking the coach park. Soon as he'd pointed me out to Kane he was gone.

-I see. . . Excellent.

-So Kane didn't have any trouble at the airport?

-Gladly, no. The Swiss are never too bothered about people leaving their country. More concerned with who's coming in. You didn't encounter any problems there, at the border?

-No. I just had to put his details on my passenger list beforehand and over we went.

-Fine. Now, to the present task. Your consignment, by the

way: it's extremely delicate but we've reinforced it and made it watertight as well. Plenty of bubble-wrap. Handle with care anyway.

-Where's it for. . . if that's. . .?

-A bank vault in Switzerland, for storage. Normally I wouldn't have asked you to do it but our man in Heidelberg was, um. . . temporarily unavailable. So I'm asking you to do the Brussels-Heidelberg leg in his stead. The password is Patrick Henry.

-I take it only as far as Heidelberg?

-Correct. That's all there is to it as far as you're concerned. Benelux is obviously no problem. It's just the Dutch-German border you have to worry about.

-Okay. So where and when?

-He'll meet you up at the castle the morning you visit it.

-Will it be the same fellow in Heidelberg?

-Yes. He's probably the safest pair of hands about, a great servant over the years. He's done more runs to Switzerland for us than anyone else. Quite the fidus Achates.

-Okay.

-Before you go. . . Just one more thing. I don't envisage any complications but *should* there be, any change of plan will be authorised by the word "Diogenes." And, um . . . do not contact me direct unless in case of extreme urgency.

-Right, Patrick Henry and Diogenes. Understood.

-Good luck. And um, well, well done with the last job.

Gathering myself, I unleash a barrage of dates and statistics about the Netherlands. It's important to convince the passengers that I know my work as a guide, that I'm not just a college boy with a couple of languages on a free holiday. I tell them about the golden seventeenth century and the Dutch and Flemish masters, do the obligatory piece on reclaimed land and polders and windmills, and at the end throw in a name I know they're unlikely to have heard of, just to put a bit of distance between myself and them. Today I opt for Erasmus. How famous is he in Sydney or Cape Town or Toronto or Auckland? Judging by their reaction, not very. Sometimes I mention Erasmus, or Descartes, or Locke – alias Doctor Simpson during his stay in Amsterdam – sometimes Linnaeus. But I never mention Camus in Amsterdam, never paint the picture of the man in the red light district writing about jenever and prostitutes and judgment. No, Camus I keep for myself. He's part of *my* Amsterdam, and their world and mine must be kept apart if the penguin man is to keep his credibility, and his sanity.

Some faces smile, some look perplexed. After all, what the hell is a Renaissance humanist, this Erasmus fellah? Most faces have already nodded off, heads lolling in the aisle, far away in the land of easier thoughts and familiar faces. Blind them with statistics or dazzle them with history, either way you end up sending them to sleep. The warm air conditioning helps as well. I switch off the mike, sit back down and watch the motorway unfold itself.

A mist hangs over a landscape of lush green fields. Gilles stares impassively ahead, his only horizon the bumper of the car in front. Now is the time I can indulge my inner thoughts. Now, if I want, I can switch on the Camus soundtrack in my head and hear the lines he wrote while he was in Holland, lines I memorised all those years ago when I trusted in Reason. Heureux et jugé ou absous et misérable, that's the line I hear most often in my head: happy and judged or absolved and wretched. The book I can leave behind in my little flat above the funeral parlour on Holloway Road but the lines come with me wherever I go. Strange to find myself thinking of that Malaysian all of a sudden. Me cramming hundreds of quotations into my head for my Finals and he'd just taken his exams and convinced himself he hadn't got a First. Engineering or something he was studying. Couldn't cope with going back to Malaysia and being judged a failure. Can't ever have said to himself well bollocks to what they think, my life is my own.

Threw himself off the top of Wessex House. A week later the results were announced and he'd got a First after all. Everybody talking of the tragedy of a gifted student and I remember thinking that I could find no sympathy whatsoever for him. Moira called me hard-hearted. She would, what with her being a Catholic. Tragedy is made by the gods, though, I told her, and this was not tragedy but weakness and stupidity on his part because he made his own happiness dependent on the judgment of others. She shook her head, said something about the Third World and called me hard-hearted again. Hard-hearted! She never saw me in floods of tears over her grave.

And come tell me Sean O'Farrell
Tell me why you hurry so
Hush a buchaill hush and listen
And his cheeks were all aglow

I bear orders from the Captain
Get ye ready quick and soon
For the pikes must be together
At the rising of the moon

There is an aspect of bliss about Gilles' face, may the gods bless him. He doesn't wear you out like the other drivers, always going on about how long they've been on the road, how well they know this, that, or so and so, boring you shitless. At least here is one who can talk of things other than buses and bums. "What you thinking about," I ask him, "if it's not indiscreet?" Carine, he says. The love of his life. She's found work at a hotel in Rennes, and do I know it? "The Altea? Sure." With its bleak view over the concrete centre commercial, McDonald's in the near distance. The same hotel where I waited for Nadette to come, where I watched the Gulf War on CNN in the evenings. Banality after banality and all the usual shite about democracy and the rights of small nations.

"And Nadette," Gilles asks, "how's she doing?" Of course, twp, twp, stupid, I mentioned her on our last tour together. The question I didn't want to hear. "Is she still with her husband and kids?" Aye, her husband, the man she'd separated from when I met her, the man she went back to after I left her. An acid sensation invades me, seeping through to the very marrow of my soul: the longing to be far away.

"Er, she's dead, Gilles." Walking away from me in that dream I have. Must have had it again this morning. Still feels fresh in the mind. Gilles suddenly anxious, not sure if I'm joking. Sees I am serious.

"Shit, that's bad news. When?" Why is it that he's the one who looks uneasy? Shouldn't it be me? More sensitive than me, less direct experience of death than me perhaps? Certain bet there.

"Oh, not so long back."

"Listen, Owen, you don't have to tell me a thing. Just tell me if you want to talk about it. I don't know what to say anyway."

The kilometres roll on in silence, and I wish the question hadn't come up. It's not an unpleasantness that should be on Gilles' mind. No, I should just have left him thinking nice thoughts about his Carine, about her back in the Altea, perhaps, imagining her in the duller moments of her job thinking ahead to his return, or trying to take her mind off just such thoughts because he won't be back for ages. Doesn't everyone in love do that, wonder what their lover is doing at that very moment, try to imagine their thoughts, wish that they really were thinking the thoughts you've just scripted in your head? I used to, at any rate. That's the world I would wish Gilles to be in right now, only I've ballsed everything up, succeeded only in making him feel clumsy.

And Nadette? They say you never get over your first love. They say. They, who know. Perhaps just this once they are right. But then, they didn't know Nadette. I've stopped talking to other people about her now. They never believed me anyway, always looked at me as though I'd been reading too many French novels.

"So how many tours have you got after this one, Owen?" Matter of fact tone. That's more like it, Gilles, me old mucker. Happy to talk about it just when I'm good and ready. How I love the French. Not like the English. Their solution to every crisis is to sit down and have a nice cup of tea.

"None. I'm retiring after this one. I'm sick of taking peasants around Europe."

"They're not all peasants. There's usually a couple of nice ones in every group."

"Yes, but it's all the rest. I've earned enough money now, so I just think it's time to move on to something different, as different as possible."

"Like what?"

"I don't know exactly."

"Boh!"

'Tis the rising of the moo-oon
'Tis the rising of the moon
And harrah, me boys for freedom!
'Tis the rising of the moon

Amsterdam approaches. I get myself ready for the usual disgorgement. This is it, knowledge as consumer product, a quick skate round the supermarket. Only the superficial is allowed, only things that can be grasped at a glance, epistemological soundbite time, culture à la CNN. These are the moments when I think Marcuse might really have been on to something after all. "Ladies and gentlemen, this street is the Stadhouderskade. The big red building is the Bank of the Netherlands. Amsterdam, as well as being the capital city, is the financial centre of the Netherlands. Ahead is the Heineken Brewery. Notice the copper vats as we go past it in a moment. We'll just turn right here. If you look left you can just see the top of Amsterdam's most famous art museum, the Rijksmuseum. That's where you'll find the *Night Watch*. Here we go then, up Vijzelgracht. Look at all the trams and bicycles coming from all angles. Population of seventeen million in the Netherlands and there are eleven million bikes. That's two-thirds of a bike per head of population. Look at the buildings on the left. Pretty damn wonky, eh? That's because they're built on piles that have subsided. And now we come to the four main canals.

"First – here we go – the Prinsengracht, take no notice of that building, it's just the Amro Bank, then the Keizersgracht. Next is the most prestigious canal, the Herrengracht or Gentleman's Canal, where people used to show themselves off on their Sunday promenade, and then the Singelgracht. Note the overhead hooks on the beams for hauling the furniture in. Floating flower market coming up but first you'll see the Mint Tower, dating from the fourteenth century. As we enter the Rokin – here it is on the right – the Allard Pierson Museum, famed for its Greek and Egyptian artefacts. Peel your eyes right and see if you can spot the equestrian statue of Queen Wilhemina. Actually she was a lot fatter than that and there on the right – pthwp! – O'Henry's English pub with the Union Jack. They've got the wrong flag but I make no further comment. There's a little, round, green urinal a bit further up on the right. You might see a pair of legs sticking out at the bottom. For men only, of course.

"We're approaching the main square now, the Dam, site of the original dam over the Amstel, hence the name Amsterdam. The locals call the city Mokum, as in ik ben een ras echte Mokumer. On the right of the square you'll see the National Monument to those who died in the War, and behind it the Grand Hotel Krasnapolsky at two thousand guilders a night, where John Lennon and Yoko Ono had their love-in for peace. So here's the Dam. The first building on the left is the New Church where they crown the monarchs and then we have the Royal Palace, built on 13,569 piles. Note the small narrow arches at ground level to prevent the mob storming the place. Amsterdam, by the way, was liberated by the Canadians, so let's hear it for Canada. . . And now we're going down the Damrak. Coming up is the red Stock Exchange, De Beurs. The red-light district is over on the right. All sorts of licentious behaviour there.

"Ahead is the Central Station built by Cuijpers of the nine thousand piles in the last century. Look at the two clocks, only the one on the left is not a clock but a weather vane. See: NZOW for north, south, east, west. Sweeping right now we have the baroque church of St. Nicholas, patron saint of sailors and Amsterdam, and then the Weeping Tower from where the women used to wave their farewells to the sailors. There's a plaque commemorating Hendrik Hudson, the famous navigator. The Hudson River in New York, that's his river. Have a good look ahead. Ignore the Sea Palace there on the left, that's just an Indonesian restaurant. Look straight ahead and you should see Amsterdam's only surviving windmill, there. The one painted by Dégas. On we go, and there's the Maritime Museum where you see the old schooner moored. The IJ Tunnel coming up was opened in 1883 and that's where we're going, under the River IJ. Life jackets at the ready."

Oof! I'm immured to it all now. Maybe the schooner's a clipper – who cares? So what if that wasn't the windmill Dégas painted? And the only reason the year 1883 sticks in my mind is because it's the year Marx died. It has nothing to do with the tunnel. Where's the harm in slipping in something like that on the sly? It's like the thief leaving behind an initialled white glove at the scene of the crime. It helps keep me sane.

The passengers don't want to understand what makes the city tick. They just want to be able to say that they've seen it, done it. It's nothing more than a set of optical resistances. Otherwise they'd have chosen to spend a week here to really get at its soul. It only took me a couple of tours to realise that anyone really interested in discovery wouldn't be on a tour like this in the first place, where you spend no more than two days in any given city. Still, the world of surfaces suits me. It helps me, too. The human propensity to put appearance before essence means that I am simply a tour guide and nothing more. It means that I can go about my real business with impunity. The people of the surfaces are fine. It's the others I have to look out for, the sewer rats, the subterraneans, all those whose natural habitat is the hidden, clandestine world. I must admit I get a kick out of this double life as well.

And come tell me Sean O'Farrell
Where the gathering is to be
At the old spot by the river
Quite well known to you and me

I bear orders from the Captain
Get ye ready quick and soon
For the pikes must be together
At the rising of the moon

My gathering will be at Heidelberg, up at the castle, the day after tomorrow. Presuming nothing goes wrong between now and then. But now at the moment means the road leading to Volendam, the little town on the Zuidersee where the locals dress in traditional costume, clogs and all. Camus described Marken — its sister town — as une ville de poupée, a toytown. The same goes for Volendam. But it's what the punters want to see and that's why every tour goes there. That's why I'm likely to bump into any number of old faces from the massed ranks of pachyderms, the legion hosts of European tour guides. The worst company, I find, are the guides of forty-something. They have this way of looking at you as though they are seeing a reflection of themselves when they, too, were at the watershed of having done too many tours. Only they did not see the moment coming, did not recognise it in time, and have stayed on the road, to become richer, certainly, but no happier than the nine-to-five people they once despised. They have all become jaded old cynics who know the price of everything, and I would rather not be a cynic.

J'aime ce peuple car il est double. There goes Camus' voice in my head again. The people of Volendam all have the head of Janus, turning one way to welcome the tourists and the other to count the money they've made off them. And not just Volendam. It's everywhere you go on these tours.

Peter, owner of De Koe, shakes my hand, presses a beer into the other and welcomes us inside his bustling restaurant. A portly man who looks like he should have been a farmer, with large strong hands and a low brow that always seems to sprout beads of sweat, he is another of the Janus people, yet one of whom never a bad word is heard, not even on the bitchy, incestuous tourist circuit. I usher my punters inside, assuring them that they can trust the establishment and that the seafood is fresh and good. "Owen, wat wil je eten?" asks Peter. He is in his element taking care of a hundred things at once and always manages to give guides and drivers the personal attention they revel in. "Raw herring sandwich with onions, please," I tell him, "and another beer."

And now to find a place for myself and Gilles. My eyes scan the section reserved for drivers and guides, settling with mixed emotions on the smiling features of Abida. I was thinking of her only the other day at the Screen on the Green when I went to see *Mississippi Masala* because Sarita Whatsername, the actress in the film, reminded me of her. There's no need to ask other people's opinion: there's an automatic consensus that Abida is beautiful. Yet the sight of her makes my heart sink. I take a seat at her table, sitting next to a man sporting a maroon tie with the emblem of a coach.

"This is Owen, from Wales," she tells him. I shake his hand and give her a peck on the cheek. For some reason she doesn't provide his name. Maybe she's having a hard time with him.

He looks like the type of driver that would think of her in the shower *and* tell the other drivers about it. In any case, Abida launches straight into shop-talk: what tour am I on, what nationality passengers, how many days, all the usual questions before she tells me all about her tour.

"Abbie, you didn't tell me your colleague's name."

"Sorry, this is Cahal."

"Not from Ireland, by any chance?" I ask him. And with a name like that not a Proddy either.

"County Antrim," he says, "you've probably seen it on the news." Could yet be a Prod.

"Dia dhuit," I say with smile, "lá galánta atá ann go díreach." There you are: God be with you and 'tis a fine day for sure. He looks baffled.

"So where d'you learn your Irish, wid you being a Welshman, or is she winding me up again?"

"In London. Where else?"

"Tuigim." He understands, and laughs on the froth of his beer. For a moment Abida looks as though she feels left out in the cold.

"Abida, a mhíle grá, my thousand loves, you don't mind, do you? Think of it as Celtic bonding." She sighs, the food arrives, Gilles arrives. "And here's another Celt, from Brittany – Gilles." The Welshman, the Irishman and the Breton. Sounds like the start of a joke. What's it the French call it? Esprit du clocher. Parochialism, the English would say, at least, those who spend their holidays in Tuscany discussing Madame Bovary over their afternoon cappuccinos. Using spoons to eat their spaghetti with. At least the food's here, so I've got an excuse for fading out of the conversation. If they're going to talk shop then I'll just do some stocktaking. And if anyone feels ignored, then tough. All this where-you-from and where-you-going stuff gets on my tits. Why is it always one of the first things people ask you, where you're from? Why don't they ask you where you want to end up?

Still, if I'd never considered myself Welsh I suppose I'd never have ended up with Nadette. A whole year paid for by the university and I had all of France to choose from, but no, fair play, Owen Morgan Parry chose to take his downy face to Brittany.

Within two weeks we were lovers. Within two months I'd moved in with her. I bought her a love spoon. She a woman of thirty and me twenty-one. Nice bit of herring, though, fair play. Good for the heart, they say. Nothing more to say to Abbie anyway, nothing that wasn't said the last time. Sipping orange juice there and twinkling her eyes at Gilles. Lovely black eyes but her only twenty-two and no fun in them. Orange juice, no alcohol, against her religion. Pakistani, born and brought up in England, a Muslim frightened of being called a whore.

After lunch I saunter through the crowds past the green slats of the Hotel Spaander, wondering how I feel about having said goodbye to Abida for the last time. But no sooner am I down the wooden steps that lead to the back of the coach park than I see her again, standing at the water's edge with a green cape slung casually over her shoulders. She says she's lost one of her passengers. My eyes slide down the slender legs in black tights and I tell her not to worry, now staring resolutely at the gravel. "They're probably still in the diamond shop."

"What's up, Owen?"

"How do you mean?"

"I mean, are you having trouble with your tour or something? Or is it me?"

"No, everything's fine."

"I mean, last time, you know. You don't feel. . .?" A searching look on her face. One of those who prefers silences to direct questions. The English in her.

"Angry? Sorry? Resentful? No, none of those things, Abbie."

"We're still friends, then?" Keen to put her at ease, I assure her we're still friends. She looks only half convinced and says she'll give me a call tonight. I watch her walk back up the steps in the direction of the diamond shop. She's in the wrong business, I tell myself. She's not a pachyderm. She wants to be judged to be doing the right thing and damn the happiness. And if she calls me tonight then I'm, hah, a Dutchman.

While the punters make the most of their free time in the centre of Amsterdam, I make my customary pilgrimage to Sheeba's on Warmoestraat, the coffee house that in Camus' day used to be called Mexico City. "Een kopje coffie, met melk," I order. My nostrils trace the source of the thick smell of ganja to the guy smoking by the window, staring serenely out at the indifference of passers-by. I like this place. Nobody hassles anyone else. It's not like the pubs in England where there's always some old wanker who butts in and takes it upon himself to give you the benefit of his experience of life. Wisdom comes with age: now who was it that came up with that bollocks first? The Bible? All that stuff about respecting your elders, the equation of age with wisdom. Oh aye, the old know the score alright, they know about life. All they know about really is their own lives, the cowering course they have charted to date, getting ever closer to death and ever more fearful of it. They've seen it all with their own two eyes, they say, but never point at the blinkers they pulled on at birth and which they never asked to have removed. Wisdom comes with age, my arse.

I'm happy all by my own. What time is it? Twenty past two: hah, ten to half before three they'd say here. Black and white poster on the wall advertising Geen gewoon indisch meisje and De honden van Slipi, a bookreading by Marion – I don't believe it – Bloem. Dear God, is there no escaping Ireland? So tomorrow we'll be in Heidelberg with sightseeing the next morning. Ample chance for me to slip away from the group to meet up with the contact. Geen gewoon indisch meisje, no ordinary Indian girl, by Marion Bloem.

And Abida? Maybe she will call tonight after all. To say

what? No point building up any hopes. She probably just wants to get far away from her tourists. All guides do it, to find a little corner of sanity away from all those who want a piece of you because they've paid the price of a holiday. And her asking me about the last time at the coach park. Still friends. After . . . say it Abbie . . . after we slept together and you opened the floodgates of guilt. It wasn't easy for you, you said. You couldn't help feeling guilty. All those broken sentences and evasions and tears and interminable silences which were trying to say that you could not break free from your family and their religious precepts. Sex before marriage, the sin the family wouldn't forgive. And you refused to accept that your life was your own. No, it was only normal that your family should claim the biggest piece of you, that your life should be the passive extension of theirs, just as theirs was of their forebears. And yet you would joyfully dance to Bob Marley like all the rest and sing along to the words about emancipating yourself from mental slavery.

The triple net: nation, religion, family. What the hell's so difficult about escaping the clutches of the net? Tout est permis, hein? Come here, Abida, read the great work of the concentric circles that was written here and recognise hell for the man-made creation it is. But no, rather than square up to it you'd prefer to call me a hypocrite and say what about my Welshness, how come I haven't escaped that? Well, I have, if you should ever care to ask. I am Welsh when I want to be. Other times I'm just as happy to be Irish, or Italian or French. I take from all, as my whim dictates, and home is nowhere in particular.

No, Abbie, into the canal with you, into the circle not of the lovers, not alongside Paulo and Francesca but the circle of the cowardly. The coward who made the great refusal. If I could risk it, I'd take the phone off the hook tonight. But I can't. Not because of you but because of Heidelberg.

The Apollo Hotel is a quiet place that looks onto the waters of the Amstel. After the evening meal I return to reception to arrange wake-up calls, breakfast and porterage for the next morning. Andy Capp taps me on the shoulder to tell me he's from New Zealand and have I ever been there? No, I tell him, never been out of Europe, me. A bit of banter about the All Blacks and he's off in the direction of the bar, a puff of smoke suddenly darting out from under his cap. The passengers are still just so many names, so many numbers. Of the thousands I've taken around Europe, I remember with any vividness only the nicest and the nastiest. The rest are mere cardboard cut-outs, a faceless, amorphous mass of lurid shorts and camcorders.

I pin up a bulletin board and head upstairs to my room with a glass of jenever. It's nine o'clock and the day is nearly over. There's just the confirmation calls. I pick up the receiver and call Germany and Switzerland, making two large ticks beside the telephone numbers on my itinerary sheet. I toast the ticks with a large gulp of jenever, loosen my tie and set the alarm for five thirty. Over the silvery Amstel the light declines and I remember Dublin city in the rare old times. The sound of a body plopping into the dark Tolka, the start of one person's journey down Acheron. My own test of fire. Could they ever trust a Welshman? A body expedited by my bullet, a single nine millimetre round from a Glock 19, Austrian-made, fourteen and one. The poor unfortunate's crime: not to have kept her silence. 'Tis the cause, 'tis the cause, my soul. Nolan putting his hand on my shoulder. – You'll get used to it. You feel sick as a dog the first time. After that, it's like shelling peas.

Patronising git. And then it was back off home with him to Germany, back to the comfortable surroundings of Cologne. Director of German operations now. Only two hundred kays from British bases, close enough but not too close so as to attract attention. First impressions, way back then. Ned Nolan. Like I'd always imagined those SS guards in the camps: capable of the worst brutality by day and all Schubert by night.

The phone rings. Reception: was it seven thirty bags for

eight o'clock departure? Yes, that's right. I replace the receiver and start to undress. The phone rings again.

"Owen?"

"Hello, Abbie, how's it going?"

"I've been trying to get hold of you."

"I was working. So what's the crack?"

"Just calling to see how you were."

"You're not thinking of coming round? I think I could squeeze in another jenever."

"Has anyone ever told you you drink too much?"

"What, two jenevers of an evening and the odd beer? Why don't you try getting fluthered sometime? You never know, you might enjoy it."

"I can enjoy myself without getting drunk."

"And I can enjoy myself without looking at a Rembrandt. It's just that I'm glad he's there too."

"Another one of your clever-clever answers."

"What was it you really wanted to chat about, Abbie?"

"Just this and that."

"And I was after thinking you wanted to come round and seduce me driver."

"Mmm. He did have nice melting kind of eyes."

"Ah, 'tis a good-looking fellah he is for sure. Only I don't tink he be from de ould sod."

"Are you taking the mickey?"

"You wanted to see if we were still friends. Isn't that it?"

"You think I'm stupid, don't you. Last time, you said I was stupid."

"Jesus, I tell loads of people that. What does it matter what I think? My word is not law. If I tell someone they're not stupid, does that make them officially not stupid?"

"I'd better go."

"Take care of yourself, Abbie."

"I'll see you some other time."

"Abbie, just one more thing."

"What?"

"Are you going to be round Amsterdam for much longer?"

"For another two months, till the end of the season."

"When you've got time enough for yourself, stop by the Westerkerk. You know Descartes' house?"

"Vaguely. Why?"

"It's right behind the Westerkerk. Take a look at the plaque above Descartes' house and read the words. It's far from being the finish line but it's a start at least."

"When do we ever get time to ourselves, Owen?"

"We had time last time."

"I know."

"Listen, Abbie, I've got to go. Take care now."

I put the phone down. Perhaps I cut her off too soon but there was really nothing else I wanted to say to her. At least I wasn't childish; self-righteous, yes, as usual, but not childish, having some smart-arse last word like telling her to go and find herself a nice Muslim boy, a nasty dig in the ribs as a parting salvo. It wouldn't make any difference either way. Reason goes out of the window with people determined to play the ostrich or the amnesiac. It's all in her own hands. Either live with whatever it is that troubles you, Abbie, and get on with your life, or look to yourself for the solution to your trouble. Ay, ay, ay, ay, ay, Nadette, why is there no-one like you? Why only these pale shades of Hades? Is it just me, or are these people already dead, the living dead, more dead than alive, blurring the division between the dead and the living? Give me some place where no-one spends their life playing these games, following all the rules whose inventor no-one can even remember, these stupid, life-corroding rules. No, I will not play any more. I put away childish things and Saint Paul with them. I am tired, and tomorrow is Day Three.

Quel autre pays où l'on puisse jouir d'une liberté si entière?
-Lettre de Descartes, 1631.

2

Gilles moves out to overtake a light blue Trabi, his first scalp on the Autobahn. "My Gaahd!" exclaims a mocking American voice behind me. "Check out that car! What is it, a tin rat or sumn?" I don't bother to turn round to see who made the comment, preferring instead to relish the sweetly satisfying thought that the parcel and I are safely in Germany. A tidal wave of triumphal ecstasy washes over me. Stop press: Parry does it again! Clandestine courier beats border! Frontier fox slips through net! It's not long, though, before my self-congratulatory smugness ebbs away and turns to dismay, a deflation of the spirit brought on not by the affluent American laughing at East German poverty but by what I saw back at the border. While Gilles was filling in the tax and mileage forms I curbed my initial interest in the poster displaying mugshots of terrorists and came upon a faded map of Germany still separated into BRD and DDR. To look at it, it had only recently been defaced. Some putrid patriot had scribbled out the border with a felt-tip pen, crossed out the name of Karl-Marx-Stadt, and replaced it with Chemnitz.

Welcome to the new Germany. The images of the euphoric night of the ninth of November are just a faded memory bordering on a sick joke whose punch-line no-one can remember two years on. The defacing patriot can gloat that the communist cancer has been lanced from his Fatherland and that the statues are being pulled down everywhere. If only it stopped there I could simply dismiss him as a cretin who has never read so much as a line of Marx. But I don't think it will stop there. Patriotism, the last refuge of scoundrels. Last refuge maybe, but the first resort for fascism. Starts with a map and ends with a Turk. Making great strides in Germany now, the fascists, specially in the East. People going over to the skinheads or clamouring for the Communists to come back.

Like a bolt of lightning, the Isle of Wight flashes up, the sudden recollection of my first encounter with naked, Cro-Magnon patriotism. My mother took me to stay with relatives and we went to see the Ryde Carnival. It must have been sometime in the early seventies and I hadn't so much as met an Irishman. Along came the procession of gaily-coloured floats carrying musicians, fairy queens, pantomime horses, scenes from Camelot, all the usual fare of country fayres. But the float that raised the biggest laugh was the one that had a group of characters all dressed as village idiots. The skirt of the float read IRISH BAWN, IRISH BREAD – STRONG IN THE ARM, FICK IN THE ED. Didn't my mother chortle her socks off! And didn't I laugh myself silly.

I remember my father too. Shaking his fist at the telly. Something on the news had got his back up and he was ranting and raving. "You should take a machine gun and shoot the bloody lot of them!" My mother told him not to swear in front of the children but he couldn't contain himself. "Shoot the bloody lot of them!" I later pieced it all together. He'd been watching the events of Bloody Sunday.

Ah, what would he say if he could see me now? If he could see me then, even, in 1981, taking Nadette to a meeting on the Hunger Strikers? She, like every French person I talked to on the subject, was outraged by Thatcher. Chairing the meeting was the man who took my Breton lectures, Per Denez. Bobby Sands was already dead. In a few days' time Mitterrand would beat Giscard in the presidentials. Two months later, on 13th July, the eve of Bastille Day, another hunger striker would die, the sixth but not the last. His family would cut the brass buttons from his battle tunic to keep as mementos. But one of them would be given away and handed on again, to me, on Sandymount Strand where the sand reminded me of Ryde beach at low tide, where once I saw my father in overalls painting the pier. On Sandymount Strand I held Martin Hurson's button in my palm and examined it. The front bore a thickly embossed harp on either side of which were the letters I and V, for Irish Volunteer. On the back, incongruously, were the words "Birmingham Buttons Limited". What would he say, my father, the Paddy-hater, the black-hater, the Pakky-hater? I don't care what he would say. I couldn't give a toss.

> Some say the Devil is dead
> The Devil is dead
> The Devil is dead
> Some say the Devil is dead
> And buried in Killarney
>
> More say he rose again
> He rose again
> He rose again
> More say he rose again
> And joined the British Army

The day brightens as we continue through North-Rhine-Westphalia. Insect corpses accumulate on the windscreen of the coach. A blue motorway sign points the way to Trier, prompting me to wonder whether it will be long before all trace of Marx is eradicated there too. But who am I to talk? I do just the same in all the deliberate omissions I make in my commentary. Take Cologne, our midday stop. Will I talk about Marx's time there as editor of the *Neue Rheinische Zeitung*? Will I even venture a small mention of Bebel, one of Cologne's most famous sons and collaborator of Marx? Not on your life! Oh no, I've been through that hoop before. Mention Marx once and you might get away with it. Mention him twice and the passengers start giving you queer looks. Three times and you might as well tie the noose yourself. It's best to pretend to be a nice liberal. The tips are better that way.

So Trier goes by the wayside, and every nasty, beastly, perfectly horrid thought with it. But fascism is different. If you don't mention it they think there's something wrong because everyone's heard of Adolf and the War and everyone knows who the goodies and baddies were there. If you gloss over that while you're travelling through Germany, then heaven knows, what if they've got a Nazi guide on their hands? So I take the mike in my hand and give a clean-shaven, loves-his-mother, nice, marmaladey overview of German history, from particularism to the economic miracle, tiptoeing gingerly – shh, quiet or you'll wake the children – up the creaking stairs of fascism.

The more I suppress all this stuff in my professional life, where the old proselyte in me sometimes aches to come out, the more it finds expression elsewhere. There was that thin-lipped public school woman I rounded on the other day when I was at some party in Islington, the blond woman with the face of a startled shrew. Giggled over her pink gin and said but how bzaahrre of me, didn't I know communism was dead? I told her about the tee-shirts on sale in East Berlin, calling for the Wall to be built up again only this time ten feet higher. Told her that as long as there's capitalism there's a case for communism. Then I called her a myopic, upper-class arsehole. A fatuous, drunken outburst. The curious thing, though, is that all this suppression has started affecting my dreams as well now. Three years studying Marxism in Florence and two years before that in Manchester and I cannot once remember dreaming of Marx or any of the others. But since I've been on the road they've started sneaking out of the dusty blue tomes and into my subconscious world.

There were two things that used to amaze Nadette about my dreams; that I could recall them in such detail, and that they would often make me laugh out loud in my sleep. I used to recount them to her in the mornings, before she went off to work, when we would share a bowl of coffee in bed. Nadette would sometimes sing in her sleep but she could never remember her dreams. After I left her, dreams became only something we wrote to each other about. The dream I had the other night, though, the night before I left on this tour, I would not have told her about. She would have worried about it.

It was a dream which started as a seminar in one of the Renaissance rooms at the Badia in Florence, all beams and frescos and cypress trees shimmering through the windows. Then one of the politics professors turned into a defence lawyer, standing there in hornrimmed spectacles and jodhpurs, smelling of dusty drawers and holding parchment notes in his hand. The basenji dog, a Portugese researcher who looked like Grimer Wormtongue, told me that this was the Court of the August Dead but not to worry. I was not on trial. I was the one being defended. It made a change, I told him. Then he got to his feet. *CALL LEON TROTSKY*, he bellowed, then, more softly, pretending his voice was carrying through the halls, CALL LEON TROTSKY, call Leon Trotsky. In came a man wearing a trenchcoat and Phrygian hat, his grey hair electrified, a pamphlet and a French novel tucked under his arm. *Fontamara* was its title. I was about to inform him respectfully that it wasn't a French novel after all but Italian, but the professor-cum-lawyer stuck out his chest and raised his finger.

-I put it to you, he began, that you were assassinated in August, were you not?

-I was, Trotsky replied calmly. In Mexico City, on the twentieth. Hurt like buggery.

-And you did, did you not, write about Germany in this, mmm, bolshevik pamphlet, dated (may it please the Court) November 1931.

-Alemania, Klyuch i situatsii. . .

-May I remind you that you are not in Russia now!

-As you wish: Germany, Key to the International Situation.

-And in it, did you not propose a united front of the organisations of, how shall we say, the . . . *lower* orders?

-Socialists and Communists together, marching separately, striking together against the fascists. The Spanish revolution had created the general political premises for an immediate struggle for power by the proletariat. . .

-Yes, yes, yes. . .

-The Comintern was caught unawares by the events. The Communist Party occupied a false position on all the fundamental questions. The materialist analysis of concrete events, hmff, my analysis that is, could have saved the lives of millions had it been. . .

-M'lud, may I remind the accused that we are not here to listen to a load of bolshie propaganda.

-Pravda eto, is that true already? Then why was I called?

-Because you did, during your sojourn in Mexico, go by the name of O'Brien, did you not?

-Maya zhizhn, my life! I did.

-And that, having taken it upon yourself to become Irish, you choose to criticise my client for the . . . services, shall we say, that he is rendering.

-His precious parcel has nothing to do with the class struggle.

-Oh! Oh! Has it not, indeed! And what if, as my client has stated, in rather regrettable language (may I ask the Court to bear with me), what if a forced withdrawal from Ireland should lead to a thoroughgoing demoralisation of the British ruling elite, the politico-military caste (I do beg the Court's forgiveness) as my client chooses to put it, and thereby hasten and enhance the chances of the Red etc., etc., etcetera.

-But what about the forces of the revolution? They have first to be organised, steeled in the combat, stripped bare of all reformist panaceas and philistine. . .

-Yes, yes, yes, but I put it to you that there is any number of badly brought up young men and (one is bound to say) women who can do that. Is my client to suffer such vilification merely because he applies himself to the circles most suited to his talents?

-Can I go now? I said I'd attend a charity Dance of Death in Mexico.

-No further questions.

-Never did like Germany anyway.

-No further questions!

The Ruhrgebiet throws up an open-cast mine stacked high with hills of brown slag and coal and the dream gives way to memories of the miners' strike. Who fears to speak of '84? I'm over it now. I'm definitely over it. But I'll never forget the bitterness I felt at the end, there, at Bold colliery, when I watched the lads go back to work at dawn. My throat begins to ache whenever I think of the miner in tears behind the banner, dragging his feet, head bowed in shame and disgust, spitting out his despair on the tarmac. Others clapped them back but I couldn't. All I felt was bitterness and a complete desolation of the soul. Anger, too, at the fact that we could have won had it not been for the betrayal of scabs, jackals and invertebrates. Bollocks to all those who said we couldn't have won. Sputa e passa! Spit and pass by. The world will not record festering amnesiac maggots like them. Sputa e passa! That was where my open political activity died. The vanguard parties were happy they'd made recruits and all bleeding-heart *Guardian* readers could be just as happy that they'd won that most monumental prize of political struggle, the moral victory. I spat and passed on to Florence.

Gilles looks up into his mirror and informs me that most of the passengers have woken up from their doze. "Autobahnkreuz Oberhausen, trois kilomètres," he reads aloud. "We should be in Cologne by about twelve thirty." "Marvellous," I say, "just keep it there, Gilles, but don't take any chances with the speed." He hasn't once mentioned Nadette today, thanks be to Jesus. It's time for some more commentary, and so I get to my feet to paint a picture of hunger in postwar Cologne, as told by Böll in *Das Brot der frühen Jahre*, throwing in bits on the Cathedral and the direct hits it took during the War, the city's Roman origins, how many billion litres of *4-7-11* are produced annually, Stockhausen and Offenbach, and Adenauer, but no, nothing about Bebel nor the *Neue Rheinische Zeitung*.

As soon as we get to Cologne the passengers head in their droves for the McDonalds by the Cathedral, just as the last lot did the time I picked up Kane here barely two weeks ago. Other buses were arriving in the coach park all the time and spilling out groups of tourists. I spotted Nolan on the footbridge with a man who had a beige suitcase at his feet, saw Nolan point over at me with a nick of the head and waited for the man to come. A bunch of Americans posed in front of their bus for a group photo with their driver and guide. My own driver, the whispy, red-bearded young Donat, came back saying he'd forgotten which departure time I'd given and then there, at my side, was the man with the beige suitcase. I jumped in before he could introduce himself or say anything which might arouse Donat's suspicion.

-Ah, now you must be John Kane, the go-show the office told me about.

-That's right, he replied, looking just a little tense.

-Donat, any chance of opening the lockers and getting this gentleman's case loaded? He's the go-show I told you about.

-No problem, said Donat.

-Nolan gone already? I asked as the driver struggled to squeeze the case in.

-Yeah. Said he didn't want to hang round long. And what's a go-show when it's at home?

-C'mon, I'll brief you over a beer. Cheers, Donat! Nice one. I grab a portion of greasy yellow Kartoffelpuffen from the Imbiss by the station and munch them on the way to the post office. After confirmation calls to hotels in Lucerne, Rome and Florence, I steer my way to the nearest bar in search of a toilet where I can wash the grease from my hands. Suitably cleansed, I take a newspaper from the rack at random and settle down with a Weissbier. The front page casts Yeltsin as the new blue-eyed boy of the West. So it's all over bar the shouting. The restoration of capitalism will be a formality. I look elsewhere and find a small column on the suicide of one Boris Pugov, former KGB man and one of the organisers of the coup. In the letter he left to posterity he said that he had seen the destruction of everything he had worked for all his life. Aye, well, Boris, you win some, you lose some. And where were you, I wonder, when they were denouncing the Trotskyite-fascist spies? In the front row of the Komsomol, pointing your finger? But what am I saying? God, Parry, sometimes you can be such a sanctimonious bastard. As if politics was a moral beauty contest. Something there about the Balkans. Takes me back, the old history books at school, Sarajevo and Prinkip and the Black Hand. Regressions of history. August 1914, mass slaughter, and Engels predicted it all in the 1891 "Introduction". The sword of Damocles, the chartered covenants of princes scattered like chaff, a race war which will subject the whole of Europe to devastation by fifteen or twenty million armed men. Word for word. Died in August, the fifth was it? 1895. Who'll celebrate his centenary come 1995? No-one, that's my prediction. No, it'll be all the end of the War crap, fifty years on instead of a hundred years back, the usual inanities and platitudes about the senselessness of war. Bit of breast-beating about the concentration camps perhaps. Massaged grief, orchestrated, cosmetic, the hymn sheet handed down from above. Churchill instead of Engels, in England anyway, the Butcher of Tonypandy. Ah fer fuck sake, I can just see it.

MEISTERRAUB. Brüssel, dpa. Laut der belgischen Kunstbehörden könne sich das verschwundene, über dreihundertfünfzig Jahre alte Skizzenbuch Van Dycks in Praha befinden. Jesus Christ, would you look at that sentence! They don't make it easy for you, do they? Just look at it. No definite article to kick off with, modal verb banging into one half of a reflexive verb, with the other half booted out to the end of the sentence. And where's the subject for fuck sake? Das blabla . . . Buch, wrapped around a disappeared three hundred and fifty-year-old adjective, that's where it is. Upshot of it all: some sketchbook might be in Prague. Talk about long-winded. Where's the weather page, for fuck sake? Nope . . . nope . . . ah, here we go.

There, Florenz, thirty-six degrees. Phew, what a scorcher. Wonder what they'll be doing right now, all the folk from the Badia? It's August, so a good few'll be back in their home countries, scattered all over Europe, like chaff. The European University at the Badia, Europe in microcosm. Three great years there. Lucky bastard I am. Founded by a Paddy, too, as Seoirse reminds everyone. Seoirse, to be sure. Landed himself a cushy job at the Commission. Shame I didn't get a chance to go for a gargle with him back in Brussels. Probably boozing at the James Joyce right now, holding court, nobody able to get a word in edgeways. Gas character. The man from Stillorgan, Brewery Road. You couldn't invent things like that if you tried. Talks like a Flann O'Brien creation. Don't know if he does it deliberately. Dear God, what wouldn't I give for a pint of plain right now! Should've had a half. This way I'll be bursting all the way down the Rhine. First Guinness opportunity will be where, Rome, spose, that boozer behind Santa Maria Maggiore, the Druid's Head. Better be off now. Don't want to get there after the punters. Leave the rest, aye. Ten marks should cover it. Who mentioned Marx?

Maybe go for a pint with Pepe in Florence. Always stays on in August, says he gets more work done without so many folk around. Loves the Irish pub, though. Few pints and he's talking about his Galicia, Breogan the hero of old and the ghosts of the Holy Circle. Good drinkers the Spaniards. More than can be said of the Italians. Wonder who else'll be there.

Must organise a session with whoever's around. Enough of this. To business.

Our charge down the Rhine proves the usual race against the clock to catch the boat at Boppard for the cruise featured in the brochure. My Wagner tape booms out on the stereo. A buxom Brunhilde in horned helmet belts out an aria, all Bayreuth and bluster, conjuring up the spirit of German Romanticism, setting the mood for the Rhineland of castles, dragons, Rheingold and Niebelungen. We sail through Bonn and Bad Godesberg, through Koblenz of the confluence, birthplace of Metternich, the man who ruled Europe but never Austria, and ever southwards we head. The sun is high overhead, the grey Rhine courses on our left and with the low green undulations that steepen here and there into terraced vineyards the landscape looks . . . pleasant. Not the place I would come on holiday, but then it is not my holiday.

A sunflash from the windscreen of an oncoming coach leaves a blind spot on my vision. Rising high on the left are the Cliffs of the Dragon, the Drachenfels, and beyond loom the seven hills of the Siebengebirge, Snow White territory. Another sunflash hits me, more painful this time. I decide to don sunglasses for my litany of castles as we approach Rolandseck. I blink hard to check the blind spot. It's got bigger. Oh, don't tell me it's a migraine. Do I feel weaker? Possibly. Slight nausea maybe. Could be the malade imaginaire, but hang on, check the fingertips. Is that numbness? Tip of the tongue. Could have been something in the Weissbier. Who'd be doing a thing like that? You're imagining it, Parry. All in your head. Faint buzz in my ears. No, not a migraine, please not a migraine. What did I do with that paracetamol? No piercing headache though. That's a good sign. But the blind spot, getting bigger by the second, fraying jagged edges, tingling colours. Sign coming up: Rolandseck. Did I read that okay or is it just that I knew it would say Rolandseck anyway? Sudden braking, lurching forward, grabbing the arm of my seat. Loud blast of the horn. Careful, Gilles.

The tingling colours have gone. I'm okay. Well, not quite. There is an unease within me that I can't quite give a name to. It's nothing physical, more like the feeling you have when someone walks over your grave. But why should it come over me now? Why here, in this landscape of olde-worlde timbered villages in pink and yellow plaster, the sort of thing you expect to see on a bottle of Liebfraumilch? I check the parcel. Now why did I do that? Ah, I know what it's all about: Rolandseck. Subliminally thinking about the legend of Roland, and Gilles blasting on the horn was the final jolt to the memory. Roland, slain by the Saracens at the Battle of Roncevaux, failed to blow his horn in time out of pride. That's the sin for which Dante put him in the Inferno. So why should that make me feel uneasy? No, hang on, I've got it all wrong. It's Ganelon that's in the Inferno, the one who betrayed Roland, in the circle of the traitors. Yes, that's it, and me thinking about the betrayal of the miners a while back in the Ruhrgebiet. That explains it. So why this unease and why check the parcel? Stress, that's it, just stress. One of those situations where because everything's going so smoothly you convince yourself there must be something wrong. Tour guide's paranoia. Relax.

"There's another Austerlitz bus behind us," Gilles remarks casually.

"Who is it, do you think?"

"He's driving a Mercedes, whoever it is."

"Ah well, we'll soon find out when we get to the boat."

"Not far now." I switch the mike on and spin out a yarn about witches that used to be burned in the market square of Lahnstein. I cast the passengers' minds forward to St. Goer, reminding them that that's where the Rhine cruise ends. Whatever they do, they are not to stay on the boat and end up coming back to Boppard. Was he famous for anything, asks an Australian, this St. Goer? Oh yes, I tell him, he's the patron saint of innkeepers and, by sheer coincidence, he was an Irishman. Canonised for curing thousands of hangovers. Used to turn water into Guinness.

Before long the stiff-legged passengers are disembarking from the coach at Boppard. I position myself at the foot of the gangplank slanting up to the boat and give Gilles a wave as he sets off to meet us further down the Rhine. A young lad from the Weinand boat company comes to shake my hand, takes my voucher and tells me we can sail in ten minutes. I count heads as they file past me. One of them asks if there are toilets on the boat. Yes, I tell her, just look for the signs. Another complains about the air conditioning. Yet another asks where we get off the boat.

At the Stammtisch reserved for guides I shake the hands of Terry and Pietro, Austerlitz colleagues who always talk about the good old days when, if they are to be believed, passengers had plenty of money and knew how to use the coach toilet. Terry sports the handlebar moustache of the quintessential Englishman, while Pietro prefers to let his Krizia suit and Rolex be his references. They seem to be in mid-conversation about another guide and they ask me if I know a Kristine, blond, from Paris.

"The Frenchwoman with the German mother?"

"Yes, indeed," replies Terry.

"I bumped into her briefly in Lourdes once. She was creating a scene with some poor receptionist. Hadn't been given enough rooms, I think." Pietro leans forward with a glint in his eye.

"If I were straight," he says, "I think I would find her attractive. Do you not think she has a certain *libidine*, eh, Terry?"

"My dear chap," says Terry, "a gentleman does not discuss such things."

The boat pulls away and a recorded voice welcomes the passengers first in impeccable Hochdeutsch and then in an

English that seems to have been learned in Edinburgh. The voice continues with a commentary that will talk of hostile brothers, an island for lovers, cats and mice, silver mines, a priest serving behind a bar, the sirens of the Lorelei and seven virgins who appear at low water. Terry and Pietro get ever deeper into tales of the road. Kristine's name pops up again, but their conversation soon moves on to talk of a new world order. It'll be good for tour guides, Terry says. No more Intourist monopoly in the Soviet Union, no more Compass monopoly in Yugoslavia, no more. . .

I sip my free glass of hock and drift away to Lourdes, the one and only time I was there, last year, Oberammergau year. I remember walking alone through the streets while my Australians from the Outback were in the night procession chanting the "Ave Maria", candles in hand, bush-hats on head. My childhood Protestantism was revolted at the sight of Brazilians garrulously jostling for holy water, clutching their plastic bottles in the form of the Virgin. I was even more revolted at the thought that Moira could come here looking for a cure to her cancer, an intelligent woman at the shrine of human credulity. She was studying French and Spanish while I did French and German. Never got to do her year abroad. She wanted to go to Granada. She could quote entire poems of Lorca. "Verde, que te quiero verde. . ."

At the age of twenty-one in the Godforsaken month of August I left Nadette to go to your funeral and I looked down into your open grave to read the copper plate on your coffin: Moira McCann, died aged twenty-one. Verde, que te quiero verde. Years later I stood on the Torre de le Vela where Mendoza proclaimed the victory of your faith over the Moorish infidels and I looked down on the Granada of your Lorca. Had you lived, I asked myself, would our friendship have endured your Catholicism? I didn't find any answer but standing there in the city of priests and nuns and cripples I still wondered at the quiet bravery with which you faced death, all withered and coughing so weakly it seemed the next convulsion would kill you. You were brave in the face of death. Unlike your hero. No, Federico was terrified of death. As they took him to the Fountain of Tears he was probably saying the rosary, perhaps even thinking about Ignacio being gored to death in front of his eyes by a bull known as Granadino. He died on the night of the eighteenth in the wholesale slaughter of that month. They shot him, but he got to his knees again and cried, "I'm still alive!" Lived with death all his life and then died alive. Near the end, your mother told me, you couldn't remember a single line of Lorca. Verde, que te quiero verde. But make no mistake, Moira. The parcel I carry has nothing to do with sentimentalism, and if it should prove to be the death of me then I will not go to your afterworld of saints and harps and virgins.

I dreamed I saw
Joe Hill last night
Alive as you and me
Says I, but Joe,
You're ten years dead
I never died, says he

Ah, the sirens of the Lorelei already. Soon be time to disembark. When first I saw that form endearing, when love absorbed my ardent soul, I cared not for the morrow. But all is lost now, and I'll not see her again, so I will go where no-one knows. I will go down among the dead men. The Ormond Hotel where we met up. A car ride out along the Liffey to pick her up at Connelly Station. Then up through Glasnevin to the Tolka Valley Park. In the dead of night. Expedited by my bullet. Nolan. The ponytail in Brussels, based in Antwerp, one face turned to London, the other to the Continent. Director of European Operations. Nice to get a pat on the back from him, though, for the last job. Nice to be appreciated. Never have known his name, just a couple of numbers I can contact him on. First time I met him he told me to call him

-Just call me the ponytail.

Puts you at a bit of a disadvantage, that. Oi, ponytail, how's it hanging? Just doesn't sound right. But why doesn't he want me to take the parcel all the way to Switzerland, being as how I'm heading there anyway? Not as experienced as the fidus Achates, eh? Our man in Heidelberg, done more runs to Switzerland than anyone else still on the scene. Demarcation, is it? His ball park. Mustn't let petty jealousies get in the way. Stay professional and make a good job of it, that's the order of the day. Cheer up, for God's sake. Iz diss a feckin wake or wha? Think of the nicer things. Think of the pint with Pepe in Florence. Look at all those smiling faces. Yes, it is lovely, isn't it? Lucky with the weather, weren't we? Think of Seoirse, that time he was on about the active service unit driving round Stoke Newington in a green van, disguised as Sephardic Jews. That's better. A genuine smile on me face now. Oisín and Donal Cohen, ehm, de Blewm Brodders from Booterstown.

Or Seoirse and me at the stadio, watching Fiorentina against Juve. I'd only known him a couple of weeks. There's me suffering from the mother of all grappa hangovers and it's hot as hell and him wittering on about his gran from Clare. The Black and Tans burned her house to the ground on account of her Fenian husband. Seoirse imitating her culchey accent: "'I wuudn't moind,' sez she, 'I wuudn't moind, but he only shot a few o' dem.'" He was off the gargle then, of course. For the whole year. Of course. And then I ran into him in the Casa del Popolo, two days later, him up at the bar with an amaretto di Saronno in his hand and a whole cohort of empty glasses in front of him. Specs all akimbo on his face.

-I'll tell you one thing, Owen: there's no-one more surprised than meself . . . to see meself here.

The Rhine cruise seems to have been a success, if the faces of my punters are anything to go by. Andy Capp strides towards the coach a few paces ahead of me, holding the hand of a woman whose profile and voice make me think of Olive Oyle. A couple of Kiwis enjoying a second honeymoon. Behind me I can hear a couple of women speaking Afrikaans. Andy Capp turns to ask me how I became a guide. The inevitable question, the one someone always asks, the answer to which flashes up like an auto-cue: when I left Florence I decided I didn't want to remain in the world of the ivory towers and I just happened to notice an ad looking for someone with a few languages and a knowledge of Europe.

"Didn't you want to do something else," he asks, "with the languages or the history?" Now, how much do I tell him? That if I ever had to work I wanted to do as little as possible? Bit risky. Maybe he thinks there's virtue in hard work. Or will I be honest and tell him I'm tired of the job and would jack it in were it not a sideline, a front for the clandestine stuff? Course not.

"I'm too much of a gypsy," I reply, "for the normal run of jobs. Not very good at staying in one place for long." Honest, at least. Now there's the young Afrikaaner at my shoulder, getting in on the conversation. "And are you married at all, Owen?" she asks. Pink Lacoste tee-shirt on, pretty in a certain way. Ah, this must be the mother and daughter from Cape Town, if my passenger list is right.

"No. Just a wild rover, Lizzy." Did I get the name right? She smiles back and asks if I'd mind posing for a photo with her mother. I wrap my arm round the mother's shoulders and pull a face. Wild rover! Playing to the image so many have of the guide as a wandering Don Juan. Me, a Don Juan! Bing! A white flash that turns red, then blue.

Our Austerlitz coach trundles out of St. Goer. Next stop is Heidelberg. There's something I made a mental note of but I can't for the life of me think what. Something to do with Heidelberg? A phone call I've forgotten to make? Something to do with the contact tomorrow morning? No, I know, a gap in the vocabulary, that was it: how to say sideline in French. Second string to your bow, the English would say. That sort of thing. Damn, I hate it when I can't remember. Look at me now, Nadette, struggling in our language to find a pissy little word I'm sure I must have heard on your lips. You the teacher and me the punctillious perfectionist. It's no good. It'll be a long shot, but the only option is to ask Gilles.

"Violon d'Ingres," he says after only a moment's reflection.

"Why's that, then, when Ingres was a painter?"

"Because he was good at the violin as well."

"And how come you know that, then?"

"You don't have to go to university to read, Owen." Said without any hint of sarcasm either. The son of a peasant, he goes on to explain, he didn't want to burden his parents with the cost of university. He wanted to make his own way without any debts. Besides, what else was there to do in hotel rooms at night but read? Try to get one of the passengers into bed like all the other drivers? No thanks! Not when he's got Carine to go back to. And what is he reading now, I ask? *Le diable et le bon Dieu*, he answers. He's half-way through it already and should have it finished in a couple of days. At least, I remark, he's not reading an English novel. What's wrong with English novels, he asks? Nothing, I tell him, if you like reading novels about the halcyon, hermetically sealed days of hyphenated Henrys, stammering Sinjuns and parasoled Prus, punting down the Cam or the Isis as they quaff pink champagne and bask in the golden rays of the sun shining out of their collective arse. All in all, they really are fine, masterly, universal works. Gilles snorts and says ta very much but he'll stick to *Le diable et le bon Dieu*.

By seven o'clock we've checked into the Gasthof Scheid, a family-run establishment tucked away in the forest to the south of Heidelberg, and by eight we're down in the restaurant sampling the complimentary bottle of Schriesheimer the owner offered us. We're in a nice, quiet little corner, all on our own. In previous years we'd have been jammed in with all the other drivers and guides but the Gulf War and the weak dollar have drastically thinned out the numbers of overseas tourists. Not even the bicentenary of Mozart's death has been able to pull them in this year. But the tourist blight has its advantages. As soon as we came upon the cabal of raucous Flems in the restaurant, Gilles and I looked at each other and decided to sit away from them. When we sat down and began unfolding our napkins Gilles said that he recognised one of their number, a certain Marcel, a nasty piece of work he once crossed swords with in Rome. For Marcel, every hotel was either owned by Jews or soon would be. C'est bidon, he sighs, so much ugliness in the world, so much unnecessary ugliness.

I ask him if he's phoned Carine yet. It's one of the first things he does on arrival: unload the bags, park the coach, phone Carine. The mere mention of her name is enough to set his eyes glistening at a faraway landscape. Within seconds he has me seeing through his eyes into a future where he and Carine will have their own house, not too far from his mother's so that they can visit her as often as they like, a house filled with the shouts of two beautiful little girls romping around outside in the garden, a house with oak beams and a big old fire for the winter. I watch him upstairs, tucking the girls into bed and telling them fairy stories till they drift off to sleep. He kisses them as light as a feather on the forehead, first one, Soazig, then the other, Armelle, whose lips suckle on a honey-sweet dream. He tidies away a toy on the floor, takes one last look at the girls and pulls their door to, leaving a shaft of light to stand guardian against ghosts and witches.

I lean discreetly to one side. Pfffrrrlp. There goes yesterday's raw herring. Don't I ever want to have children, Gilles asks? No, most definitely not, I answer. He doesn't ask why I don't want children. He just raises his eyebrows, shrugs with perfect Gallic nonchalance and says each to his own. While he avidly scrapes the last of the strawberry ice-cream from his dish I try to imagine what sort of father he would be. A good father, I decide, caring and loving, devoted too, with a boyish smile and playful voice that would light up any infant's face. The sort of father who would leave little presents around the house for the kids to find. Not like my own father. The only things he left around the house were the scent of greasy hair and dark corners where I cowered with my sister, both of us sick with fear at the thought of his belt. Sometimes Mum would intervene, putting herself between my father and us, and he'd go away chastising her for mollycoddling us. If I could be a kid again, Gilles would be the sort of father I'd choose for myself. I can't ever be convinced that fear is a good thing to be brought up with. God-fearing is so innocuous compared with father-fearing. But one day I fought back, determined to protect my sister and bolstered by the thought that cowering fear was worse than taking a good beating. It didn't work. I caught him with a blow to his ulcerous stomach and I thought I'd killed him. That was the most frightened I ever was.

I go to pour Gilles some more wine but he holds his hand over his glass. It's not that he doesn't like the wine, he says. No, it's really quite good. Nothing to compare with an average white Fleurie, of course, but really quite decent nonetheless. It's just that he's got to think of his job. Okay, so he doesn't want to be a coach driver for the rest of his life – unlike that crowd over there – but for the moment he'd rather hang onto his job. "Ah, while I think of it," he says. "You know what my English is like, but didn't you say on the way down that Heidelberg was a Celtic city?"

"Yeah, well, originally. Why d'you ask?"

"It's just something I hadn't heard before. So why don't I feel at home here, if it's Celtic and I'm a Celt? I mean, as far as I can see, it's just German and there's an end to it."

"I'm bollocksed if I know the answer to that one. Do you feel a Celt in Brittany, then? There's many a Breton I've met doesn't feel in the least bit Celtic."

"Of course I feel Celtic in Brittany. How couldn't I? You know, my grandfather was one of those who went to the Fontaine de Barenton in the thirties because there was a drought and people still thought that Merlin could break the drought. That's the kind of stock I'm from."

"Amazing."

"You know the Fontaine de Barenton?"

"Vaguely."

"My grandfather used to tell me stories of being punished for speaking Breton at school. They used to hang a clog around his neck."

"Same sort of thing used to happen in Wales."

"Excuse me for interrupting you, Owen." Suddenly hanging over me is the pallid face of a man whose breath smells of coffee. Lanky fellah stooping down. Christ knows what his name is. Big, gangly, lanky fellah with a beard and shifty eyes. "I mean, I don't want to spoil your meal. . ."

"No, fire away."

"I just wanted to ask you something."

"Sure."

"It's just, okay, will we get a chance to see Dachau tomorrow? I mean, you were talking about Worms and Little Jerusalem and how the Jews were poisecuted there. Kristallnacht and all that." Fast-talking New Yoik accent. The only New Yorker on the list, one of the single rooms, come on, what's his name? Fucking stupid question anyway.

"Dachau? Er no, it's not on the itinerary I'm afraid."

"But you know, okay, if we cut something else out, I'm sure there'd be others who'd want to see Dachau too. Like, it's just, I'm only running the idea past you, see what you think, okay."

"No, I'm sorry, Mr. Miesepeter, we just can't do it if it's not on the itinerary." Looking at me like I'm some kind of insurance salesman trying to take him for a ride. I just know he's going to be trouble.

"Oh, okay . . . No, I was just asking."

"Sorry to disappoint you." Face lighting up, probably just because I remembered his name.

"No problem, Owen." He straightens himself and lopes off in his sensible tweed jacket.

"Dachau!" Gilles whispers. "Did he ask if we could go to Dachau?"

"Yeah. I told him we couldn't."

"I should hope so too! Lose three hours there and we wouldn't get to Lucerne till midnight. Incredible. He should try asking that Marcel about Dachau!"

I try to tempt Gilles with a digestif but he wipes his mouth and says he's going straight up to his room. He doesn't want to get collared by the Flems. Either you impose French on them – and he can quite understand their not liking that – or you spend half the time out of the conversation and never knowing what they might be saying about you on the sly. No thanks, he says, he'd much rather have his head in his book for an hour or so and then get an early night. I decide to go with him. Icy Flemish stares greet my nod of acknowlegement as we pass by and amid the laughter directed at our backs I catch "jeanet", the Flemish word for poof.

We unhook our keys from the rack at reception and take the stairs to the first floor. Gilles still can't get over Mr. Miesepeter. Does he think we have all the time in the world to wander round any place that might take his fancy? This is a coach tour, a group tour, with a set itinerary and he should realise that. He should have another look at his brochure. I should watch out for him, he warns, unlocking the door to his room with one hand and balling a fist with the other: velvet glove, iron fist, he says, that's how to treat Mr. Whatsisname. Aye, I smile, and wish him goodnight. I lock the door behind me and take my briefcase from its hiding place under the bed, springing open the catches and lifting the lid. Uppermost is my black clipboard, decorated with two white oval stickers, one bearing the F for France, the other YU for Yugoslavia. It looks like Mr. Miesepeter will be the first for the clipboard treatment tomorrow. Under the clipboard are two maps, a book of vouchers, reams of rooming lists, a glossy Austerlitz brochure and finally, wedged safely into a corner alongside a couple of tapes, the bulky, innocuous yellow parcel wrapped round with Sellotape. It bears an address which I know to be fictitious. And that is all I want to know about the parcel. Tomorrow morning, up at the castle, I shall be rid of it.

3

My eyes stare blindly into the darkness. My left hand feels a swollen sex and I try to remember what I dreamed of, but this time my dreams have already taken flight, leaving behind only the fading image of a tear running down Nadette's cheek. My eyes ache when I turn on the light. I blink, and peer at the face of the clock, whose hands indicate five thirty exactly. The air outside my bed feels inhospitably cold but I force myself to get up and wander about the room still half-dazed. The only sound is my feet padding on the wooden boards. Flipflap.

It was just half a year ago, in February, that I journeyed to Rennes to see Nadette, for the first time in ten years. I'd phoned her from the TGV and arranged to meet her in my hotel room the next morning. And so I waited. Each time the hotel cleaning women passed I heard the sound of leather against heel. At first, I thought it was Nadette coming, but after a while I could recognise those busy footsteps with near certainty, up and down the corridor, up and down. Flipflap, flipflap.

I had showered early and gone back to bed to wait for her there, watching the Gulf War in TV-silence for fear of not hearing her when she knocked. My hopes were caught in that nomansland between unbridled optimism and the dark chasm of disappointment. So many times in the past she had said she would come and never did. So many times she had said she would be sure to phone and I had stayed in all night, only to go to bed with the memory of her voice ever more distant. It was always the same story: either she couldn't get away from her husband or she was chained down by something to do with the kids. Flipflap, flipflap, flipflap. Women's voices in the corridor but not hers.

I was glad that I had finally made it back to Rennes, that I had at last done what I told Pepe the Spaniard I would do on that night when we talked about our loves as we wandered back from the Irish pub, bouncing off the walls of the Via Masaccio. "But I'm serious, Pepe," I kept insisting, "I really *am* going to go back and see her." Now I was to see her again and it felt as though I would be closer to her in age somehow, even though she was still nine years older than me. I found myself surveying the years since I'd left her to carry on with my studies. I was content, I concluded, content with all the things I'd done: all the marvellous friends I'd made, all the laughter they'd given me, all the places I'd been to, all the discoveries and adventures. Staying with Nadette would have consigned all those things to the status of a stillborn foetus. I was happy with my life. It was then that I resolved the only thing left for me to do was never to allow myself the time to become old, sad, and embittered. I hoped to God it was not too late already.

Flipflap, flipflap, more silence, and then the sound of a knuckle against wood. With a white towel around my waist and butterflies in my stomach, I opened the door. It was like letting sunlight into the room. She was now forty but still glowing with that same elusive something which made me think of the last hum of a lofty bell tower at the siesta hour, sombrely majestic and alone. Her hands were cold against my skin, but light, soft, and inquisitive. "You have the body of a young girl," she said. I gave out a small laugh, amused at her quixotic choice of words. Her hand slid through the overlap of the towel. "Apart from one detail." She undressed by the window in the grey light of a Brittany morning that had suddenly become resplendent.

I held her face in my hands, felt her lips against mine, felt her soft auburn hair on my chest, on my stomach, then my hips. I was transported back to our days and nights together on the rue Charpentier and clichés ran through my head: symphony, harmony, and requiem. It was all like a homecoming on a desert island. But when she eased herself away from me and sank her face in the pillow I felt a shudder. Ridiculously, I thought she was laughing and I asked her what was funny, but when she turned back to me I saw a tear spilling along her nose. She brushed it away but another welled up and scored a fresh path down to her chin. I told her I loved her. It only seemed to sadden her more. "Je t'aime, moi aussi," she said, "je t'aime, Owen. Putain, je t'aime et je t'aurai jamais, pas vraiment." She had said all sorts of things to me before but never had she said this, that she would never really have me. But she was right, and both of us knew she was right.

It was after my last moments with Nadette that I started dreaming of Kynddilig, every once in a while at first but now it's almost night after night. He always appears against some hideously modern backdrop, like the centre commercial at Rennes, an NCP carpark in Manchester, or the lobby of some hotel. Nobody else notices him, this figure that seems to have stepped straight out of the pages of Tolkien. Only I can see him. Sometimes he speaks to me in Welsh, sometimes in English, but he invariably begins the same: "I am Kynddilig the Guide. I am no more a stanger in a land I have never seen than in my own." It is the Kynddilig my mother used to tell me of when she would read me bedtime stories from the *Mabinogion*. He was Arthur's guide, a friend of the likes of Merlin, Taliesin, and Gwrhyr Interpreter of Languages who knew every tongue. It was he and Kei who rode on the back of the great salmon of Llyn Llyw, the oldest and wisest creature of them all. When Arthur's army went to the otherworld of Annwfyn in search of the life-renewing cauldron, Kynddilig was one of the seven that returned. In my dreams Kynddilig always tells me that if I wish to go to Annwfyn he can take me there. He is the only one that knows the way. He stands there with his long white beard and long white hair. His weatherbeaten face looks at me and waits for my answer. He leans on his staff of elder as though tiring under the weight of the long white mantle he calls Gwen. Sometimes I want to tell him that the otherworld is the only place left for me to go. But he always disappears before I have given my answer and his last words are always: "Your father's coming." Like the last time, a few days ago, he was warning me about a castell coch which stood near a mynydd sant. But as soon as I asked him what red castle and what holy mountain, he disappeared and only his voice was left saying, "Your father's coming."

Kynddilig is the last thing on my mind right now as we plough our furrow toward Heidelberg, one coach among scores of coaches all making for the same place. At least with Heidelberg there is nothing to hide. There is nothing about the place which stands out in the foreground of my mind, no associations that link it with nasty marxists or unsavoury chapters of history. Nestling on the banks of the sleepy Neckar, this place is pure feel-good factor. You see smiles on punters' faces here you'd never see in Rome. They feel safe. They have no reason not to. This is the city of Bunsen, inventor of the burner, the city of the Student Prince, of the drinking and duelling societies, of the pillaging French of 1689. This is the city of the renowned and redoutable Perkeo, the court dwarf who drank fourteen litres of beer a day. No, the only thing I have to hide today is my business with the contact.

We drop at the coach park and I lead the way up the steep cobblestones, past the Königstuhl funicular, keeping one eye on the passengers while I look around for the man I'm supposed to meet. We have a bright, sunny morning to keep everything nice and pleasant, thank God. There's nothing like rain for putting a sour face on tourists. I can even afford a wry remark about the Japanese gentleman taking a photo of a real, authentic, Heidelberg litter bin. One click of the camera and he's scurrying off to catch up with the rest of his group. At the entrance to the gardens I point out the archway built overnight as a surprise birthday present for Elizabeth Stuart, the nineteen-year-old wife of Friedrich V. I can't help but add, casting my eyes heavenwards, that although she was Scottish, these are still known as the English Gardens. By the moat that used to be filled with bears I relate how an Englishman once fell in and got eaten; Palmerston sent an official letter of protest, complaining that English subjects were not being protected well enough. Rows of pigeon-chested statues of past rulers line the pink facade of the castle courtyard, and below them, equally stiff, rows of Japanese tourists pose for a group photo.

Zum großen Faß: I indicate the way to the giant wine vat made from 130 oaks and lead on to the rear of the castle for the view over the Neckar and up to the Philosophers' Way. The Japanese, just said cheese, swarm into the rear courtyard and huddle around the footprint made, so legend has it, by an adulterer leaping from one of the regal appartments above. I raise my voice to point out a couple of spires and the turrets of the Karlstor, remind my passengers of the departure time and tell them they're free to do what they want. A man points a lens at me. Click. Yep, that's him alright. No money belt or shorts. Ordinary man-about-town shoes, not trainers or sandals. No lost, searching, what-am-I-supposed-to-be-looking-at-now look. No dashing to the edge like the rest to get a shot of the view. About my age, brown hair, and damn good-looking with it, the bastard. He could easily be mistaken for one of the official photographers were it not for the can of Fanta bulging out of his jacket pocket, a slovenly detail which they would never allow. He lowers the lens. "Suchen Sie jemanden?" he asks in a German that bears the heavy stamp of an Ulster accent. "Ja," I reply, "Patrick. Und Sie?" "Henry," he answers and shakes my hand. He looks a bit heavier around the jowels than usual. Taking a small plastic bottle from the other pocket, he undoes the white cap and shakes out a pill. Sunlight catches on a ring or bracelet and throws back a scintilla of silver as he pops the capsule into his mouth. "Wizhdom teyth," he explains and washes it down with a gulp of Fanta. "M'on antibiotics. Pain in the fokn arse." Aaaa, that's why he was temporarily unavailable.

"There's something wrong with Paddy Henry," he continues. "You've got to hold onto what you're carrying. I can't take it."

"What?!"

"I can't take it."

"Says who?"

"Says Diogenes."

"Shit."

"I know. You're to give it to someone in Lucerne. Rendezvous is Bahnhofstraße, outside the Post Office. I don't know what the fock's going on. There's no time, no description of the contact. That's all there is: Bahnhofstraße, outside the Post Office. Bit of a pisser for you if y'ask me."

"Too right."

"Play it by ear, that's all you can do. And keep your wits about you."

"I hope there isn't any film in that camera there."

"Course not, my friend. It isn't me you've got to fear."

"Diogenes didn't say anything else?"

"No. Sorry. Well, mustn't hang about too long. Go n'eirigh an bóthar leat!"

"Aye. Slán now." He leaves. And may the road rise up to meet you too. I like not this. Something is rotten in the state of Heidelberg. I want to run after him to find out more but it's pointless if what he says is true. So it's me all the way to Switzerland now. Isn't that what I wanted anyway? Yeah, but from the outset, not like this with no time, not knowing who I'm supposed to meet. Uncharted waters. Shit. All of a sudden I've got a nasty feeling about this job.

Having once more gathered my flock together on the coach I do a head-count and give Gilles the signal to move off. While he edges gingerly down the hairpin road Mark Twain once walked up I study my trusty Hallwag map of Germany to see whether my hastily formed contingency plan is feasible. It looks as though it is. We can still do the obligatory stops at Titisee in the Black Forest and at the Rhine Falls. It's just that our routing will be a little different from the usual one. It lacks the streamlining of the normal routing via Freiburg, the one that everyone follows, but that's precisely what I want. Left there by the Ulsterman, looking out over the Neckar and wondering what to do now, I had dire visions of the enemy lying in wait for me at every turn. It could be that someone is after the parcel who should not be after it. And if that's the case the only thing I can do is try to throw a spanner in their works, introduce a sudden variable into the equation in the hope that it might momentarily throw them off balance. It might do no good at all but nothing is lost if it doesn't. I'll tell Gilles that I've heard there are terrible tailbacks along the usual routing that could cost us dearly.

"Via *Stuttgart*?" intones an incredulous Gilles when I put the proposition to him. "You must be joking!"

"No, I'm serious, or do you want to risk losing a couple of hours?"

"It's not normal."

"Normal, schmormal! I thought you came from the land of Danton. You know, de l'audace, de l'audace, et encore de l'audace!"

"And you know what happened to Danton . . . Do you know the way, because I've never done it that way before?"

"Do I know the way? Does the Pope shit in the woods? They don't call me Kynddilig for nothing."

"Who?"

"Never mind. Allez, what d'you say, Gilles?"

"Oh, okay, if you're sure you know the way."

"Don't you worry about a thing."

"Just tell me where to turn right and where to turn left."

"No problem."

Aye, I know the way alright, Gilles, and I don't even need the magical skills of Kynddilig. I've been over this route so many times before, in my head. This time we just do it in reverse. We go Karlsruhe, Stuttgart, Gottmadingen, Schaffhausen, Zurich. It was Lenin who went the other way, from the obscurity of exile in Switzerland all the way to the Finland Station and triumph. I've covered that route so many times that in my wilder moments I can convince myself I was actually there with Lenin, travelling through war-torn Germany in the sealed train with the rest of the comrades, all courtesy of the German General Staff, and the Machiavellian machinations of Comrade Parvus.

Sometimes I see myself there, on 9th April, at the Hotel Zähringerhof, a ghost borrowing time from the future. All the comrades are there for the farewell gathering. Comrade Oskar Blum throws you a glance. He's the one you suspect of being a police spy, an informer. You ignore him and spare a thought for Herr Adolphe Kamerer, your shoemaker landlord. He gave you a pair of good strong hiking boots as a parting gift. No more will you see the cramped rooms of number fourteen Spiegelgasse, the lane of the mirrors. No more will you smell the sausage factory when you open the window. No more will you smell the dung of the Tuesday cattle market. There were two beds, one table and two chairs, all second-hand.

Suddenly your eyes are filled with Inessa's furtive smile. Most of your intimates call you Starik, the Old Man, but she calls you Volodya. You remember the time when you sat with her in the Café Odéon. She pointed at someone and told you it was Herr Joyce. He sat alone at a table drinking coffee and reading a newspaper, occasionally dabbing at his eye with a handkerchief. On the wall behind him hung his hat and cane and the long black overcoat with leather gloves dangling from the pocket. But you were not interested in Herr Joyce. You only had eyes for Inessa, the woman who would always make you melt when she played Beethoven's Appassionata on the piano. Time was short. She had to catch the evening train back to Clarens and you wanted to drink every second of her company to the last drop. You watched her as she sipped her white wine. After forty-three years, Nature had given her chestnut hair a few gentle brushstrokes of white and her large, grey eyes were as captivating as the first day you saw her, seven years before in Paris. She would be with you on that train to Russia but she would not stay with you in Petersburg. After the workers mobbed you at the Finland Station, she left for Moscow, and you felt that the moon had suddenly come between the sun and earth.

"This exit?" asks Gilles.

"Yep."

I present Stuttgart as a bonus, a little diversion we've staged to give the passengers a glimpse of the city that is home to Porsches and Mercedes, standard-bearers of German affluence. In case this is considered too mundane to warrant the diversion, I have Gilles take us to within camera range of the Staatsgalerie so they can say they've seen where one of Germany's most important art collections is housed, albeit only from the outside. But the fidgeting Mr. Miesepeter is underwhelmed. He is not in the least impressed by Stuttgart being Hegel's birthplace nor that the young Schiller was educated here. All the time I can see him thinking well if not Dachau then why for Chrissakes Stuttgart? As Sod's Law would have it, today he's in the front seat, eyes bearing down on me. He looks like one of those passengers who counts everything in dollars. One who worships value for money. One not happy with his life. Probably lives in fear of laughing at the wrong time. No, he's definitely not happy. I wouldn't put it past him to start circulating the story that the only reason we fell upon Stuttgart was that we took the wrong turning and got lost. Well, if that's how he wants it, if he wants to be a thorn in my side I'll make sure he gets the worst room in every hotel. Petty and pusillanimous of me, but effective. Where will his value for money be then? Or even better, how about a dose of ritual humiliation? Expose his weaknesses before the assembled company. Just a mild dose to begin with, a shot across the bows. Get my retaliation in first.

"And while we're on the subject of art, I wonder if anyone can guess the thematic link between Stuttgart and Florence. Any ideas, Mr. Miesepeter?" He fidgets again and rubs the moist grey shadow on his upper lip, the only exposure of a neatly trimmed beard. His eyes dart back and forth across my face, desperately trying to read my intentions.

"Stuttgart and Florence . . . art. . ."

"I'll give you a clue: Judith, the good woman of Bethulia."

"Judith and Holofernes, you mean?" Shit, he's not supposed to know that. What's he doing knowing that?

"That's right."

"Oh, right, I get it. Florence . . . Judith and Holofernes. The Donatello sculpture." Bastard. "Stuttgart . . . now then . . . Oh I get it, there's sumn to do with Judith and Holofernes in the Staatgalerie?" Bastard, bastard, bastard.

"Is the correct answer!" Scrofulous, syphilitic bastard. "Well done . . . Yes," you cock-sucker, "there's a painting by Cranach on the same theme in the Staatsgalerie. Let's hear it for Mr. Miesepeter!" A ripple of applause washes through the coach. He turns to acknowledge the acclaim. So much for my shot across the bows. Hoisted, I'm inclined to think, on my own petard. I invite him to tell the story of Judith and Holofernes. Eagerly he takes the mike.

"Okay, well, okay, I don't know much about Cranach . . . More of a MOMA man if you know what I mean . . . Okay, Judith . . . in the Bible it says there was this guy Holofernes, a Philistine general who went to conquer the Holy Land. And, like, he swept all before him. Really successful guy, you know, kinda upwardly mobile before it was fashionable. So it's all going well till his army lays siege to the town of Bethulia, where there's this woman Judith? And like, the town's ready to give in but Judith persuades the elders to let her go and see Holofernes in his camp. Like, he's all macho and everyone's terrified of him but she figures all men have a weakness . . . You know . . . Guess she was right . . . Okay, so she goes into his camp and he sees her and thinks . . . Like she's a good-looking woman, you know. Ahum . . . Yeah, right . . . So he lets her come and go as she pleases. I mean, no, I don't mean it like that . . . Ahum . . . Right . . . Okay, so one night, she's there serving him wine and dancing for him and flirting and all that stuff, and he thinks like this must be Christmas and Thanksgiving come all at once. So she keeps plying him with wine and he doesn't realise how he's really starting to tie one on because his mind's on other things . . . Guess that still happens a lot now, right? Okay, so he has one pitcher of wine too many and falls asleep. And like that's when Judith takes his sword and cuts off his head and sneaks out of the camp back to Bethulia. So when the soldiers wake up and find their general dead and decapitated there's one hell of a panic. Like, big time. So all the soldiers flee and Bethulia's saved. I guess that's kinda it."

A star is born. Chuck Miesepeter is no longer the loner in the single room. He's one of the crowd, one who knows his stuff. He looks like he's just started enjoying his holiday. He will remember Stuttgart with fondness now. Stuttgart was his big moment. Problem solved.

She stepped out, I stepped in again,
I stepped out, she stepped in again,
She stepped out, I stepped in again,
Learning to dance at Lannagan's ball

Switzerland lies a tantalising fifty metres away. But we remain at a standstill. The Bavarian border guard seems to be taking an unwarranted interest in our French number plate. Images of Steve McQueen's frantic attempts to get over the border leap to the foreground of my mind as I stare at the limp

Swiss flag on its pole, yonder, jenseits, on the other side. Oh, come on, what have the French ever done to you, apart from lay waste vast tracts of Bavaria? Come on, just wave us through like a good fellow. He comes round to my window, looks up and asks what nationality passengers I have. I show him the passenger list. Stonewall face on him. "Südafrikaner?" he asks. "Yes, five of them," I tell him, "that's not going to be a problem is it?" He returns the list and rests a hand on his revolver. "Ausweise!" he orders. I put on my most ingratiating face. "C'mon, you don't really want their passports, do you?"

"Nicht ihre Ausweise. *Ihren* Ausweis will ich mal sehen. Und den des Fahrers auch." God's teeth, what the hell for? Steve McQueen tangled in the barbed wire. Is that how it's going to be for me? Gilles asks what the delay is about.

"He wants to see our passports. Mine and yours."

"Why?"

"How should I know?"

"I've never had to show my passport at any border before."

"Me neither. He must be having a bad day. Bavarian wanker." Gilles twists to get at the briefcase behind his seat. I hoist the money belt up my trouser leg and unzip it. Now, which passport do I give him? The real one? Might be better to give him the false one if I'm in trouble. Quick, decide which one, black or burgundy? No, go for the genuine article. There, one nice, warm British passport. The guard gives Gilles' passport a cursory flick though and turns to mine.

"Und Sie heißen wohl Parry?"

"Yes." And why shouldn't I be called Parry?

"Engländer?"

"Actually, no. Welsh." He gives a dismissive, sour-faced look and waves us through with an imperious "Durchfahren!" Gilles releases the brake with an asthmatic gasp and trundles forward. Come on, Gilles, get your foot down and let's get out of here. Second gear, yes, that's it, thank you. Twenty metres to go. Why did he ask if I was called Parry? Magpie up there. Bad omen. One for sorrow. There another one about? Can't see one. Sorrow it is then. Come on, ten more metres and . . . wonder if it had anything to do with the parcel. Someone onto me already. Five more metres and . . . yes! Oof! Fuck off Germany. You can't catch me now. Never been so glad to be in Switzerland before.

"He took a long time over your passport, didn't he?"

"Aye, he did. It could be that Moroccan stamp I picked up last year. They always take a second look when they see that."

"But why did he ask for our passports at all?"

"Search me, Gilles."

"I suppose that's one thing about this job. After a while nothing surprises you any more."

"Mmm."

Within half an hour we're at Schaffhausen. The passengers admire the thundering waters of the Rhine Falls while I take in a deep lungful of fresh air, relieved that the border is well behind us now. At my side is a smallish guy who said his first name was Leahman, a good ole Georgia boy. Looks a bit like the guy off *The Late, Late Show*. Baseball cap pointing up to the top of the falls. Mouth open.

"Wow!" he says. "To think this is the place where Sherlock Holmes fought with Moriarty!" No, no, it's, oh never mind. Don't want to disappoint him. Reminds me of that other American at the Pitti Palace, puzzling over the Martyrdom of Saint Sebastian. Looked at the body of the agonising saint, all shot through with arrows, and asked me if he was killed by the Indians. Priceless. Then there was that woman complaining it wasn't fair, all those paintings and sculptures of the Madonna and Child. Glad I asked her what wasn't fair. Could barely control myself when I heard her say it wasn't fair because the baby was always a boy.

Leahman. Strange name for a first name. Said the Black Forest reminded him of Georgia. Didn't tell him I'd been there. Georgia on my mind, where no-one bats an eyelid at the sound of gunfire coming from the forest. Deer-hunting they'd think. That green card you have to fill in on the plane to get into America. Question B of the U.S. Department of Justice, answer yes or no: have you ever been or are you now involved in espionage or sabotage or in terrorist activities? Like you're going to say oh yeah, I'm just over for a spot of basic training, and I just lurve your policemen. Taught the basics, that's all. Christ, I'm only a courier.

We soon abandon Schaffhausen and its wonderfully fresh air for the stale, air-conditioned environment that somehow smells of rubber. I unfold a picture of Switzerland which is pure stereotype: chocolate, yoghurt, watches, cowbells, yodeling, William Tell. It's not that I'm avoiding contentious descriptions of the real Switzerland. It's simply that I don't know what the essence of Switzerland is. I have never been able to penetrate this land of carefully cultivated surfaces. It is a land of secrets, a land that defies stethoscopes. We all know about the post-nuclear cities bored into the mountains, we all know about the hidden art treasures and the Nazi gold and the numbered accounts. But what of the rest? I can't help thinking a monumental joke is going on, and the joke's on us. The Swiss seem to invite parodies of themselves, to thrive on them, even. A warrior nation that on countless occasions has repelled the foreign invader when hopelessly outnumbered, a nation whose mercenaries are legend, whose armies drew the admiration of Machiavelli, and yet they invite us to distill all this into the quaint, innocuous image of the Swiss Guards outside the Vatican, costumes by Michelangelo, luvvy. If there's a hard edge to anything, they manage to take it off. Few associate Nestlé with anything nasty. No, Nestlé melts cosily on the tongue to become Nestles and the Milky Bar Kid. Mention Switzerland to anyone and people conjure up images straight from a muesli packet. Heidi, now there's another thing. How could any self-respecting nation actively promote Heidi and still hope to be taken seriously? Unless they're actually taking the piss, killing themselves laughing at the fact that we think the joke's on them. For me, this land is pure conspiracy.

So I give my punters the full monty, tell them everything they want to hear. I can't tell them my joke theory of Switzerland because I'm not sure it's right, so completely do the Swiss have me confused. All I know is that the punters will just love going up the mountain tomorrow, adore the Swiss folk music at the Stadtkeller in the evening, gorge themselves on Swiss chocolate. This is what they have come to Switzerland for. This is what brings the side-splitting shekels in.

The fast-track Transit signs pull us through tunnels and along high-sided flyovers that afford only the briefest glimpses of the city of exiles. Zurich! The city of Joyce, of Lenin, of Rosa Luxemburg. City of towering intellect. People remember Joyce here, and Lenin, but who ever remembers Rosa? Twenty-one years old she was when she was the brilliant young student at the University, one hundred years ago, and I have often pictured her walking – no, limping – along the banks of the Limmat on a Sunday afternoon, her arm threaded through that of the adoring Leo Jogisches. I can imagine the bonnet she wore, tied under her chin with a ribbon, and the ankle-length white dress. I can imagine Jogisches' face reddening with jealousy at her typically casual announcement that she intended to marry a German worker, any German worker, just so she could acquire German nationality. But her face, then, her 1891 face, that's the problem. No sooner do I try to recall the face of serenity and quiet beauty, the face you see on the cover of biographies, than it fades and dissolves into her final face, the 1919 face, bloated, deformed, hideous. One eye, half-closed, has been wrenched down her face, probably the result of a Freikorps rifle-butt crushing her cheekbone. This is the face they fished out of the Landwehrkanal one icy-cold Berlin morning. Probably they raped her, too. Why not? To the trolls of the Freikorps she was not the author of the *Mass Strike* and

Reform or Revolution, one of the most gifted intellects of her generation, no, she was the Jewish bitch, the red whore. Why would they stop at rape?

Why did she step out to lead the workers of Berlin? She must have known the odds were overwhelmingly against the workers and that there was a price on her head. Other comrades tried to persuade her to get out of Berlin, but she still went out to face the drums in the night. She was forty-seven years old then. Perhaps she knew her time had come, that the appointment with death could not be broken. Or perhaps she was broken, in spirit, knowing that it was her own beloved SPD, the party she had risked her life for, the party of the workers, that was training its guns on the Berlin workers. She was killed by the Freikorps but it was the SPD which signed her execution order. Just like Danton, killed by her own. Sobering thought, that. I just hope Lucerne won't be my drums in the night. I'm nothing in comparison with Rosa, but all the same I'd prefer not to be killed by my own. In Zurich she was Anna Matschke. In Lucerne I think I'll be Aaron. I won't use my other name, my fine Irish name. Only two people, maybe three, know that name.

What is this shit with the parcel? Was yer man in Heidelberg to be trusted? Well yeah, a priori at least. The safest pair of hands around, the ponytail said, the fidus Achates. But what about the one I'm to meet in Lucerne: can they be trusted? Like a game of chess. The Greek gift, beware the Greek gift. The adversary nudges his bishop into an exposed position. You take it, and then, wham, out of nowhere he has you in checkmate. The death of the king. But who's the bishop, who's the king, and who the hell am I? Wasn't even given a time for the meeting in Lucerne. No time, no description, no nothing. Play it by ear, the Ulsterman said, that's all you can do. And keep your wits about you. Too bloody right I will. What exactly am I carrying? Not supposed to ask that question but even so, can you blame me? Whatever it is, it can't be entirely harmless. But how harmful is it, could it be, and to whom? The ponytail wishing me good luck back in Brussels: he's never done that before. Later.

Frau Zwingli welcomes us to the Hotel Central, six kilometres outside Lucerne. She is a slender woman of an age you wouldn't dare ask who always wears her black hair tied back. The golden jewellery and the light tan suggest a woman who is living comfortably from tourism. But then, who isn't in Lucerne? Once we've sorted out the room numbers and brought the passengers in to take their keys, she offers me a beer from the bar. "Ah!" she says, stopping in her tracks. "There was a message for you." "From the London office?" I ask. She smiles with a suggestive lifting of plucked eyebrows and reaches behind the desk. "I do not think so. She did not say much over the phone." I take the note and read: "Mein lieber Cicero, I look forward to seeing you again at midday." Teenage porters come in lugging suitcases, followed by Gilles, who asks me his room number before going off to wash the coach. "When did she phone?" I ask Frau Zwingli. More importantly, why the fuck did she phone at all? "About half past four," she replies.

I take to the bar and sit down with a beer to write out a bulletin sheet with the schedules for the next two days. At least we've got two nights in Lucerne which gives me more time to work in. And then we're off to Venice, Italy at last. But why the hell did she phone, leaving a message with a third party like Frau Zwingli? You never know who else could be listening and in these circles it pays to be paranoid. Anybody with a bit of gumption could find out which hotel I'm staying in. It doesn't exactly defy the powers of invention. That's why there's normally only two days between picking up a parcel and getting rid of it. And that border guide asking if I was Parry. There's something seriously wrong. Or is it the opposition that phoned? Ah, now there's a thought. Bad news either way. If it *is* the opposition, then it's really bad news.

Could be a breakdown in the network. The work of an informer perhaps, a viper in the bosom? Would explain the change of plan at Heidelberg. Wish we weren't using Patrick Henry as password: give me liberty or give me death. Bodes ill, what with that and the magpie . . . Make doubly sure the contact is bona fide tomorrow and get rid of the parcel as quickly as possible. Then it's their problem. I'll have done my bit and covered my tracks. But how to make sure, with no name, no description, just the password? At least I know the contact's a woman but only because Frau Zwingli's told me. Think on your feet, mun. That's why you're a tour guide, the problem-solver, remember. Can't contact anyone in the network to get help and risk putting others in the shit. Too short notice as well. Not authorised to, not at this stage anyway. Only in case of extreme urgency. So if I can't contact them, then what can I do? Backed into a corner here. Caged. Trapped.

Having pinned up the schedules on the noticeboard, I escape up to my room. Whichever way they turn, my thoughts on the parcel reach nothing but dead ends. Maybe if I take my mind off it with a bit of television and let someone else's thoughts fill my head for a moment, I'll be able to look at the problem in a fresher light afterwards. It's just turned nine; there might even be some more fall-out from the Soviet Union. I press the button on the remote. The caption in the top left-hand corner confirms that this is the news alright, the German-language version. The screen shows a sequence of drawings in a hue of faded ochre that seem all to depict the Madonna and Child and then, just as I'm thinking of skipping channels, comes the infinitely more arresting image of a haggard old woman with a hooked nose, her head and shoulders covered like a nun's. My curiosity aroused by this woman, I turn up the volume. She leans forward in her chair as if trying to struggle free from the lines of sloping hand-writing that threaten to engulf her. The voiceover says she is

Sophonisba Anguissola, an artist who in her time the equal of Titian was. The sketch shows her at the age of ninety-six. Ironically, the voice continues, Van Dyck also painted her portrait, the whereabouts of which are also unknown. Also? She disappears and I cannot even remember her name, only that it had the sound of the rustle of satin. I aim the remote at the screen again but halt when I hear the name of Diogenes and see him there, on screen, seated in toga with his name clearly written above his head. It is the only drawing in the collection inspired by classical antiquity. The *Italian Sketchbook* remains missing, the voice concludes. No ransom demand has yet been made. The screen switches to the head and shoulders of a newsreader. And now, business news. . .

My own parcel-picture begins to emerge from the shadows of the dead ends. This must be the same story reported in the newspaper I glanced at in Cologne, the one that told of the theft of a Master that had, allegedly, found its way to Prague. Laut der belgischen Kunstbehörden . . . according to the Belgian art authorities, it said, from whom it was presumably stolen. Van Dyck's sketchbook, over three hundred and fifty years old, it said. And then there was the ponytail saying how delicate my parcel is, extremely delicate, sealed up in bubble-wrap and made watertight, destined for a Swiss bank vault. A Swiss bank vault, aye, where better to store a stolen art work? Already millions of them knocking round Switzerland, never seen the light of day for decades. But hold on. Of itself, this does not mean that I am the bearer of Van Dyck's *Italian Sketchbook*. Admittedly, I did take possession of the parcel in Belgium, but let's not get carried away with ourselves. For one thing, how big could this sketchbook be and would it fit into the parcel that can so easily be hidden inside a jacket pocket? And why would we want to steal that sort of thing from the Belgians and put their backs up? But at the forefront of all this stands the name of Diogenes. Diogenes. No, this is too much to be coincidence.

Fuck, what, shiiiit, I'm carrying a priceless art work and the world and his wife are going to be after it, the big-time boys all tooled up to the teeth and they'll stop at nothing to get hold of it. Contract killers, even. I'm a dead man already. Shiiit! No. Du calme, du calme. Deep breaths. Right, there's one sure way to find out if it's the Van Dyck and that's to have a look at it, take a peek. Problem: if it is, and it's over three hundred and fifty years old, what condition's it going to be in? What do I know about handling fragile works of art? Even if I'm really, really careful I could end up destroying it altogether. No. I'm stuck with it. There must be another way out. Think.

Think about my strengths. What have I got? Think back to the seminars on power, all the Machiavelli we poured over at the Badia. Where are you, Niccolò, when I need you? The beast, how does it go again. . .? As a prince is forced to know how to act like a beast, he must learn from the fox and the lion; because the lion is defenceless against traps and the fox is defenceless against wolves. I will be the fox and the lion. But a lion has strength and if I cannot contact the network what strength do I have? I need a resource base to draw from. But I haven't got one. I'm all alone in Switzerland with no-one to help me and I've got to meet some dodgy contact tomorrow. What would you have done, Niccolò? You used to go home at night, take off your soiled rags and don the courtly clothes more appropriate to the world you were about to enter, the world of the great men of the past, where you felt completely at home. You would pace up and down through the night, conversing with Agathocles, Alexander the Great, Philip of Macedon, Petrarch, Savonarola, just as I do with my marxist ghosts. You would listen to them, and they you. It was only the people of Florence who would not listen to you. The people of Florence. Ah now! There's a thought.

The nearest public telephone is about five minutes' walk from the hotel. I lift the receiver, insert enough coins for a lengthy conversation and dial a number in Florence. The long tones of purgatory sound. Come on, you piss-heads. Pick the fucker up. There are more tones, and then that impeccable West-Brit voice, "Pronto. Bar Fiasco."

"Declan, you old fucker!"

"Oh my God! You're not in town, are you?"

"No, I'm not in town. Listen, is Steve there, by any chance?"

"Er, yes. Do you want a word with him?"

"God, there's not much gets past you, is there?"

"Piss off, you . . . Steve! One second, he's just coming. Steve! There's a nasty surprise for you!"

"Thanks, Decky. So nice to be loved."

"Hello?"

"Stevie. Speak in Welsh, and just listen. It's important, yn bwysig iawn, okay."

"Okay. Oes rhywbeth. . .?"

"Just listen a sec. I've got a message for the Celtic lad from Spain. You know who I'm talking about?"

"Erm, there's only one person here who fits that bill. Shall I get him?"

"No, it's better if I give you the message in Welsh. Damage limitation, you know."

"Are you in some kind of trouble, Owen?"

"No more than usual."

"Anything I can do?"

"Just translate this for him and don't tell anyone else: Breogan, cyfarfod dydd Gwener, un o'r pnawn, yn y dref ble roedd. . ."

The message, like the parcel, should be watertight. Steve will have understood everything apart from the reference to Breogan, so his innocence in my sordid affairs cannot be compromised. Any uninvited ears would be unlikely to understand Welsh and even less likely to know who Breogan was. And even if they did happen to know he was a Celtic hero there is absolutely no possibility of their knowing the significance of the name for myself and Pepe. Not that Pepe knows my fine Irish name, but he does know of the clandestine work I do because I let it slip one night when the grappa loosened my tongue. That night Pepe told me not to die too young because he'd miss me too much, but he swore himself to secrecy and said that if ever I was in a fix and needed his help, I should just mention Breogan. So Breogan it is.

4

"It was the celebrated writer, Samuel Langhorne Clemens," I begin, "who came here and was so moved by the Lion Monument that he said that anyone who does not weep on seeing it has no soul. Does the name ring any bells?" Before me is a sea of bemused faces, the becalmed waters illuminated only by the sudden beacon flash of Leahman's features. "Mark Twain!" he shouts out, just beating Chuck Miesepeter to the answer. A brolly-hoisting city guide passes by with a nodding "Grootsie mittenan!" and stations herself at a convenient gap for her tourists to fill. As she will soon do, I recount the story of the Swiss Guards massacred at the Tuileries defending Marie Antoinette against the Paris mob. Grootsie mittenan, I muse as we troupe back to the coach, what a strange form of greeting, half-French with the mittenan for "maintenant", and half German with that curious derivation from "grüßen". And there's another thing: why do so many Swiss towns end in – ikon? Dietlikon, Pfäffikon, Gerlikon, Effretikon . . . you'd think that'd be more Greek than anything else. I have asked but never got an answer. Sing-song Effretikon, grootsie mittenan. No, decidely, I'll never get to the bottom of the Swiss. And as for yer fella Twain, just can't fathom him either. What was it so moved him about the Lucerne Lion? All those Swiss dying in a foreign field? What's so bad about dying in a foreign field anyway? Wouldn't think it'd make much difference to your death.

After dropping a few passengers in the centre of town we speed off towards Stans. Gilles bets that with the low-lying cloud we won't be able to see much from the top of the

Stanserhorn. He's never been up a Swiss mountain, he says, always been stuck below waiting for the punters to come back down. Mount Pilatus, Titlis, Rigi, Stanserhorn, it's always the same story. Besides, he doesn't imagine it to be as good as the Pyrenees. At least there, you have the sea as well. Switzerland is too locked-in, too encircled. "T'as raison," I agree, and wish he'd chosen another day to bring up encirclement. Cicero, the contact called me. Didn't he come to a sticky end too? Or no, didn't he foil a conspiracy or something, rather than end up the victim of one? Within half an hour we're at the tiny town of Stans. There's something touching about the way the passengers get off the coach and then try to suppress their child-like haste to board the little red train that would not look out of place in Trumpton. I pay for our tickets and take my habitual place as temporary shotgun at the front of the train. The old driver steps stiff-limbed aboard and from beneath the shiny peak of his black cap raises an obligatory "Grootsie!" This is all he ever says to me. His disinclination to conversation, I prefer to think, does not arise from his being a miserable old sod who's just counting the days to retirement, but from the well-founded conviction that I'd have the divil of a time understanding a blind word he'd say. The ascent begins. Before us stretches a sinewy grey cable, vibrating on its rollers, pulling us gingerly up the sharpening incline. Fresh green pastures begin falling away to left and right, dotted by solitary reds and purples and whites.

Mum would have known the names of all these flowers and she'd have smiled, huh, clutching her handbag, and said this is lovely. Lovely, the word that was always on her lips when she came to see me in Italy. The Leaning Tower: lovely. Siena: lovely. The view from Fiesole: lovely. Seoirse, Dario, Nereo, all my friends at the Badia: lovely. It was just Florence: lovely . . . but dusty. Made her bad eye weep, the dust. So much I still wanted to show her. So many more lovelies I wanted to hear her say. A simple woman, really. Simple, in the nice sense.

So euphoric when I made it to university. The chance to escape the working class and that was it, her proudest achievement, that one of her children had made it to university. Tears by my Ford Anglia when the day came to go. You write first, she sobbed, you'll have more to write about. Tears of sadness, fair to say, but tears of achievement. Against all the odds she'd managed it. Made fairground toys at night for pin money. Slave labour. I saw the boss's Merc once, and his tan. It's called surplus value, Mum, not that you ever saw it that way. Scrimped and saved and kept the gas fire off, pretending it wasn't cold when it was. Embarrassed about my free school dinners because she didn't like charity. And all that without Morgan Owen Parry, died when Owen Morgan was ten. Sent her money out of my grant for the bills. Put the fire on whenever you want, Mum. But you didn't, did you? No surprise when the cause of death came as pneumonia. You never knew how ridiculous it all felt, that morning in August when it was hot and, yes, dusty, and I wound my way down to the bus stop. Urgent message waiting for me at the Badia. I wound my way down and recited the words "today, mother died, or perhaps it was yesterday" and it felt ridiculous and absurd, but the words, at least, were right.

The train slows alarmingly, as though it has run out of the necessary puff to make it the last ten metres. But we finally set foot on terra firma, only to abandon it again for the perils of the cable car. The guard slides the door shut and presses a button. Knuckles whiten on the handrail, and up we go. Up, up, and ever upwards. Trees and cows begin to take on the dimensions of a Lego landscape. A jerking of the jaw clears the blockage in my ears. I am not one for heights. They put the shits up me. How anyone can derive pleasure from hang-gliding or parachuting or bungee-jumping is quite beyond me. At least I'm used to the cable cars of Switzerland, though, and my prime concern is for the fears of my passengers, but only because I have been blamed before for having subjected them to terror unbearable. But it's the pylons that get me. Were it not for the pylons I'd ascend the mountain like any true son of the Alps, with utter indifference. It's just those moments when the car lifts over the pylon and then plummets for what seems like several seconds, in reality barely one. Here we go now. Huu*uuup*, and *aaaaaaarrrgh!* Balls shooting out my mouth at the speed of light.

> From Bantry Bay to Derry Quay
> From Galway to Dublin town
> I never seen such a grand colleen
> As the girl from County Down

My legs are still a bit shaky from the cable car descent, but at least in the ride back from Stans my testicles have regained the weight God intended for them. Most of my passengers dive straight into Bucherer's, the imposing department store dominating the Schwanenplatz, Lucerne's equivalent of Harrods or Macey's. Others go to change money. None of them seemed disappointed that the summit of the Stanserhorn was wrapped in a blanket of white mist, just as Gilles had predicted. If anything, I think they quite enjoyed the atmosphere of mountain hide-and-seek. Now it's my turn. I compose myself, wind up my senses to maximum alertness, and set off for my rendez-vous with the contact, the mystery female who called yesterday. She might already be waiting at the post office on the other side of the river, whoever she is. Passing the Schwanen-Café, I pretend not to have seen the bearded face at the window and carry on, only to be caught up moments later by the same Bill, yet another Austerlitz colleague. I shake his hand, genuinely pleased to see him again, only wishing that our meeting fell at a more convenient moment. "How you doing, Bill?" He pushes his glasses back on his nose. He is dressed as always in his elegant black suit and white shirt. Together, we must look like something out of the Blues Brothers.

"Great," he answers. "Yourself?"

"Yeah, fine."

"Where you heading?"

"The bank. I've got to sort out something to do with the Finalba credit slips."

"Oh well, I'm going that way too." Shit! "So what tour you doing?" he asks. We turn the corner by the river. I think of taking the long way round via the Spreuerbrücke to stall for time.

"The Cavalcade, shortened version, missing out Austria, thank God. Yourself?"

"The Grand. Thirty-two days! Although, at the moment they look a pretty nice group, so I'm hoping it turns out okay. Early days, though, early days." The Kapellbrücke stands before us, the wooden bridge with the water tower you see on all the brochures of Lucerne. I decide against taking the Spreuerbrücke: it would look decidedly odd. I try to steal a look across the river to see who might be waiting by the post office but my view is blocked.

"Yeah," I say as we walk up the steps of the bridge. "Still, I had a Grand last season and it worked out just fine. Best group of the season in fact. Just don't count the days, that's the secret." Shit. How the fuck am I going to get rid of him without?

"Are you doing the Stadtkeller tonight?" he asks.

"Yeah. You too?"

"Yep. But we're in fucking Entlebuch, would you believe?" My eyes flit over the triangular pictures wedged into the roof of the bridge. Scenes from the lives of St. Ledger and St. Mauritius. Indecipherable gothic script. If I don't go into the bank with him he's going to think something's up. If I do, it could frighten the contact off.

"Entlebuch?" I commiserate. "I was stuck out there once." Amid the bodies milling along the bridge I spot the head and shoulders of someone in white. It can't be. No, for a moment there I thought I saw Kynddilig, standing with his arms folded as though intent on blocking Bill's path.

"God, what a pain, though! It's a good job I booked the Stadtkeller for the second night. I booked it for the first night once and then I got a hotel change at the last moment. Never again, Owen, I can tell you."

"Yeah, I always book for the second night as well."

"By the way," Bill continues, "I saw Kees on the road, you know, the Dutch guy. He's arriving this evening. Lucky sod, he's in the Hotel Flora, right in the middle of town. He'll be at the Stadtkeller tonight as well, back for some more Swiss folk night punishment."

"Oh good," I reply. "It'll be good to see him again. I like Kees." A tramp shuffles past in a dirty white overcoat. He must have been the figure in white I glimpsed a moment ago. Hang on, though, what's a tramp doing in squeaky-clean Switzerland? Don't they throw them out here? And in a leather overcoat? Bill stops suddenly.

"Shit!" he exclaims, rubbing his forehead. "I've forgotten to pay Gübelin a call. I suppose I'd better do that now. You never know, one of my pax might just buy a Rolex there. You been already?"

"Yeah."

"Listen, I'm going to shoot off back now. I'll see you tonight anyway."

"Okay, Bill," I say, turning to watch him retrace his steps along the bridge. The tramp has disappeared, and soon Bill, too, is swallowed up in the flow of bodies. I give myself a shake and tell myself to concentrate on the business in hand. Check the parcel. If the contact's not bona fide I'll say I don't have it on me and stall for time. Don't want it falling into the wrong hands. I take a deep breath and stride out. The bells of the Jesuit church chime. Midday. I'm late.

I always try to get there early when I'm meeting a contact, to get a feeling for the place, see how the land lies. Besides, I prefer to see the contact coming before they see me. It makes me feel more in control. Down the steps and left along Bahnhofstraße, must't hurry. Last time I was down here was taking Kane to the station.

-Sure you got your passport?

-Aye, such as it is. Listen, Owen, I'm not out of the woods yet but whatever happens, I owe you one.

I wait by the entrance to the post office, standing crane-like with a foot against the wall. A woman drags a wailing toddler past and shouts, "Schreh nöt so luht!" Schrei nicht so laut, could that be? Don't shout so loud? Concentrate on the job, Owen. The fox and the lion, Owen, fox and lion.

"Ach, Cicero," I hear a woman's voice exclaim, "da bist du endlich!" Lips are pressed against my right cheek and I turn to meet the beaming face of a young blond woman.

"Ja, da bin ich," I mumble hesitantly. Yes, here I am, and who are you, I wonder. She threads an arm inside mine. "Where now?" she asks.

"I know a restaurant not far from here." We start back up Bahnhofstraße, looking for all the world as though we have known each other for ages. We could be Rosa and Leo on the banks of the Limmat.

"Your name?" I ask in a low voice.

"Effi."

"And I'm Aaron. Not Cicero, please."

"Good. By the way, Patrick Henry in Heidelberg says hello."

"Excellent." Good sign, that. She knows the password. But what about Diogenes? A notice by the Jesuit church mentions Loyola's quincentenary. We cross over the road.

"Which restaurant are you taking me to?" Effi asks.

"Valentino's, on the Weinmarkt. It's an Italian restaurant, Effi." Swans preen themselves at the water's edge. At the brow of the half-dozen steps that rise to meet the Reuss-brücke the white outline of the Hotel Gutsch appears in the distance, looking down disdainfully from the crest of its wooded hill. I suppose Effi could be just as suspicious of me as I am of her. Speaking to me in Hochdeutsch. Doesn't necessarily mean she's not Swiss.

"They're very accommodating at Valentino's," I tell her, "because I always leave a huge tip so they should give us a nice friendly welcome." Besides, there's a back door onto the street through the kitchen. One quick side-step and you're out in Fischmarktgässli. "Good," she replies in a neutral tone, "although I'm not very hungry." The river flows ever faster, hurtling towards the wooden weir. The path along the river narrows. Single file only here. Effi frees her arm. Ahead, I can already see the relief of the crucifixion on the central pillar of the Spreuerbrücke. Medieval fortifications come into view over on the right, the other side of the river. That'll be the Männli Tower, then the Luegisland Tower then the fucking hell, Owen, take your mind off the tourism bit and concentrate on

"Couldn't we have taken the Reuss-brücke, Aaron, to get to Weinmarkt?" I try to reassure her with a smile.

"It's just that I like the Dance of Death along the Spreuerbrücke here." No, that wasn't the right thing to say. "Besides, it's noisier and I like the noise." She stops to stare at me, her green eyes decidedly hostile. Pretty, though.

"I am not wired, Aaron, if that's what you're thinking. You can search me if you don't believe me."

"No, that's . . . that's not necessary." We turn left around a sharp corner then right up the steps leading onto the bridge, to be greeted with the smell of fresh, crashing water mingling with the deep reek of oak. Hideous skeletons appear overhead, laughing and dancing all the way along to the other quay. The bridge bends round. You would have to shout to make yourself heard above the rush of the weir. Another set of steps leads down onto a cobblestoned street decked out with flags of all colours. More flags than usual. Celebrating the eight hundredth anniversary of the Everlasting League of Swiss cantons. Now, let's see: don't want to get lost and make a dick of myself. A right and a left, fountain of the wine market, Metro snack bar on the left then Valentino's on the right by the Hôtel des Balances. Yep. Here we are. *The Last Supper* on the façade up there. Could maybe have chosen a better setting. Hôtel des Balances. Hotel of the scales. Used to be the palace of justice.

The waitress plants a bottle of Fleurie on the table and goes to attend to other customers. I catch snippets of conversation in Italian, German, French and American. Let the game of chess begin. "So, Effi, what are your instructions?" Yes, she is pretty. Straight blond fringe. Olive green jacket. A firmness in her eyes. The thought of searching her. I pour out the wine. She leans forward.

"To inform you, Aaron."

"*Oh!* Ma guarda chi c'è!"

I look up and acknowledge the salad waiter, fresh from the kitchen: "Sergio! Ti vedo in forma."

"Eh, come sempre, sai."

"To inform me about what, exactly?" She clears her throat. "You are to retain the package. Someone will contact you in Rome."

"Jesus. . ." I whisper through my teeth.

"The contact will meet you at the Cafe San Pietro, on the morning of your second day." I feel my jaw begin to drop. Another three days! Jesus, Mary and sodding Joseph!

"That's excellent. Just great! At a place which just happens to be swarming with every kind of guide under the sun."

"If you say so. I don't know the place."

"And then what?"

"Then. . ." She shrugs. "Then, I don't know. These are the only instructions I have to give you. It isn't my fault and if I could help you any further I would, believe me. I'm only telling you what I was told."

"Yes, yes, I know it's not your fault. I'm sorry if I gave that impression."

"Forgive me for saying this, but I'm glad I'm not in your

shoes. If there's. . ." I begin to laugh. "What is it?"

"Oh, I'm sorry, Effi. It just struck me as an odd way of putting it." I see the waitress approaching with our order.

"Putting what?"

"I don't know. Your sympathy?"

"Allora, linguine con pesto per la signora, ed un bel risotto di mare per te." I smile and wait until she is out of earshot.

"There's something wrong, isn't there, Effi? With the operation, I mean." Her eyelids close for a moment.

"Yes."

"Can you tell me what it is? It might help."

"I cannot tell you what it is because they didn't tell me. But they did tell me that it was serious. Very serious. And they're counting on you to make it a success. I can tell you one thing, although. . ."

"Don't, if you're not supposed to."

"Although I'm not sure if it's relevant. I wasn't supposed to be your contact. I was only told at the last moment."

"That's why you phoned?"

"Yes. I had to."

Aye, the fox and the lion, and what happens now, Niccolò? Who is telling the truth? Who do I trust? Wonder where she's from. Swiss perhaps. Not Irish at any rate. Germanic in her looks and in her answers, thank God. Perhaps Austrian. Or maybe a combination of the Germanic and something else, like who was it Terry and Pietro were talking about on the Rhine cruise? The one shouting at the poor receptionist in Lourdes, aye, Kristine. Effi: maybe comes from eftechia, is it, Greek word for happiness. Doesn't look all that happy.

"Have you been enjoying the celebrations, Effi?" She looks up from her plate with some surprise.

"Please?"

"The Everlasting League celebrations."

"No," she says, suddenly sanguine, adopting the kind of smile reserved for a stupid question. "That's not till next week." And then her face changes. The fox has struck. So you are Swiss. How else would you know that? "Do you know," she says, shifting uneasily in her seat, "why this place is called Valentino?" Change of subject, defensive move, Effi. Don't overdo it, Owen. Swiss, eh?

"I suppose someone here has a penchant for the film star. Maybe they originate from the same town as him. What I mean is, no, I don't know."

An uncertain smile, tucking into her food. Feel free to underestimate me, Effi, if you be from the opposition. Nikki i thanatos, victory or death: I will be like the women of Souli, dancing over the precipice to eternity, indifferent to death, the Greek women who refused to become Turks. Or like the real Valentino, the one Niccolò called Valentino, Cesare Borgia. Aut Cesare aut nihil inscribed on his sword: either Caesar or nothing. Now there was one who would not settle for mediocrity. I'll declare war on the lot of yez. Sipping her wine. Subtle lips. Hint of lipstick.

"There is one final thing," she says, "and it is very important. You must not break cover."

"You mean I should stay with the tour?" Her smile is broad and warm.

"That is your cover, isn't it?"

"Aye, it is, for better or worse."

"Do you know what you will do now?" she asks. Is she genuinely concerned? I detect a slight tension in her eyebrows and notice that they are a couple of shades darker than her hair.

"Er no," I reply. "Not exactly. But I'll think of something. At least, I hope to God I do."

"Don't get caught."

"I don't intend to."

"I wouldn't like that."

"I think I would like it even less. All the same, it's a bit of a tall order, having to hang on all the way to Rome."

"I know you can do it."

"How do you know that, then?"

"An intuition. Not female intuition, *my* intuition."

"And does your intuition tell you anything else?"

"Yes."

"And what's that?"

"That you will get caught."

"Ah." That bloody magpie. No, she's just joking. Certain coquettishness in the play of her eyes. Playing to her strengths. Ring on her finger there. Two hands clasping a crowned heart.

"You aren't married, then, Effi? Just making small talk, you know. That's a claddagh ring you've got there, isn't it?"

"No, I'm . . . I'm between relationships at the moment. I live in Frankfurt. And you?"

"London."

"Do you like it there?"

"Not really, but it has its good points. It's mainly an Irish area but we've got everything really, Asians, West Indians, Turks, Greeks, a bit of everything."

"Have you been to the West Indies?" Ah, right, steering well clear of anything Irish, taking the conversation to the other side of the world.

"No. Maybe one day, if I'm not caught."

"Oh, you should go. I was there last Christmas, when it's their summer. Saint Lucia first, and then I went to the French islands. You wake up in the morning and it's just like being in France. The letter boxes are the same, the street signs with all the same names of famous Frenchmen, the banks are the same. And there's a statue of Joséphine in the square called the Savanne and, well, she was born in Martinique so it makes sense. But the nights are the best. I've never seen so many stars in the sky, stars I hadn't seen before, so big, so bright, but so many. It's like a deep, black diamond mine over your head. You really should go. I'm sorry . . . You must be sick of tourists telling you holiday stories."

"Ah, y'know. . ."

You have plundered many nations
Divided many lands
You have terrorised their people
You rule with an iron hand

When I proposed coffee Effi said she had to leave. She
didn't say why and my asking would have suggested an
unwarranted curiosity in her affairs. I wished her well and took
a good look at her as she walked towards the door: olive green
summer jacket tapering in at the waist, white skirt, slender
calves marred only by the red patch of recently crossed legs.
Apart from a slight heaviness in her gait, there was nothing
uncommon or surprising in her externals. She would have
blended in almost anywhere. It was rather Giovanna the
waitress who surprised me. She must have seen me observing
Effi. She can only be in her mid-twenties and yet it was with
the tone and countenance of a mother giving advice to a son
that she bent towards me and said, "Never trust a woman who
dyes her hair. Non so se mi spiego." And she said she understood when I asked if I could leave by the back door. But then,
is Giovanna's advice to be trusted? After all, she did once
confess to supporting Juventus.

Gilles, however, is an uncomplicated case. He tells me that
he called Carine from the telephone exchange on Bahnhofstraße this morning. It couldn't have been all that long after I
met Effi on the corner. He is elated. They had a long talk and
for the first time Carine told him that she wanted to have a
baby. They had discussed the matter before, in the abstract,
but this time she had her heart set on it. He says it was a good
job the booth was sound-proofed otherwise half of Lucerne
would have heard his cry of delirium. "You don't know what
it means to me, Owen," he sighs, with a peculiarly beatified
look on his face. Obviously not.

Once everyone is off the coach I lead up Ledergasse in the
direction of our evening's entertainment at the Stadtkeller. A

voice behind me comments on how wonderfully clean the streets are here. And what will they think of Italy, I wonder? Okay, so there's the Pantheon that Michelangelo said must have been built by angels, but the mess! The noise! The chaos! Punters always prefer Switzerland, because the people are polite, they all speak English and the streets are clean.

A buxom Heidi in folk costume shepherds my passengers to their places. The hall is already filled with punters sitting expectantly at tables laden with litres of beer and copper fondue pans. The stage is draped with huge Swiss flags and has for its backdrop the projected image of an Alpine idyll. Saving a seat for Gilles, I sit down in the corner reserved for guides and drivers, far from the spectacle we've all seen countless times. "We meet again, D'Artagnan," says Bill, shaking my hand. "Sorry I had to rush off like that this morning." He reminds me of St. Paul, jutting beard and fiery eyes. Only the sword is missing. A kind of designer St. Paul, only nice. Beside him sits Kees the Dutchman, loosening his tie. "Hi, Owen," he says, and with another tug, "I don't know why we wear these fucking things, choking ourselves to death all day."

"Because if you don't," says Bill, "it means that you don't care about your appearance and that means you're sloppy, and therefore a sloppy guide."

"It's alright for you," Kees retorts. "You don't even have to shave in the morning. There's another pain in the arse for you."

"And what's wrong with growing a beard?" says Bill, stroking his own with pride.

"What, and look like some Wild Man of Borneo like you?"

"He might be a swagbellied Hollander," Bill tells me, "making piles of money out of the business but he does like to whinge."

"Whinge?" says Kees. "You should have heard one of mine this morning up at Heidelberg." Pulling a parsimonious face, imitating a whining American accent. "'I thought we were going to see a proper castle. Newswansteen's a proper castle but this is only the shell of a castle.' *That* was whinging."

"So what did you say to her?" asks Bill.

"I told her it's pronounced Neuschwanstein."

"Ooh, dear, dear," says Bill, wagging a finger. "No tip for you there. Ah!" A fondue pot is placed before us. Kees rubs his hands and rolls up his sleeves. Bill skewers a piece of bread in the basket. Kees takes hold of his fork and points it at a face in the hall.

"That's the woman over there. If she carries on like that I think I'll inject her case with battery acid. Then after her first wash back in the States she'll have clothes looking like Emmental cheese."

The music starts up on stage, a hurdygurdy ensemble in costume plucking, blowing, and tinkling away with disinterested gazes. I introduce Gilles as he takes his seat next to me. He had some trouble parking the coach; still, he says, what does that matter in the wider scheme of things? And did I remember to order the steak for him?

"Here, you're Irish aren't you, Owen?" says Kees all of a sudden. He must have taken me seriously the last time.

"Sometimes. Depends who I'm with." He waves away the nuance like a troublesome mosquito.

"I saw in the paper this morning about an Irishman being stabbed to death last night in Heidelberg. Terrible, isn't it?"

"Terrible if you were him, I suppose. How come he was stabbed? Did it say?"

"Not really. Something about it might have been neo-Nazis."

"I thought it was the Turks they were after," Bill interjects.

"Did they say where he was stabbed?"

"In the back, I think."

"No, sorry, where in Heidelberg?"

"Do you think the poor guy cares what part of town he was killed in?"

89

"Just asking."

"Bunsenplatz, I think it said."

"They'll be killing people for having long hair next," says Bill.

"And did the paper say how old he was?"

"What, you want his biography? I was only reading the morning paper for God's sake." Don't push it too far.

"But you know how everyone in Ireland knows everyone else. It could have been someone I know."

"I don't know. Thirty-something. Thirty-three?"

"The year of sorrows," Bill intones.

"I'm sorry, Gilles," I say, "are we cutting you out of the conversation?"

"No, no. You talk, I eat."

Yes, you eat while I think. Bill and Kees getting stuck into the nosebag too. Killed by Bunsenplatz. Could it have been the guy I met, the Ulsterman? Why am I going all goosepimply and thinking about Kynddilig again? And imagining I saw him in the flesh today when it was only a tramp. Fact is I *wanted* it to be Kynddilig, so he could cast a spell and get rid of Bill for me. I'm losing my marbles. Have to keep a firm hand on the tiller. But, shit, the Kynddilig dream where he warned me about the red castle, y castell coch. The red castle by the holy mountain and dear suffering Jesus that's Heidelberg. Original settlement on the site of a pagan temple. Heilig-berg, holy mountain, mynydd sant, God's teeth, and the castle *is* red. It is. Warning me that the guy was going to be killed? No, it can't be. But Bill did go off in the same direction as the tramp and, God damn it, it *is* strange seeing a tramp in Switzerland. They just don't have them. Well, maybe Zurich, but not toytown Lucerne. Could it really have been Kynddilig? Get a grip, for God's sake, Owen. I am a dialectical materialist, a logical, rational marxist. Can't be doing with all this Celtic mysticism. And that funny feeling that came upon me in Germany when I was thinking of Ganelon the traitor? A presentiment? A nasty forethought?

The audience runs through a yodel chorus with their hostess. After the third chorus she points into the crowd and cajoles reluctant individuals into joining her on stage. They form a line, all looking self-conscious, folding their arms or hiding their hands in their pockets, trying to act normal. None of them knows that they are about to be invited to produce a note from the six-foot Alpenhorn, nor that they will have to try a solo yodel, least of all that a two-litre glass of beer is already being prepared for them behind the bar.

"Bill, I couldn't borrow your mobile phone, could I?"

"Of course."

"Can I phone outside Switzerland on it?"

"All over Europe. What, you phoning ahead to Venice?"

"Yeah. I'm still two twins short at the hotel. You know the story."

"God yes, you'll need to get that sorted out."

"Sure you don't mind me using your pride and joy?"

"What are we here for if not to help each other on the road?"

Sweet tranquility comes to meet me as I close the door on the Stadtkeller. How the hell do you use these things? Pull out the ariel? And what's the code for Heidelberg again? Six two two one and then Thomas's number. Please be in, Thomas. If he doesn't know the full story then I don't know who does. Ah, at least it's ringing. C'mon, c'mon. Did I not pick you for every game we played in Florence? Okay, so I could have passed the ball to you more often. But didn't I buy you three pints of Guinness that time we beat the butchers of Greve, one for every goal? C'mon, c'mon, Thomas, don't let me down.

5

"Welcome to the Valley of No Return," Nadette announces with a smile, "autrement dit, the city of Heidelberg." I walk on beside her, down a street full of ghostly faces coming and going, faces behind their masks, pale corpses without rest. The night air is dimmed by shades of pink and ochre and all the clouds have turned blood red. Just now it seemed to me I heard a scream passing through nature. "What are you doing?" I ask her. "I'm doing your job," she answers, "just like you do. Kynddilig said I could. And this street is called Karl Johan." "No it isn't, Nadette, it's the Hauptstraße and this is the Holy Ghost church." She frowns. "Okay, okay," I say, putting an arm round her bare shoulders, "it's Karl Johan." "That's better, Owen. I'll leave if you want me to." "No, no, carry on." She scurries ahead of me to creep up behind an unsuspecting man. The hem of her yellow skirt tightens around her buttocks. She thrusts her microphone over his shoulder. "Pardon, Monsieur, do you know Aidan Flynn?" "Never heard of him," he replies gruffly. Laughter from a studio audience rings out. "And have you heard of Thomas Rhenish?" "Aye, he'll be the journalist from hereabouts. Studied in Florence with yer man." Applause. Nadette waves back at me, still following behind the man. It's good to see her enjoying herself. "Do you know what was in Owen's parcel?" she asks him. "You'll have to excuse me, Nadette," he says, "but I don't speak French and I'm after being stabbed." More canned laughter. "Do you know where to die?" she asks cheerfully, playing up to the audience. "Oh aye, just by Bunsenplatz over there." Don't get too far away now, Nadette. I quicken my step. The man falls to the ground by a statue of a slave grimacing in his chains. Nadette kneels beside him and lifts his head. A pool of blood begins to form around her knees. "Why is he dying, Owen? It isn't fair." Her auburn hair drapes over his face, covering his features. "He's dying because someone stabbed him and Thomas says it wasn't neo-Nazis, sozusagen." I want her to hug me instead of him but she stays clutching him in her arms. "I don't want to die sa samhradh," he murmurs. "Qu'est-ce qu'il dit, Owen?" "He doesn't want to die in the summer," I explain, trying to make light of the situation. A scream pierces the air. "Is that the banshee?" he asks with a fearful start, and then relaxing again, submitting to his fate, "My time is worn out, past, críochnaithe. . ." He doesn't have the strength to continue. Nadette presses an ear to his mouth and listens. He convulses and coughs. She loops a mesh of hair around her ear and turns to me, her face bespattered with freckles of blood. "He says you must look after Aidan Flynn." "Tell him I'll do that," I assure her. She whispers in his ear. He coughs again. "We'll have to go now, Owen," she says sadly. "No stay, Nadette. We can go to Tangier together. You can sunbathe. Don't leave me again." "I have to bury him in the Valley of No Return. Et puis, it was you who left me, Owen." I suddenly realise that she is dead. Should I break the news to her? No, it will only upset her and then she'll definitely leave with him. And she looks so beautiful like this anyway. "Je t'aime, tu sais," I whisper, and blow a kiss. "Regarde, Owen!" she says, pointing behind me, "voilà Kynddilig." I turn round but see only a deserted street and when I turn back Nadette has gone too. There is only the man bleeding to death by the stone cold statue of the man in chains. And a piercing scream in my heart.

Our morning landscape is one of mountains and ravines, glaciers and waterfalls, a harsh, rugged terrain mirrored in the steady flow of uncompromising Germanic place names: Amsteg, Gurtnellen, Wassen, Wattingen. Scuttling ant-like along the bottom of the Reuss Valley, you cannot escape the impression of your own insignificance before Nature. Hemmed in between plunging gradients of fir or pine, you feel infinitessimally small and transient. Nature dominates you. It has age over you. It has size. It has permanence. Even the castles clinging to the bare, brown rock, tenants of a mere six centuries or so, look down with misty disdain in the certain knowledge that they have seen far better than you. What are you compared to the great, glinting armies they have seen sweeping through the valley? You are just one little speck of no moment or import, a flea heading south to easier climes, where it belongs. And then you come to the St. Gotthard tunnel, seventeen kilometres of tenuous penumbra burrowing through the stifling granite all around you. Above you, a mile of rock presses down. Your fate is in someone else's hands, the gods', the engineers', the mountain's, who knows? All you know is it's not in your own hands. And just to reinforce the all-pervading sense of alienation, there's one final touch, a sublimely Brechtian coup de théâtre. Every five minutes a voice from the tunnel interrupts our radio to ask us kindly to keep our speed to eighty kilometres an hour, thank-you very much. It even interrupts me when I'm talking on the mike, letting everyone know precisely who's in charge. The effect is disconcertingly eerie. But the mountain is magical as well as threatening. While we have been in the tunnel the Zauberberg has cast a spell. Suddenly the country finds itself in different clothes. Gone are the sombre, dowdy rags. It's time for colour and flamboyance. The Valle Leventina we burst into rings out with names like Airolo and Faido, Giornico and Personico. Biasca! Lodrino! Bellinzona! It's as though we're already in Italy and listening to one of those over-excited football commentators. Cadenazzo! Robasacco! Rivera! And AUSFAHRT has become uscita. At last we are sliding down the umbilical cord to Italy.

I am in buoyant mood, having told myself that if there are going to be any problems today I will confront them when they happen and not worry about them in advance. The only thing I have to concentrate on is the contingency plan for the parcel. As for omens, magpies, dreams and Kynddilig, they can all take a back seat today. The border crossing at Chiasso holds no fear for me either. I just know it's going to be a doddle. Another day, another border: that's all there is to it. It matters not one jot that it all went horribly wrong for Mussolini at Chiasso. So what if it was the place where the Duce turned impotentate? So what if Chiasso was the nemesis that led straight to Milan's Piazzale Loreto, where he and Clara Petacci would end up dangling from a meat hook like chickens at the market, spat at and kicked by the partisans? So sodding what? If Chiasso's a bad border for fascists, then it must be a good one for Commies like me. End of story.

Crouching beside me is Lizzie, the South African who way back on the Rhine enquired whether I was married. She asks if I can get Gilles to turn the air conditioning up. It's just a little too hot back there, she says. I relay the message to Gilles and seize the opportunity to ask Lizzie if she'd do the Romeo and Juliet balcony scene with me when we get to Verona. Before she can decline, I hand her a couple of dog-eared photocopies and tell her it'll only take a couple of minutes to do. "Okay," she says with a bright, oxen-eyed smile, "I'll be your Juliet." Thanking her, I turn my eyes back to the road and decide that, yes, I do find her attractive, but no, my chances of seducing her are zero. Besides, says a pompous voice in my head, it would be wrong to abuse my position of authority. Another voice says bollocks, you know full well there's no such thing as right and wrong and anyway all's fair in love and class war. I leave the voices to slug it out and rise to give the passengers a salutary tale of the evils of grappa that spills over into the art of coffee drinking in Italy. Ah, the caffè corretto! The macchiato, the lungo, the lungo-macchiato, the caffè-latte, and remember, I tell them, seeing the border coming up, an Italian would not be seen dead taking a cappuccino at any time other than breakfast.

The Swiss guard waves us straight through. The Italian stops us. "Don't forget to smile at him now," I tell the passengers and make way for him to step on board. He's a middle-aged man with a nice, lovingly tended pasta belly. I watch him stroll up the aisle, scrutinising the passengers from behind his sunglasses, a slimmed-down version of Pavarotti. Some steal a look at his gun. Others try not to look guilty and succeed only in looking guiltier than before. Lizzie flirts with him. Chuck Miesepeter looks away. The guard asks Leahman for his passport and flicks through it casually. Could Leahman be the fiendish mastermind of an international drugs operation? The guard hands him back the passport and ambles back down to the front of the coach. There's something he's not happy about.

"Tutt' apposto?" I ask, everything in order? He gives a shrug whose meaning could be one of a thousand things. But I have an idea what it might mean. I reach behind my seat and pull out a pristine Austerlitz touring bag wrapped in Cellophane. "Ecco, capo," I say, "perhaps someone in your family could find a use for this. Omaggio della casa." "Molto gentile," he replies, then, as if remembering himself, straightens, salutes, and leaves with the bag tucked under his arm. We are safely in Italy.

We roll on. I wait for their stunned gazes to plummet over the edge and down to the expanse of shimmering blue that is Lake Como, wait for them to digest the beauty of the place, then begin my introduction to our sixth country. "Abandon all assumptions," I warn, "all ye who enter Italy. There are three fundamental rules to be observed in Italy. *First*, time is not what you think it is: immediately means in fifteen minutes' time, now means sometime in the next hour and today means sometime this week. Four o'clock is six o'clock in Florence, seven o'clock in Rome and any time you like in Naples. *Second*, if anything is simple, make it complicated. *Third*, there are no rules in Italy. All ye who observe not these rules shall be cast into the infernal pit of confusion, wrath and eternal waiting for the bill. Here endeth the lesson."

They seem not to believe that in Italy you pay more for sitting down at a bar; that the green man on pedestrian crossings is mere decoration; that you can suddenly become invisible when faced with a barman; that you have to buy special paper if you want to report something to the police; that it takes either a year or a fortnight to get a passport, depending on who you know; that Neapolitans prefer to wear a tee-shirt with a diagonal black band across it rather than wear the seatbelt itself. They seem apprehensive about the country all of a sudden. I smile. This is how I want them. I want them to be utterly dependent on me in this land of chaos, in partibus, where nothing is as they think it should be. If they are dependent on me they will behave. I relax in my seat, stare at the blank road and go over our route in my head, content to leave Gilles to the pleasures of whatever music he has on his walkman.

So: Milan, Bergamo, Brescia, Verona. Autostrada all the way. And then on to Venice. Lake Garda just before Verona. Mustn't forget to mention that. Known as Lake Benaco in Dante's time, the lake of augurs and seers. Give Mantova a mention too, might as well. Founded by Manto, mother of Virgil. Feel me eyes drooping. Stay awake, Owen. Important business to be thinking of. Coup de pompe, that tiredness that hits you out of the blue. Keep the eyes open. What if Pepe says no? Taking it for granted he'll say yes. Shouldn't take my friends for granted. Hate that word: shouldn't. Snakes on the road, white serpents' dots all the way to Verona. Augurs and seers. Wish I was a seer now. Come in handy, that would. Could figure out what the story with the parcel is. Could see whether Pepe will say yes or no. Could see who's lying in wait for me. To be a Calchas or a Polydamas, or that fella down in Hades, the one with his marbles, the one who told Ulysses what he had to do. Was that Teiresias? Think it was. Teiresias, father of Manto. Back to Mantova again. Going round in circles here. Down and down into the circles of hell. Le cercle des . . . traîtres, the last circle. Inferno's the best place. Got all the juiciest sins. Purgatory boring. Paradise sickly sweet. No, inferno for me every time. Feel more at home there, down among the sinners. Stay awake. Seers and augurs and snakes and sinners. The snakes of Teiresias. Struck them with his staff and turned into a woman he did. Said they enjoy sex ten times more than men. Can't be true. Can anyone enjoy sex that much? Dot, dot, dot, dot, dot, there they go. Ophidian dots. Droopy, heavy, dots. One dot for every sin. All my dots piling up. Sin is in the eye of the beholder, thus spake Pelagius. Who the hell's Pelagius, they say, the ones who talk of sin. Morgan, you wankers, that's who Pelagius was, Pelagius alias Morgan. Forgotten what I was going to. Falling asleep. Pelagius, Morgan, me. Fifth century. Self-obsessed, Pepe said I was. My greatest sin, he said. Aye, but, Pepe, we can live without sin. That's what Morgan the monk said. Course you can if it doesn't exist in the first place. That's better, winning the battle against sleep now. Got it beat. Pelagius-Morgan, springing open the prisons in the fifth century, the prisons that count. Didn't want to release the prisoners, he wanted to stop free men from rushing in. Mesmerising road. The nature of sin, the sex of angels, what's the point? Me, sneaking and snaking my way across Europe. Effi the seer, said I'd get caught. Rome is where I'll get caught. That's Owen the seer for you. Shit. Coup de pompe. Annwfyn. Anne ooh vin. Sliding away. Can't fight it any more. Take me there, Kynddilig. I am ready.

"On prend Verona-Sud, c'est ça?" The sound of Gilles' voice sends a bolt of fire through my head and jolts me back to the land of the living. God, are we at Verona already? I must have nodded off for a good while there. Yes, I tell Gilles, Verona-Sud's the exit we want, and immediately realise by the sardonic expression on his face that he knew that all along. Acknowledging the debt I owe him for waking me up in time,

I begin my introduction to Verona, city of Petrarch and Dante, the Roman settlement on the River Adige, all the usual stuff that flicks up like so many index cards at the mere mention of the name. As soon as we drop, I gather everyone together and lead them through an opening in the city walls to a street where cars lie ready to pounce at the lights. Crossing over, I stop briefly at the amphitheatre to explain that it's the third largest Roman arena in the world, after the Coliseum in Rome and the one in Libya. A young paninaro in yellow Lacoste tee-shirt accompanies me the next dozen or so paces to ask if I have any tickets for the opera. I tell him I have none. Disappointment writ large on his face, he taps my shoulder and lopes off. I walk backwards to check on my flock, then, turning round, scour the corners of the Piazza Brà. If I were lying in wait for me, that's where I'd be.

Clutching Act Three, Scene Five, Lizzie walks beside me as we skirt the amphitheatre and turn into a busy Via Mazzini. "It's a shame we don't have longer here," she says, "it looks really pretty." A sweet woman and a discerning woman, and will you stop thinking about Teiresias's snakes, Owen? The shouts of market traders can already be heard coming from the Piazza delle Erbe. We make a right turn down Via Capello, where the significance of the small opening on the left is indicated only by the number of people blocking it. A party of Italian schoolchildren argues over gelati at maximum volume. A young man in sunglasses with the profile of a boxer stands away from them, smoking a cigarette and holding open the pink pages of *La Gazzetta dello Sport*. Hand held high, I lead on through the mêlée into the courtyard of Giulietta Capuleti. Already there are eager hands fondling the breast of the brass statue of Juliet, burnishing it even further, giving my noble lady an unbecoming brazenness.

I cup a hand over the breast and concentrate hard on the first male face I come upon, that of Andy Capp. He puffs on his roll-up and gives me a laddish grin. If you rub Juliet's breast,

I inform them, you'll be lucky in love. Faces tilt up to the balcony. Lizzie tells me she's ready. Eyes and camcorders train now on us. She swallows and begins. "Wilt thou be gone? It is not yet near day. . ." Her voice is clear and confident. Only the black-bordered sheets betray the trembling of her hand. We lurch through the scene, burning out night's candles, tiptoeing over misty mountain tops, beckoning welcome death. We reach the end of our extract. "More light and light," I lament hammily, "more dark and dark our woes." I go to plant a Puritan's kiss on her cheek, but Lizzie turns at the last moment and the kiss lands uncomfortably close to her lips. Her mother says nothing. She seems interested only in gobbling up the moment on celluloid. After the bows and the applause, I tell them when to meet me back on the coach and abandon Lizzie to go in search of the boxer. He is still there. His white T-shirt reads: ITALIA '90, Il Gioco del Calcio. A plastic Standa bag hangs from his wrist, containing, most likely, a bunch of keys, today's *El Pais*, and a packet of Winston. "Pepeeee!" I hold out my arms to greet him. He smothers me in a hug and stands back to take a good look at me.

"Que tal, coño!"

"Grand, Pepe, de puta madre. No, I tell a lie." The light brown hair of his crown bristles in a sudden breeze. He removes his sunglasses. His soft grey eyes seem troubled by the news that all is not well with me.

"Que pasa, Owen?"

"I'm not at all well cos I've got a thirst on me you could photograph and if I don't get a beer quick I'm going to peg out." He laughs and pulls me off my feet in another bear-hug. We joke our way back along the Via Mazzini. He tells me who of the old guard is still around in Florence, relates a few of the latest scandals there, says that temperatures have not dipped below thirty-five for a month, stops me when I ask about his thesis. I usher him to a table outside a bar on the Piazza Brà. Here, at least, the prices are bound to keep my tourists away.

There is a faint jingle of metal as he plonks his bag down on the table, covering it with his football paper. "Senta!" he calls out with the practised authority of one used to living in Italy, and orders two large beers.

"You don't take your jacket off?" he asks. "You must be roasting your pelotas in this heat."

"Not just yet, Pepe. Once I've explained things." Wanting to break him in gradually, I begin with a very general summary of events so far, from the contact in Heidelberg to the meeting with Effi in Lucerne. I cannot tell him about my hunch concerning the Diogenes coincidence; he is safer not knowing that name. It is a name that could be wrenched out of him. He listens attentively and then says,

"I don't see what the problem is, Owen. You have a packet, you don't know what it contains for sure, but you want me to take it to Florence for you. I mean. . ."

"What?"

"I mean, if you want me to take it, I take it. But why didn't you post it to me? Why do I have to come to Verona?"

"And leave the parcel to the tender mercies of the Italian postal system? How do I know it won't end up in Palermo? There's no telling *when* it would reach you either." He laughs, admits the point.

"Sí, es verdad, pues–"

"There's something you should know about the Heidelberg man. I found out from Thomas that he's dead, stabbed."

"Joder! No!" He checks himself. "You mean Thomas in Heidelberg, Thomas Rhenisch?"

"Yes. I phoned him again this morning and found something else out. The fingernails of the dead man's right hand were missing."

"La hostia!"

"Precisely." I leave a lengthy pause for digestion before continuing. "As it is, you won't have to cross any borders so nobody's going to search you . . . So that's no problem."

"They tortured him because of the parcel?"

"That's what I think. I'm trying to tell you how it is, Pepe, just so you know what the deal is."

"But someone knows you have the parcel now, yes?"

"At least two people."

"And no-one would know that I have it?"

"Only me . . . And you don't have to hold on to it for long."

"Why?"

"The parcel is watertight . . . impermeable, hermético, whatever. The earth in Florence is as dry as a bone in any case, so if you put it in a metal box and bury it, it should be safe. Bury it tonight, when it's dark, in the grounds of the Badia, the bottom end by the via Roccettini, between the wall and the goalposts. Use gloves so there's no fingerprints. Then, nothing and nobody can trace the parcel to you . . . That's what I'm asking you to do for me, Pepe. As far as everyone else is concerned, I still have the parcel . . . Whatever you decide, take this anyway." I hand him a tightly folded oblong of pink banknotes under the table. His face tells me I'm offending him.

"I don't want money for doing it!"

"It's to cover your train journey. Two hundred thousand."

"It didn't cost that much."

"So buy yourself a few pints and treat Stevie as well."

"Just let me think. It's a lot to assimilate, you know." "Yeah, sure. Take your time, Pepe."

He rummages inside his bag and produces a crush-packet of Winston. With a hard flick on the base a single cigarette shoots up. He puts it to his lips and lights it, not bothering to offer me one because he knows I'd only refuse. Winston, not Ducados. Not the stereotypical Spaniard I'm asking him to be, charging off like Don Quixote on a hare-brained quest. Pepe looks to the sky for inspiration, shields his eyes against the sun, curses the heat. He snorts through a nose broken long before I knew him.

"You know," he says, "you won't believe this: that arsehole Seoirse, he told me he used to be in the IRA. He's so full of bullshit. He wants you to think he used to be the El Cid of Ireland. He's just a . . . un cantamañanas."

"A chancer."

"Yeah, a chancer. *But* you're the one who's taking the chances. The difference is you do it and say nothing; he does nothing and pretends he was some kind of hero."

"Hold on, Pepe, I'm still an arrogant bastard, okay?"

"Okay."

"Anyway, Seoirse's never a man to let the facts get in the way of a good story."

Two frothy yellow beers are served up by a waiter whose attention is focussed not on us but on the women at the next table. Pepe lifts his glass towards mine. "Salud!" he says. "Salud!" I respond, and we drink together in a silence I find unbearable. I don't want to put any pressure on him but time is short.

"So you'll do this, Pepe?" He looks me straight in the eyes, weighing his decision.

"I'm here, no? Capullo! Of course I will. I was up to my dick with my thesis anyway." My heart leaps into my mouth and once again I see shining in his smiling eyes the incorruptible jewel to which the name of friendship is given. I point at his bag. "Listen, is that another newspaper you've got in there?"

"Well, it's *La Nazione*. I only got it to see what films they're showing for the Estate Fiesolana."

"It'll do." I take the parcel from my pocket, slide it into the bag and pull out *La Nazione*. I finish my beer and look at the time. Pepe sees I have to go and rises to give me a rib-crushing embrace. I tell him I'll see him in four days' time to check everything's okay. "And, hey, thanks, Pepe." I wish him safe journey back to Florence and take my leave, dumping *La Nazione* in the first bin I find. If there wasn't any news of the

Van Dyck in this morning's papers, there's bound not to be any in a provincial daily.

We grind away the tiresome kilometres of a relentlessly flat and unchanging plain steeped in a heavy mixture of haze and pollution. Signs glide by telling us that Venice is creeping closer but it feels as far off as it did this morning, as distant as the green hill without a city wall. Wavy red-tiled roofs on peeling walls that once were white appear in clusters by the roadside, their dusty, darkened shutters locked tight, hiding the naked bodies that sleep within on clammy sheets dreaming of diaphanous bottles of cool, blue mineral water. The only movement is the paper-chain fluttering of clothes on the line, a faded grey shirt here, jaded overalls there, and wizened brown tights everywhere. Those who have missed out on their siesta – Milanesi for the most part – throw themselves into a teeth-clenching vengeance, zipping past us in the fast lane in their Alphas and Audis and Autobianchis, not even sparing a gesture of contempt for the steam-roller in their yawning wake struggling to make it to the hotel by five. A three-car accident, obligatory, it seems, on this stretch of the A4, funnels us all into one lane and by five o'clock we are still no further than Padova-Este, crawling behind a maroon Ducato van with a Torino plate whose rear doors bisect the words MATERASSI MORFEO. It's just gone six when we hobble into the driveway of our hotel, and after a huge bowl of aglio, olio, peperoncino, washed down with a bottle of wine and a couple of Stravecchios to make sure I get straight to sleep, after writing out a bulletin board, after arranging wake-up calls, and after telling Lizzie as tactfully as possible that I'm really too weary to go for a swim in the pool, finally my head hits the pillow with a thud.

"You may as well come in," I say to the men in tweed jackets who have just thrust their identity cards into my face. The numbness of sleep suddenly disappears when I realise that they might have lied about being police. "I hope you haven't got my driver up as well," I remark, looking at my alarm clock. "I don't want to appear uncooperative, but after all it is three in the morning, and I have a very busy day tomorrow, I mean, today."

Perching myself on the edge of the bed, I invite them to sit in the armchairs. They look a little unsettled, perhaps because I haven't bothered to put anything over my boxer shorts. The man on the right with the moustache is impressively tall even sitting down. His short dark hair shows signs of a curl struggling to get out. He must be in his late thirties and reminds me of Luciano, the ex-Carabiniere I used to know in Florence. Since I didn't catch the names they gave I decide to think of him as another Luciano. He folds his fingers in his lap and leans back in the armchair. It looks like he's going to let the other one start with the questions.

The man on the left is much smaller. Although greying at the temples, his hair is otherwise black and curly and, with the small round lenses of his gold-rimmed glasses, he bears a striking resemblance to photos of the young Gramsci. Leaning forward, he rests his elbows on his knees and adopts a regretful countenance. "Just a few questions, Dottore Parry."

"Sure, fire away." The unflappable Brit, yes, one way of playing it. Nice and courteous, disarmingly courteous.

"What do you do when you aren't working as a tourist guide?"

"Not a lot. I like to drink Guinness and play pool. I live in London."

"We know," interrupts Luciano, who makes a steeple with his fingers to stress that he knows. "And we know that you visit Ireland regularly."

"I visit a lot of places regularly, on tour and off tour, including Ireland. It's my itchy feet, you understand."

"Do you know a man called Fleenn Ayeedan?"

"Aidan Flynn? Yes."

"And have you ever visited him in Dublin?"

"No, I can't see any reason for visiting him there because he lives in County Antrim. He owns the little pub in the middle of the village. Are we talking about the same man?"

"Ayeedan Fleenn lives in Dublin, Finglas Road, number twelve."

"Well, I know Finglas Road, but an Aidan Flynn of Finglas Road, no. It's a very common name in Ireland."

"Signore Parry," asks Gramsci, "you will have no objections if we search your room?" Ah, Signore is it now? Dropped the Dottore to make me feel less important.

"None at all," I tell him, flopping backwards and making a pillow with my hands. I hear objects being moved, zips being pulled, jars being rattled.

"Could you open your briefcase, please?" asks Gramsci. I get wearily off the bed, spring open the catches and show them an open briefcase. Luciano looks through passenger lists, bulletin sheets, hotel lists, maps, vouchers, optional excursion lists, turns over a book of adhesive labels, fiddles with a black marker pen. He closes the case. He looks under the bed, in the wardrobe, frisks through my clothes, still to no effect. He shrugs his shoulders at Gramsci.

"Signore Parry," begins Gramsci. "We shall not detain you any longer."

"I know," I say as I usher them to the door. "There was obviously some mistake."

"We are sorry," says Luciano.

"Not at all." God, that was quick, I think to myself as I close the door on them. There's a faint smell of lavender in the room: ah, the mosquito machine. Now what was that all about? They knew Aidan Flynn but they didn't know who he was. Thanks be to Jesus for Pepe! Seems like several packs of hounds are out after me. But who's master of the hunt, or is there more than one? Another knock at the door. Are they back already?

Gilles is dressed only in a white singlet and floral boxer shorts. "Owen, you won't believe what's just happened," he blurts, stepping straight past me. "Mais c'est pas possible! Who do they think they are, these people?!"

"I've no idea." This time I sit in the armchair with Gilles at the foot of the bed.

"They asked me hundreds of questions. How long I'd been doing these tours, where I lived, who my friends were, how long I'd known you, where we were going next, the trouble they could make for me. They said they'd sent someone to talk to you as well."

"They did. Two of them."

"But three o'clock in the morning, for Christ's sake! Do you realise?! Trois heures du mat! Who do they take themselves for, Starky et Utch? They searched my room, just like that, without even asking if they could. God, I hate the police!" But were they police, Gilles? First question. "And they wouldn't tell me what they were looking for when I asked them. Three in the fucking morning! I should have hit them, I should have."

"So they searched your room too."

"Yeah, and they asked if you'd given me anything to keep or if I'd given you anything, and I told the guy that if he didn't tell me what the hell was going on I'd put my fist through his face. I mean! I threatened to call the consulate and everything. What the hell's going on, Owen?"

"I don't know. My guess is it's something to do with drugs, as though we'd be stupid enough to carry that sort of thing around with us. Maybe somebody gave them a false tip-off."

"But who'd do that?"

"Christ knows. Maybe somebody harbouring a petty grudge against you or me. You know how this work can drive people over the top, how people let little things get out of all proportion."

"Bastards."

"Maybe it was one of those classic police balls-ups."

"But why should it be us they end up coming down on? And if it was a balls-up, you can bet your life there'll be no apology. They're a law unto themselves, the same everywhere. They just put on a uniform and they think they're God."

"Your ones had uniforms?" Gilles waves a hand.

"Well, no, but you know what I mean."

"Yeah, sure. Listen, Gilles, just don't let them get to you. Try and get some more sleep. You need your sleep."

"How do you expect me to sleep now, at this time of the morning? Are you just calmly going back to bed, then?"

"I'm going to try."

"Three in the morning!"

"It's better than eight in the morning."

"How can you say that?"

"They could have come at eight in the morning and fucked the whole day up for us."

"Spose so."

"Just go back to bed, Gilles. Don't let them get to you. Just think of Carine, eh?" I give his shoulder a reassuring squeeze.

"You don't think they're going to charge in on us again somewhere else?"

"I shouldn't think so. Not once they've realised their mistake. Hey, we mustn't let the passengers know what's happened. It could be very unsettling."

"Huh, you're worried about the passengers. They didn't get woken up in the middle of the night!"

"Come on, Gilles. You're not going to let a couple of arseholes with badges ruin the tour for us, are you?" He sulks for a while. I notice a large blue scimitar tattooed on his right shoulder. Just like Judith's sword, poised over the head of the sleeping Holofernes. "What time is it now?" he asks, indignation still burning bright in his eyes.

"Half three."

"Half three!"

Gilles eventually returns to his room, leaving a trail of invective behind him. It is all one unholy mess. For fuck sake, I was nearly caught there. Didn't realise the danger was so close.

Too complacent I was today. Those two were obviously looking for the parcel. Which means that I'm only one step ahead of them. Half a step, more like. Police, my arse! But who were they working for? My lot or the other lot. It's got to be an informer. All this confusion, all these crossed lines of communication, that points to an informer stirring things up, muddying the waters so nobody knows who's who any more. Or maybe my lot think I'm the informer, the turncoat, and they're trying to get the parcel back before I do any damage. Or maybe the informer's told them I'm the informer. Effi saying they're counting on me to make it a success. But even if I do manage to clean things up I'll still get a bollocking for acting on my own initiative with the parcel, giving it away to Pepe, someone not of the fold. That could get me into even deeper shit. I just can't make any of it add up. It's like playing chess on a board where the squares keep changing colour, where knights act like bishops and pawns like queens, chopping and changing all the time, nobody doing what they should be doing. Not being able to lift your head to see if it's still the same opponent you're playing.

Still, at least Pepe should be back in Florence by now, tucked up in bed, oblivious to all this. Far away. If they're onto me, at least they're not onto Pepe. At least he's safe, thanks be to the gods. Thank Christ I contacted him when I did. Only supposed to be back-up. Didn't have to use him but could if I needed to. Pulled in cos all the signs were pointing the wrong way, case anything else went wrong and now it has. The Heidelberg guy and now this. Back-up without portfolio, Pepe, my flexible friend, one beacon of beauty on the shit-brown landscape. Slán abhaile, Pepe, and make dreams of gold.

Aidan Flynn knows no sin
Send him off to Annwfyn
Give him neither march nor hymn
Only anger's violin

6

A private motoscafo bound for the Piazza San Marco chugs away from the quay. Only the pilot, Mauro, and myself are on deck. The passengers are all below, peering out of windows, getting their first glimpse of the city of water. Mauro rests his wrist on the wheel. Deep lines score criss-cross patterns on the weatherbeaten hide of his neck. I cannot see his face, though I imagine it staring impassively ahead, marvellously indifferent to my presence. A crane hoists metal containers from a ship anchored at the dock. I read across the Greek letters on the blistered stern: Thalassa, Athina. God, I love this city. It feels good to smell the salt air laced with the promise of sea beyond and to feel the vibration of the sea-churning engine in my feet. And there's the lagoon excursion to look forward to as well, more salt air wafting in the face, with lunch at a seafood restaurant on the island of Burano. A nice relaxing afternoon where I can have time to myself while the punters get pissed. But can I afford to relax, after what happened this morning? No, I need to be on the look-out all the time. Still, I feel surprisingly fresh and alert despite the scant hours of uncertain sleep. I'll just have to write off the lost sleep as a bad job. If need be I shall be like Kei in the Welsh legends, who could go nine days and nine nights without sleep. There's one thing, at least, about Venice which stands to my advantage. It must be the easiest city in Europe for shaking off anyone following you. The channel broadens and with a couple of downstrokes of his hand Mauro eases us into the Grand Canal. The Angel of the Redeemer, darkened against the fresh blue sky, brandishes its sword at the church of the Gesuiti across the water. I find myself thinking back with fondness to my first time here, a week spent wandering the bridges and canals alone. I remember the difficulty I had finding the Peggy Guggenheim collection, hidden in a labyrinth of narrow streets intent on disorienting me. And then there was that morning when I was abruptly brought up at the edge of the canal and I simply could not figure out why the wooden bridge that had been there only the night before had vanished into thin air. It seemed I was the only person who didn't know what was going on, the only one who had not been let in on the secret. They'd told me about the pickpockets in Venice but nothing about bridge-thieves. Life went on around me as normal, and I decided that it must be normal here for bridges to disappear in the night.

My heart sinks, though, at the sight of all the activity around San Marco: the thousands of feet tramping across the square, the figures tiptoeing fearfully into gondolas, the flying rats swooping down en masse to feed from a foreign hand, the bodies crammed against the handrail of a passing vaporetto. It is as though I can already smell the Ambre Solaire, hear the gondoliers' English, see the striped tee-shirts with 'Venezia' scrawled across them in sloping letters of red or green, underpinned perhaps with an 'Italia' just in case they forget where Venice is.

The Palace of the Doges looms up, the seat of power and intrigue, conspiracy and denunciation, inching its way towards me. In the foreground, twin columns stand like the Pillars of Hercules, the signal-pillars warning men not to go beyond. We disembark and while I wait for my passengers to gather round the column of St. Theodore I see a tourist in a black tee-shirt, shuffling through the postcards he's just bought. In khaki shorts, white socks and sandals, he must be a tourist. Straining my eyes to read the lettering on his shirt, I discover it's in German and – oh, how wonderful – it says: I want my Wall back, only two metres higher. If only that shrew-faced woman were here now. I want to rush up and shake his hand but Lizzie nudges my elbow and says that Mauro's trying to tell me something. Ah, so that's the last of them off. I lead off with a spring in my step and a song in my heart.

Ice cream stands and souvenir vendors clutter the way. The piazza has been reduced to a mass of flesh milling ankle-deep in pullulating pigeons. Venice in August is every bit a trial of patience as picking your way through the rush-hour tube when you've got an urgent appointment to meet. I cannot remember a time here when I have not fulminated against the slowness and aimlessness of all these bumpkins, these back-packing, Coke-swilling incumbrances whose heels get caught in your shins, who stop dead right in front of you for no justifiable reason. Only this time it's different. This time I feel that every last one of this ambling, dawdling, clogging mass is a friend, covering me, camouflaging me, protecting me. It feels good, too, to be short. "He wanted a dollar but I got him down to fifty cents," relates with pride a nasal voice of indeterminate sex. Ho, hum. There are four city guides around the Campanile alone, four guides with four groups, a hundred and sixty people struggling to hear their guide above the other three. The battle of the microphones. "Cette loggia, d'inspiration florentine. . ." "And the priests would be suspended from the Campanile in cages. . ." Good for them. "Bemerkenswert sind auch die Pferde, die man. . ." Die man was? Talking about the four horses of the Basilica no doubt. "Kagadeska sui. . ." No chance understanding any of that. "My wallet! My God, where's my wallet?" Oh dear. Welcome to Venice.

People shuffle forwards at the entrance to the Basilica and present themselves for inspection by the Catholic decency police. No shorts! No bare shoulders! Nothing worldly! Don't want to go upsetting the Saint, now do we, Madame? Is that *your* rosary, Sir? On the square described by Napoleon as the most beautiful drawing room in Europe a woman grimaces beneath the pigeon picking grains of corn from her hair. Ach y fi! The Saracen's hammer sounds the half-hour on the Torre dell' Orologio, causing zoom lenses to swing round like tank guns. Past the piazzetta dei Leoni we go, the only place where tourists can sit without paying. Already giving out under the heat or the sheer oppression of numbers, they guzzle mineral water like there were no tomorrow. It's all a far cry from Tintoretto and Titian and Canaletto and the Radio Four short story.

We weave through a couple of side-streets and halt on a bridge to take photos of the Bridge of Sighs. I do a quick head-count. By some miracle all are present and correct. Proceeding into the shaded patio of the Vecchio Murano glassworks, we climb a stone staircase to the first floor and enter the furnace of a room for a demonstration of glassblowing. As the last of the passengers files into the room I escape into the office, where, on seeing me, the pert, lipcoated Tizzy holds out a hand for me to kiss, all the while issuing instructions to someone on the other end of the phone. I plant a light kiss on the back of her hand, noticing a small crescent of sweat on the armpit of her blushing pink dress.

"Tiens!" comes a voice from behind. I turn to find Kristine sitting in a corner, balancing a clipboard and calculator on her knees. We kiss à la française. Blond hair stiffened into respect-ability. "I'm going to the Gatto Nero with you for lunch," she says. "Isn't that good?" Large blue eyes drawing back, somehow discomforting. The woman of Lourdes.

"I couldn't have chosen better company myself," I reply, and inwardly cringe at the inanity of my words. Change of subject called for. "Er, Terry and Pietro were talking about you on the Rhine."

"Really?" She looks flattered. "What did they say? Good things, I hope."

"Pietro said you had a certain *libidine*, I think."

"Who's talking sexy?" Tizzy interrupts. "How are you keeping, Owen?" I tell her I'm fine. "You're at the Gatto Nero with Kristine."

"Yes, she's just said." She offers to get me a beer from the fridge but the phone rings again so I help myself to a can of Nastro Azzurro. Kristine packs her clipboard and calculator into her Louis Vuitton attaché case. What, then, is my itinerary, she asks? Her face hardens as I reel off my list of towns and hotels. "So," she observes, "we are going to be in parallel all the way to Paris."

"Ah."

"You look unhappy."

"No, I don't mind, as long as you don't go checking up on everything I do."

"I've got only one condition, the usual."

"That I don't make your passengers jealous of mine because I'm doing extras."

"Exactly. Well, now that we have that established we can be friends."

"Fine. It's just that I hate people checking up on me."

"If you have nothing to hide you have nothing to fear. The important thing is for both of us to do a good job."

No, I don't like her. Too stern by half. Kristine gets to her feet and pays Tizzy the money for the lagoon excursion. She must be something in the region of five foot nine, slim without being bony, a little heavy on the make-up. Smartly dressed in skirt, tights and blouse, she gives the impression of being pretty despite the tell-tale signs of lack of sleep. She leaves, saying that she will meet me at the quayside of San Marco at eleven fifteen exactly.

"Was it something I said?" I ask Tizzy as soon as we are alone.

"Oh, she's probably just stressed out."

"Isn't her mother German?"

"You think that explains it? Don't be daft, Owen. She's French through and through. Can't you tell?"

Within the half-hour I'm exploring Venice's back streets, just following my nose, working on the principle that if I don't know where I'm going then nobody else can. There's plenty of time to get back to San Marco, ample time to savour that rarest of pleasures for the guide: getting lost and not having to care about the consequences. This is wonderful, these streets that suddenly turn into cul-de-sacs and the bridges that lie tantalising out of reach. Any but the true Venetian would feel like a fish out of water here, surrounded, hemmed in by names that seem to belong elsewhere, that sound more Spanish than Italian, like the Calle larga San Marco or the Calle di Magazen. And pity the poor infidel, assaulted at every turn by saints and monks and angels. If anything, it reminds me of the Catholic gauntlet you run in Seville where every other street is named after a virgin. What was that one that made me laugh? La Virgen de la Huerta, aye, the Virgin of the Vegetable Garden. Counted over thirty different virgins there. Stifling city, Seville. Scrawny old moggie creeping round there. So many cats around Venice. Good way of keeping the rats away I suppose. Whole piazzas of them sometimes. Nine lives. There's a point, if cats have nine lives, do they say life begins at three hundred and sixty?

And what does this one say? Calle degli Assassini. Well would you Adam and Eve it. Bar-Tabacchi. No harm popping in for a quick beer. No, that Nasty Azurro has put me off beer. Ah, I know, a caffè corretto, yeah, something to put a bit of beef into the day. "Sì, mi dà un caffè corretto con grappa per cortesia?" Oops. Must have said something wrong there. Probably sounded far too polite. Can feel all the eyes in my back. Just like walking into a pub in Limerick with a Dublin accent. You're not from here are you, boy? Can't understand their Venetian dialect. Days of the week is all I know, zioba for giovedi and sabo for sabato. Mmm, and you boys never knew a kinder Florentine, did you?

Three monkeys on the shelf behind the bar. See no evil, hear no evil, speak no evil, the mafia's omertà. Be better used as a mascot for the English intellectuals, so-called: see nothing, hear nothing, speak only bollocks. Amis Minor writing about Auschwitz, backwards. Backwards! Stunning profundity. And all the others spouting shite like after Auschwitz, darling, poetry simply is not possible. Or quoting Hannah Arendt. Ignatieff, eff for fuckwit on the telly trying to bend his sixth form brain round fascism and nationalism. And looking so intellectually *intense*. Schoolboy asininity, Marx would have said, schülerhafte Eselei, like he did with Bakunin. Folk coining it in hand over fist for talking diarrhoea. Mediocre minds for mediocre times.

Ah, there we are. Can smell the grappa coming off it already. Give it a stir. No, boys, I'm obviously not an Italian because I won't put half a ton of sugar in. Feel about as welcome here as Daniel in the lions' den. Pinching the cup between index and thumb. Mmm, great coffee, though, not like they serve up in the trendy bars on Upper Street, weak as piss. All the English there sitting out on the terraces pretending to be cosmopolitan. Drinking pastis with fizzy Perrier. If they're so cosmopolitan how come they haven't mastered washing up yet? Never rinse when they wash up, just plunge it all into the soap suds and straight out on the draining board with it. Soapy-toothed English. Mind you, the Welsh are no better on that score, or the Irish. That's what they should have done during the War when they suspected someone of being a spy. The English should have got their suspected Germans to make a proper cup of tea, and the Germans should have made the English wash up. A lot quicker all round. Aye, great coffee, comes up and says hello. Grappa lingering in the nostrils. Excellent. Couple of thousand should cover it. Time to play Theseus again.

A trail of broken arrows daubed on facades points the way back to San Marco. Occasionally I come to a junction where the choice is either straight right or straight left and there's no arrow to tell you which is the right way. But I seem to be guessing right for the most part because I soon pick up the arrow again. If need be I can always ask the way from someone in jeans, or someone carrying an Italian paper. Usually sorts them out from the tourists. Before long I find myself in familiar surroundings, taking a diagonal line across St. Mark's. Kristine is already dancing around under the column of St. Theodore, trying to count her passengers, getting hot under the collar because they keep moving. I tell my passengers to embark and do a count below decks. Everyone's there. They're a good group really. Very disciplined. Kristine's passengers get on and when her blond head bobs up from below she informs me that all hers are there too. We pull away, churning past the imposing outline of La Salute and, beyond it, the Customs House with the figure of Atlas bearing the weight of the world on his shoulders.

Kristine asks if I want to do the commentary: she doesn't feel like doing it. I suggest we toss a coin to decide and it falls in my favour. She looks tense. Fresh beads of sweat appear on her forehead, poking through the Max Factor. Either she's feeling the heat or she doesn't feel confident about doing the commentary. It shouldn't be too difficult. San Giorgio first, where the heads of state meet, then Santa Maria della Pietà further down on the left, the Arsenale mentioned by Dante and the naval museum, San Francesco del Deserto, the islands of the mental asylums, Marco Polo airport, all that sort of stuff. Throw in an anecdote for each one and who's going to complain? Or talk about the Moses Project to save the city from sinking. Or if you're really stuck there's the *Merchant of Venice* and *Othello*. Hell, there's no need to pull that face, Kristine.

There's little point trying to listen to Kristine's account of Venice. The loudspeakers are all below and besides, even if the engine were silent, the wind swishing across the upper deck would snatch away any words not shouted. People wave at us from a vaporetto. Now why do they do that? Just because they're on a boat as well? Oh alright, where's the harm in it? I give them a wave back. Kristine's oblique look accuses me of acting like a dumb tourist. Is this the guide she's been lumbered with all the way to Paris? Poor her, poverina.

Callipygian, isn't that the word for nice buttocks? Something to do with Aphrodite somewhere down the line. Kallos, beauty, coupled with pugé, buttocks. James Bond in *Moonraker* parting the San Marco crowds with his hovercraft gondola. Making the beast with two backs, Iago called it. Forget it, Owen. Out of your league. Santa Maria della Pietà on the left, Vivaldi's church. There's another word: mariolatry. Marco Polo airport further down. Suppose they'll be celebrating Columbus next year. They're welcome to it. The *Niña*, the *Pinta* and the *Santa Maria*. More mariolatry. Bringing Christ to the savage, oh, and the small matter of all that gold.

Every kind of vessel is out on the lagoon: speedboats, ski jets, yachts, fishing boats, a police launch, a liner bound for Greece. Time begins to pass more lazily. Kristine takes a seat and taps figures into her calculator. She seems pleased with her total. "Ecco ci qua," says Mauro after a while. Kristine presses the microphone into my hand and says I can do the last piece. She stands close to listen. Already checking up on me when I've told her not to. With an obliging nod, I relate that we are now approaching the island of Burano where they grow the odd vine and artichoke. They also produce some of the finest lace in the world. But above all it is a fishing community. The houses, too, are very distinctive, painted in bright colours so that the fishermen can pick out their own houses when there's a mist on the sea. Each family has its own colour, thus the houses in red belong to the Antonioni family, the houses in blue to the Busos, the greens to the Bertis, the yellows to the Baggios, and the oranges to the del Cazzos.

At the restaurant we are given a table for two, tucked away in a corner where Italian is the only tongue to be heard. Our passengers are in the next room. Above Kristine's head hangs a reproduction of Magritte's *Empire des Lumières*. Along the walls are other paintings, mostly maritime in inspiration, with arrangements of nets and fishing tackle to give the place the salty sea-dog look.

"You were making those names up," she comments half-way through the antipasti.

"I wasn't. They're authentic names, only they just happen to have all played for Fiorentina. Apart from Signore del Cazzo, of course."

"I don't like football."

"Ah."

"It's macho."

"Not in Italy, it isn't."

She raises disbelieving eyebrows and turns the conversation to work, safer ground. At a guess, I'd say she were in her late twenties. Probably popular with the male passengers, unpopular with the female. She tells me she speaks four languages, that she's done thirty tours, that she's glad to be back in the league of the big companies after having been passed over by them for the last two years due to some injustice she does not expand on. She says that she has lived in Spain and spent some time studying English in Manchester.

"Really? I lived there for a time." Her real passion is animals, dogs and horses. Anyone who doesn't like animals doesn't like humans. When she was younger she trained hard at a school of tauromachy in southern France but she decided to give it up. But then, you can't succeed at everything. It's a question of knowing what you want to succeed at. Take touring: she's pleased to have made her mark as a guide because it's not an easy job and you have to be good at so many things, not just languages. Though she has a bit of trouble understanding the Australians, some of whom have given her bad evaluations in the past for her English.

"I shouldn't worry about that too much. It's the same for Anglophones when they work with the Québecois." But at least it pays the rent and it's not just her flat in the eighth district of Paris, no, she's got other financial burdens and everyone thinks you must be rich just because you live in the eighth.

"Is work very important to you, then?" Of course it is. How else can you survive in this world? Especially when you've got obligations and responsibilities and it's important to do your work well because there's a thin line between the ups and the downs and nobody ever gives you anything for nothing.

"Friends do." Oh dear. She looks at me as though I am trying to trip her up, as though by disagreeing I am saying she's wrong, and if I'm saying she's wrong then I must be taking her for a fool.

"You think so?" It's not that she doesn't have friends, of course, no, she's always lending out money but how long is it before they ever give it back? Six, sometimes ten months later, just like oh, I forgot to give you your money back, Kristine. Patatipatata. No, friends are fine, it's just that they have their limitations like everyone else and you can't always believe what your friends tell you either.

I opt for the frozen grin between mouthfuls. It's easier than painting on wide-awake eyes like they do in the cartoons. Perhaps I should have said, "My friends do," instead of the stupid generalisation. Comunque! Nothing can detract from the excellence of this food and this wine. Magritte there, now there's an old cobweb. The postcard Nadette said reflected her feelings for me. Magritte's *La Victoire*; an island with a door ajar, a cloud drifting in through the gap, or maybe drifting out. On the back she wrote: ceçi représente EXACTEMENT ce que tu me fais vivre. I didn't really understand and she didn't explain, but that was typical of her, the card in the first place and then no need to explain a thing. Nobody does such things, they say. They say you imagined it or that sort of thing only happens in French films, but no, that was Nadette. She said I would think of her if I went to see *37'2 le Matin* and I did.

And it's all a question of being positive. If you don't think positively then you won't get anything out of this life. She went on a course called Putting People First and it really helped her, helped her think of her life in a positive way. And it was really useful for all those stressful situations on the road like when you get a sudden change of hotel and have to break the news to the passengers.

"Tell me something, Kristine: how do you decide if something is negative or positive?"

"It's obvious."

"Well. . .?"

"You mean you can't tell the difference between positive and negative?"

"No, I honestly can't. I mean, what if you're tested positive for AIDS?"

"Then it's a question of the way you approach it. If you're negative, then you might just as well curl up and die on the spot."

"Oh."

"You don't agree."

"Sounds like ersatz religion to me."

"It's humanism. I take it you're not religious, then?"

"Nor a humanist."

"You should think about it more. Maybe you'll find something you agree with."

"Kristine, I have thought about it."

"And you think it's wrong?"

"No, I think it's bollocks."

"I have to say I find you arrogant, Owen." Aye, well, there we are again. I am arrogant, and arrogance is not allowed. Arrogance means you're too sure of yourself and people don't like you being too sure of yourself. We should all be humble, like the good Jesus in the Garden of Gethsemane when he asked that the cup be taken from him. No, at the very worst you should disagree nice and politely so that no-one gets

122

offended, even if they are talking the most arrant dross. You must not infringe the sacred conventions that are there to cocoon people from frightful, beastly nastiness. And if I were less sure of myself, would they feel more sure of themselves, more secure? And if so, in the name of all the gods why?

"Are you married, Kristine?"

"Yes."

"Any kids?"

"I've had two children. And you?"

"Gloriously single with no kids."

"You'll want to have children at some stage."

"Ah, you even know my thoughts."

"Children are what you leave after you."

"I care not if I live but a day and a night, so long as my deeds live after me. That's what the Irish warrior Cuchulain said. And why should you want to be leaving something after you?" She puffs out her cheeks; clearly, I am being impossible. "Why do you want there to be some reflection of you in this world after you're dead? As though there's some part of you that isn't dead. Isn't it just a vainglorious grasp at immortality? And why choose children to do the job for you? At least Cuchulain settled for his deeds."

"You want to have children. You just don't want to admit it."

"To bend another being to my will? To fashion them according to my own image? To see them as an extension of my own existence? No thank you, Kristine. I'm not so arrogant as to want to play God."

"You sound like a robot."

"Some more wine?"

"You will grow old and lonely. I will have my children."

"So they're an insurance policy, are they? And what if they end up not liking you? You can't tell me it doesn't happen."

"They give you love. And they enrich you. Every day you see the world in a new light. Every day is a new discovery, for them and for you. But I don't expect you to see that. You've never had kids. You don't know what it means."

"I've never stuck my prick in the fire either."

"I wonder if you even know what it is to be loved. Anyone who hates the world as much as I think you do is incapable of giving love . . . or receiving it."

"Something of a peremptory judgment, isn't it?"

"Have I touched a soft spot then?"

"I don't have any soft spots." Her blue eyes widen. She dabs the corner of her mouth with a napkin and sits back in her chair.

"Perhaps I shall prove to you that you do."

When she comes back from the toilet the conversation lurches straight back to work, as though everything that has been said is dead and buried, declared null and void. We discuss arrangements in Rome. I shall be in the Palazzo Aurelia on the via Aurelia, while she will be in the Hotel Globus on the viale Ippocrate, the other side of town. But we shall be following identical schedules, starting with the Italian evening at Gino's tomorrow night. In Florence we'll be sharing the same hotel. She asks if I have anything planned for the night in Florence, any extras for my punters. No, nothing like that, I tell her, already thinking ahead to the night out with Pepe at the Fiddler's Elbow, downing a few pints together. Best not to mention that to her. Don't want to have her tagging along and spoiling the evening talking about work all the time. And then after Florence it's Nice, two nights, Lyon, one night, and finally Paris. That's that sorted, then. Beam me up, Scottie.

In the afternoon, while my punters are plying the canals of Venice in their gondolas, I buy a copy of *Il Manifesto* and install myself at a table in the Florian. A glance around the room reveals no undesired faces, no guides, no Austerlitz tourists, no Kristine. No sign either of Gramsci and Luciano. The chances are I won't run into them again. Their trump card was the element of surprise and they've already played it.

124

No, the opposition will probably take a different tack next time. I order another caffè corretto, this time with Sambuca. Kristine would probably say it's madness to pay ten thousand lire for a coffee, but it's not the coffee I'm paying for, nor the pianist tinkling away on the ivories out on the terrace, it's the tranquility, the chance to be alone and unmolested.

I light myself a cigarette, take a drag and press it into the crook of the ashtray. A couple sitting at a nearby table look to have had a row. She sits there with ram-rod back, holding a book in one hand. He sits next to her absorbed in a copy of *Le Monde* with a pipe hanging from his full, red lips. Sulking each other out. That's no way to spend a holiday in Venice. There's nothing about the stolen Van Dyck sketchbook in either the international or cultural pages of *Il Manifesto*. The story, it seems, is already old news. Either that, or there's been a news blackout. The possibility of my having anything at all to do with the sketchbook looks more absurd by the hour. My course of action, too, seems increasingly questionable, a blind panic brought on by nothing more than a tenuous coincidence. But whatever its actual contents, the fact remains that if I hadn't got rid of the parcel, it would have fallen into the hands of Luciano and Gramsci last night. But what to do in Rome, now that I have no parcel to pass on? What if the contact comes direct from the ponytail and demands it there and then? One thing's for sure, whatever happens: I'm not giving it to anyone till I'm certain who they are. Oops.

My cigarette falls from the ashtray to the floor. Immediately I reach down to pick it up but pause at knee level, confronted with the sight of the woman's hand inside her companion's flies. Straightening myself, I concentrate hard on some article about Mike Tyson and the rape case, but it's no good. When I'm absolutely sure I can get away with it, I look over the title of the woman's book: *A la recherche du temps perdu*. Proust at the Florian? Of course, one of his old stamping grounds. Pipe-sucking poker-faced Proustian. What's going through his mind, I wonder? The tinkling bell of childhood? Is she his Albertine? Does he even know her name? Two souls indulging a fantasy, or is it just one? Perhaps this is the only love he requires. Touching.

On the fourth of July eighteen hundred and six
We set sail from the sweet cove of Cork
We were sailing away with a cargo of bricks
For the grand City Hall in New York

'Twas a wonderful craft, she was rigged fore and aft
And oh how the wild wind blowed her
She'd stood several blasts, she had twenty-seven masts
And they called her the Irish Rover

The passengers all look dead beat by dinner time. Gilles, who started the day by putting a gallant face on a bad mood, is in fine form now. Once he'd given the coach a good wash and cleaned out the toilet he was as free as a bird, with plenty of time for a nice long siesta in the coach. It made up for last night's fiasco. He telephoned Carine but she was busy. He'll call her back later on. He had lunch with Kristine's driver, a Flemish guy by the name of Koen who spoke passable French.

Gilles is philosophical about our two tours running parallel. It isn't ideal, he says: this Koen struck him as the kind of driver who thought he knew everything because he'd been on the road for twenty years and that kind of driver usually turns out to be a right "casse-couilles", a pain in the arse. But as long as they don't interfere with our way of doing things he can't foresee any reason why there should be any friction. And what do I think of Kristine, he asks? Is it true, as Koen said, that she has the looks of a film star? She isn't at all unattractive, I say, but half the time she looks like she's after sucking a lemon. She rubbed me up all the wrong way, I tell him, not a woman who's travelled down the road of life very far. Ah well, he says, you know what they say: opposite poles attract. He can just see me sneaking up to her hotel room in Rome for an illicit assignation. There's a definite twinkle in his eye, perhaps there to disguise a deeper, more brotherly concern for my wellbeing. Perhaps, after Nadette and all that, he is only trying to say that a fling wouldn't do me any harm at all, that it's time to stop grieving and get on with life. Rubbish, I say, and in any case we'll be in different hotels in Rome, she in the Globus and we in the Palazzo Aurelia: you couldn't get much further apart. He frowns and says there must be some mistake because Koen said he was in the Aurelia as well. Gilles remembered the name because the last time he was there they fleeced him over the phone bill. Well, Kristine most definitely told me the Globus, I assure him. Perhaps Koen is just getting senile, he jokes. It doesn't matter much to him either way; he's just counting the days till he's back in France. Once we've got Rome and Florence under our belt it'll be all downhill from there, plain sailing all the way.

Then the ship struck a rock
Oh Lord, what a shock
The boat it was turned right over
Turned nine times around
And the poor old dog was drowned
I'm the last of the Irish Rover.

7

We'd already paid the obligatory visits to the Trevi Fountain and the Piazza Navona, and I'd taken my group to Gino's restaurant, a stone's throw from the Termini station. The waiters, a couple of young bloods called Casparo and Giumbini, had installed the passengers in a downstairs room where they could enjoy the eating, drinking and carousing I'd promised them on their first night in Rome. For my own part, I made the mistake of sitting next to a guide from another company who proceeded to tell me that the greatest freedom of all was money.

As soon as Gilles arrived from parking the coach I introduced him, but having forgotten the guide's name already, mumbled something without consonants hoping I'd get away with it. When Gilles screwed his face up and asked me to repeat it, the guide himself proclaimed his name loudly and clearly, going on to divest himself of a wealth of auto-biographical detail for the assumed benefit of my unfortunate driver. I suspect that the man was simply trying to impress, with his fluent French and knowledge of various one-way systems in Yugoslavia, and I was busying myself trying to devise a polite way of getting rid of him when into the restaurant walked Kristine.

I found it odd that she should give me just a single kiss on the cheek rather than the more customary two. Even Gilles must have found something strange in it for he commented that the only proper way of greeting someone was to give the four kisses, as is the practice in Brittany. The guide stood up and insisted on kissing the back of her hand. I think I did make some attempt to find out which hotel she was in but it was clear to see that the other guide was hell-bent on having her undivided attention. Gino, the owner, came to welcome us all in his gravel-raked voice and, having fulfilled the duties of the host, drummed his fingers on his portly girth to signal that he'd better get back to work.

No sooner had Kristine's driver, Koen, appeared than he and Gilles were deep into a conversation about a component that it was always useful to keep in the toolbox because if you ever broke down and needed to get hold of a new one you'd be off the road for a week. So what with the guide telling Kristine how to cook the perfect carbonara and Koen describing the topography of Salzburg with wide arcs of his fork, I decided the only course of action was to let the vineyards of Frascati tell me their own stories.

As the evening wore on, I rose to check on my group downstairs. Kristine stopped me with a hand on my wrist and asked if there was anything the matter. I looked into the soft blue ovals of her eyes and did my best to assure her that all was well with me. She seemed unconvinced and told me not to drink so much. "You're not sulking then?" she whispered close to my face.

"No, not at all," I replied, and for a reason which still escapes me I kissed her forehead. On the stairs I met Andy Capp's bad-toothed wife who recounted excitedly how one of the waiters had pinched her bottom and wasn't the place wonderful! Below, I was hailed by a chorus of half-cut antipodean salutations and joined the revellers in a toast. The musicians came in and played a few tunes. Andy Capp's wife returned from the toilet and lunged squealing at Casparo's bum. I stayed for a chorus of "O Sole Mio", la-la-la-ing the bits I didn't know, then made my retreat. Upstairs, when I was paying for my group in the office, Gino mentioned that there was a message for me. I unfolded the chit of paper. At first I was at a loss to make head or tail of it, until I realised that it was a message in Irish recorded by a hand which had tried to impose Italian sounds on it. Even though tacked onto the end of the preceeding word, the source of the message was, however, clear enough: Seoirse. And he was telling me to be extra vigilant because I was in danger.

I thought back to that conversation we had years ago. On Sandymount strand we walked along, Seoirse making ten-to-two footprints in the sand. "There's someone here thinks your tourist work could be useful to us," he said. "Even if you're not on for it, there's something I'd like you to have." He gave me a button he said came from a Hunger Striker's battle tunic. I thought about the proposition. I knew that, if I chose this course of action, Trotsky's spectre would come to haunt me at every turn, thundering against individualism and opportunism and such like. But a more important consideration came inexorably to the fore, more powerful and frightening because of the void that it suddenly opened up. What if I did *not* take up this opportunity? What would there be left? When would I get a chance like this again? When the revolution came? But the revolution might never happen, at least, not in my own lifetime and I knew that in my lifetime I wanted to fight, aye, to the bitter end. I wanted that oldest of human cravings: revenge. Revenge on those who had declared open class war on us and won. Who else was there fighting that smug English ruling elite who, with all their forelock-tugging collaborators, had ground the miners into the dust and pissed and shat on the hopes of an entire generation, my generation? What other avenue was there, in a country where there was no Communist Party and where the Labour Party had ceased to exist in everything but name? There was nobody else. It made political sense, it made sense for me and my life and my anger, and yes, I said, "Yes, count me in."

I put the piece of paper in my back pocket and rejoined the company at table, where Kristine was being treated to a critical insight into Kant's Categorical Imperative. I informed Gilles that everything was fine with the group and made the acquaintance of a fresh bottle of Frascati, puzzling to no effect over the reason for Seoirse's message.

When it was time to leave we rose as one and led our reluctant passengers outside to wait for the coaches. The other guide took Kristine away to one side. Keeping one eye on Kristine, I chatted to an exuberant Lizzie, all dressed up to the nines but looking a little the worse for wear. She hadn't expected the Roman Night to be anything near as good as it had turned out, "but life is full of surprises, Owen, isn't it?" she said with a twinkle in her eye. A battered red rose dangled precariously from Andy Capp's ear. I was just about to take another drag on my cigarette when, out of the corner of my eye, I saw Kristine jerk her knee into the Kantian's groin, leaving him to skulk off round a corner with a categorical limp. Her face was incandescent with rage.

"Didn't you tell him you were married?" I asked her.

"Some people's egos are so big they never listen to such things. I hate violence but there was nothing else for it."

She seemed to calm down remarkably quickly. It couldn't have been the first time some old bore had tried to get off with her, and I admired the way she dealt with it. Koen arrived shortly afterwards with Gilles close behind. "I'll see you tomorrow," she said, breaking into a smile as she boarded. But there was no kiss, either Breton or otherwise.

It was when I was waving goodnight to a lift full of singing passengers that I noticed another bulletin board taped to the wall alongside my own. At the bottom was Kristine's name. Reception confirmed that it was one and the same Kristine and that she was in room 317. A hitherto uneventful day was now replete with intrigue. Why she had lied about our being in different hotels remained a disquieting mystery but I decided the last thing she needed just then was another interfering man keeping her from her sleep. At all events, the important thing for me was to focus my thoughts on Seoirse's message and the meeting with the contact at the Cafe San Pietro the next morning. Indeed, so wrapped in these thoughts was I that when I opened the door to my room I didn't notice anything different. Then, on the bedside table, I saw a silver bucket with the neck of bottle of prosecco craning out of it. On my pillow lay a single red rose. I searched on the floor, under the bucket, even pulled back the blankets, but I couldn't find an accompanying note. I remembered Lizzie's words about life being full of surprises but persuaded myself that she hadn't been alluding to this. The image of Judith's sword flashed up, only this time it was poised over my own head, and I could see myself kneeling there, primed for the coup de grâce. I picked up the phone and dialled 317.

"Pronto."

"Kristine, c'est Owen."

"Qu'est-ce qu'il y a?"

"Umm, this is going to sound a bit strange perhaps, but there's a little mystery in my room."

"You're telephoning me at this time of night to tell me about mysteries?"

"Sorry," and I put down the phone, cringing again at my ineptitude, although relieved and thanking the gods that I'd not even suggested that *she* might have been the anonymous donor of the gifts. And what about Seoirse's warning? I took the bottle and twisted the cork carefully, pressing down hard to prevent the bubbly from erupting. A thick white vapour rose out of the rim. I ran a finger around the inside and held it to my nose. It smelled . . . of prosecco, not of almonds or anything sinister, just prosecco. Holofernes opened his eyes again and smiled.

I decided to leave the question of the prosecco in mid-air and dialled Seoirse's number in Brussels, only to get his answerphone telling me first in Irish and then in French that he wasn't there. There was little point leaving a message, and I cursed the answerphone for being there instead of Seoirse. He had a kind of sixth sense for danger, something he liked to trace back to his ancestors of Clare. So even if it were mere presentiment on his part, it must have been powerful enough to warrant his intervention. We trusted each other implicitly, Seoirse and I. He'd once told me that I was one of only a handful of good souls with whom he would trust his life. It was understood between us that whatever happened, even if it went against the rules, I would watch his back and he mine. There was a dry knock on the door. At least, I joked to myself as I went to open it, I am armed with a bottle of prosecco and I know how to use it. Kristine stood there with folded arms, shaking her head and muttering under her breath. "You," she said, pushing me aside, "are the worst case I've come across."

"I'm sorry about phoning you, Kristine. You haven't come to shout at me, have you?"

"Oh, I see you've opened the champagne without waiting for me."

"You sent the champagne?"

"Of course." Her eyes glowered with the obvious. "Who else would send champagne and a rose to a stubborn idiot like you?" She flopped on the bed and covered her forehead with her wrist. "I could not believe it when you put the phone down on me. Are you that easily discouraged? Or are you afraid of women?"

"I didn't know there was anything to get discouraged about."

I went to the bathroom and fetched two glasses. As I poured out the prosecco she sat up on the bed and leaned against the wall. Was she French through and through after all, as Tizzy had said? She certainly had the quality of unpredictability, and I like that. I gave her a glass. She took it, clinked it against mine and took a sip, her eyes devouring my face all the time. I took a mouthful and, not really knowing what to say, thanked her for the gifts. "It's ages since anyone's given me a rose."

"God," she lamented, "there's something so cold about you, something you're frightened to let out. Like tonight, you let me sit there and suffer that idiot on my own without saying a word, clammed up in your own little world."

"Perhaps I preferred that world."

"You're one of those intellos, aren't you, that doesn't know the meaning of action."

"Ah, so you *have* come here to shout at me."

"No, I'm here to prise you out of your shell."

"Oh, I see." Exasperated cheeks puffed out.

"I had it all nicely planned. You didn't even see me on the road on the way down. You didn't notice my group in the hotel. I arrange the champagne for when we get back from Gino's, keeping everything a secret to make a lovely surprise for you, and then you go and ruin it all. You don't come to my room, no, you phone me, and then after two words you hang up. What is it that makes you so timid, or so frightened?"

"But why did you do all that? I mean, why me?"

"Listen, we have so little time on the road to ourselves. Why don't we make the most of it?"

"But why me? Just because I'm there, like the mountaineers say?"

"Why do you have to know? My reasons are my reasons. You never know, I might even tell you what they are. After."

The glimmer in her eyes I could only compare to the translucent blue of the grotto at Capri. The hair that fell down to her shoulders made me think the fair Rhiannon had stepped out from the pedestal pages of the *Mabinogion*. And her smile was how I'd always imagined Mata Hari's, mischievous, dangerous, tempting. Through the centuries I could hear Galileo screaming for the fleshpots and, as if to tell me that it was not all in the mind, part of me began to warm to her, uncontrollably. The qualities of the beast again. I thought of the couple in the Florian and decided that if she had her reasons, then I had mine too, and they were not noble.

Seóthó, a thoil! ná goil go fóill.
Seóthó, a linbh, a chumainn 's a stór,
Mo chúig céad cumha go dubhach faoi bhrón
Tú ag sileadh na súl 's do chom gan lón!

"What are you singing there?"
"An Irish lullaby. We are supposed to be sleeping."
"You sing out of tune, Owen."
"About a hungry baby."

Do gheobhair 'na bhfochair sin lomra an óir
Thug Iason tréan don Ghréig ar bord,
'S an tréan-each cuthaig mear cumasach óg
Do bhí ag Coin Chulainn, ceann urraidh na sló.
Seóthó, a thoil! ná goil go fóill.

She told me she used to have an Irish friend in Paris, but
Sheelagh went home to Dublin. They corresponded for a
while but then the letters just dried up, as though she'd just
disappeared off the face of the earth. You get attached to
someone and then they leave. They write, then they don't even
write any more and they might just as well be dead. Her last
tour had started in Dublin and she went to the address near
Connelly Station but no-one had ever heard of Sheelagh
O'Flynn.

"And then there was Johnno." A lover, an Irishman, a
bastard who had left her pregnant. She had an abortion, the
second abortion she'd had. He spoke Irish, too, but never sang
her lullabies, not even in the wrong key. He only used to speak
Irish when he was in a rage because he knew she wouldn't
understand. She spoke four languages, but not Irish. Friends
and lovers, they all have their limitations. And how did Johnno
fit in with her husband, I asked? She didn't want to talk about
her husband, and it was hypocritical of me, she said, to be
singing about a starving baby after all I'd said about children
on Burano.

And you shall have the Golden Fleece
Which brave Jason brought in a ship from Greece
And the spirited swift horse, young and sturdy
Of Cuchulain, the leader of the hosts.

Hush, darling! Don't cry just yet.
Hush, baby, my love and my treasure!
My five hundred sorrows, as I lament
That you are crying and your belly's empty.

Kristine's body twitched but it didn't seem to disturb her sleep. I tried to will myself to sleep but got nowhere. Why was it, I wondered, that whichever woman I slept with, she always got to sleep before I did? But everything was nice and cosy, a little bit too hot but what could you expect in Rome in August with two in a bed? She shifted again and turned to lie facing me, sending up a warm waft of sex in the sheets. It was, I think, that primeval, carnal smell which Nadette delighted in calling "l'odeur de faune" which finally lulled me to sleep.

That night I dreamed of an obelisk set high on a hill in the distance. Around it people were circling three times and after the third time they vanished behind it. In the foreground I saw Kynddilig sitting on the banks of a ford, playing a game of gwyddbwyll with another. He looked up from the board and greeted me. "May the gods be good to you, Owein! Have you found the countess of the fountain yet?" "No," I said, "she is lost in the fountain of tears." "My name is Macsen," said the other, "and may the gods be good to you in this my city of Rome." "Emperor," said I, "can you tell me why they are circling and how is your game of gwyddbwyll?" He removed his laurels and they shrank to the size of a man's toe. "Imagine this is my king," he said, "and these are Kynddilig's warriors." He removed the golden buttons from his tunic and they became warriors in blood red brocade, riding sturdy horses with long black manes. "I have to get my king to the edge of the board before he is captured by Kynddilig's warriors hiding in the forest." "I see you have nearly succeeded," I said. "But the game is not yet won," said Kynddilig. "You should watch closely, Owein. The Emperor knows my warriors are hidden in the dark forest but he does not know where. When I am ready the Emperor will have to guess at the name of the forest and if he guesses wrongly my next move will capture his king."

I sat cross-legged beside them and watched them play. The sky was blue but a cloud was drifting across the sun. I lost my balance and fell back into the water in a silent splash. I struggled for breath until I realised I did not need to breathe and through the water I could still see Kynddilig and Macsen. A salmon spoke to me. "Such a fine May Eve it is," it said. "Ask them again about the obelisk." "But they will lose their concentration," I answered. "Then ask me. There is no secret I do not know." I span in the water and scratched by back on a reed. "Why do they circle three times," I asked "and then on the third disappear behind the obelisk?" "Because three is the number," said the salmon, "and without that number you cannot enter Annwfyn. You are not hiding a net in your pocket, are you? I hate nets." "No," I assured him, "I have no nets. And tell me: what is the name of this ford?" "Ford or ffordd?" he replied and gurgled out a bubble. "Ford, as in rhyd, not ffordd as in road." "You answer well, and the ford is called the Tolka," he said.

"Does it lead to the station of the man in the wheelchair?" I asked. "It does and sure wasn't he shot by Welshmen in the downcoming of Easter. Now take this ring and give it to Kynddilig."

There was a bright green ring between his thick pink lips. I recognised the ring but I knew that the salmon would not be able to explain until I took it, so I prised the ring from his mouth and held it tight in my fist. "But this is the ring of Rhonabwy," I said. "He was careless with it," the salmon said, "and if you value my words you should not be careless tomorrow." "Is there a need of the ring on Kynddilig, then?"

"He needs it. As long as he wears Rhonabwy's ring he will remember everything but once he casts it into Thalassa his own time will faint away and there will be nothing to remember any more. Now go, before the water gets too hot."

I took the ring to Kynddilig and he slipped it onto his finger without once looking up from the game. It glinted with an even brighter green now that it was on his finger, as though it were happy to have at last found its rightful place. He looked at Macsen. "Now, Emperor, what is the name of the forest?" Macsen studied the board and thought hard. Kynddilig winked at me and stroked his beard patiently. The sun went down and came up three times before Macsen answered. "Thalassa!" he decided. "Emperor," I said, "how can a forest be named after the sea?" "No," said Kynddilig, "it is not Thalassa. Will you guess, Owein?" "But I am not playing gwyddbwyll." "Answer anyway!" shouted the salmon. "Maxentius," I guessed, "after the Emperor here." "No," Kynddilig said gravely, "it is Paimpont. You should have known that, Owein." "Do not be sad," said Macsen, "I have lost my king and you have lost your love but it was nice of you to think of me."

8

Her face is changed. She must have one of those faces that takes time to come to life in the morning. It is pale, as though night has drained it of blood, not completely, but enough to raise the pallid standard of death or sickness. Her lips are dull, devoid of colour, barely darker than the rest of her face. Thin crescents have been scored into the paper-thin flesh under her still closed eyes, and they, too, I feel sure, will have lost that opalescent radiance of last night. I have seen this face before. It was Nadette's face, the time she fainted on holiday in Spain, unable to stand the agony of the bull any longer. So many times it had dropped to its knees in exhaustion, only to get to its feet again, vomiting blood into the sand but still facing its tormentors in its desperation to live. The sword the matador plunged deep into its heart failed to kill it. Even when the stiletto was stabbed into its skull for the coup de grâce, even when the nine inches of steel were twisted round inside its brain, still the bull's big white eyes blinked. A hind leg twitched when the horses dragged it away and it was then that Nadette's auburn head thumped into the back of the man in front of us. I pulled her back by the armpits and supported her neck with my hand. Her face frightened me. Gone was the soft, gentle face of vitality, gone were the golden features that promised to break into laughter at any moment. Her skin had taken on a macabre mixture of grey and green. Her shoulders convulsed and she made ugly noises as her cheeks sucked in air and for a moment, in my panic, I thought she was going to die. A young woman, a stranger, wafted her face with a fan and while sympathetic hands offered bottles of agua a faint pinkness began to appear in her face. Tears of delayed shock spilled out of her eyes as she came round. No, she wasn't going to die at the bullfight, yet at that moment I had a chilling vision of her in the future, dying in my arms, just like this. It seemed I'd just been through a dress rehearsal of her death.

But she didn't die in my arms. She died in the Forest of Paimpont, the most enchanted place in Brittany, in the most mundane of manners: a car crash, her daughter told me. She thought Nadette must have fallen asleep at the wheel on the long road from Rennes to Finistère. I knew that Nadette had a friend in Finistère and that she would often take off on the spur of the moment to go and see her but I couldn't help remembering the first time we passed by the Forest of Paimpont. Travelling along in her little black Mini and thinking the world was in the palm of my hand, I told her the story of Merlin and Viviane, how he had fallen in love with her and taught her the secrets of his magic, how he was still there in the enchanted forest, weeping tears in the Fontaine de Barenton, trapped for all eternity in the prison of air that Viviane had made for them both so that they should never be parted. A sadness seemed to overcome Nadette when I finished the story, but she made light of it and turned to ask me if I'd ever heard of a part of the Forest of Paimpont called the Val Sans Retour. I said I hadn't and asked her how it came to have a name of such finality. All she said was, "I know why it's called the Valley of No Return," but she never did tell me why. Now I think I know the meaning of the place, or at least, the meaning it had for Nadette. But I shall never know for certain.

And there's Kristine, lying there. Does last night mean we're lovers now? Long limbs all akimbo making sharp angles in the sheets. Why does the praying mantis come to mind? Eat their lovers after the act. Suicidal males. As if reading my thoughts, Kristine wakes with a jack-knife start, her head snapping sideways to look at the alarm clock on the bedside table. I make to greet her with a smile that says hail lover well met but her eyes show only an intense indignation. "Putain de merde!" she bursts out, "Why the hell didn't you wake me up before?"

"You said to wake you up at six, Kristine. It's still only ten to. Sleep well?"

"Oh, I see *you're* all ready. God, you look like a bloody priest like that."

"I'm out of white shirts. I take it you don't like my all black look."

"Pfff!" She rummages in the sheets, finds her body at the foot of the bed, her bra caught on the bottle of prosecco, picks her skirt and blouse from the floor and disappears into the bathroom, to emerge a few minutes later making a bee-line for the door. Definitely not a morning person, I conclude, as it closes behind her fleeing form. Not one for post-coital post mortems and questions like, "Do you still respect me?" It's just as well: I don't know what to think of her. Why did she single out me to sleep with, this woman with the husband and kids? I thought only Nadette did that sort of thing, with me at any rate. Could be she regrets it already, storming out like that. At least she didn't say "See you at the Cafe San Pietro". Maybe she'll choose to avoid me there. I hope so. I don't want her getting in the way of my business.

Kristine does not show herself at breakfast, nor is there any sign of her bus on the way down the Via Aurelia. Only when Gilles and I are already pulling away from the entrance to the Vatican Museums do I see her bus approaching with her at the front, mike slanted to her face, pointing to the spot beneath the mighty walls where her passengers are to queue up. She does not acknowledge me. Either she's avoiding me by deliberately arriving after us or her group is not as punctual as mine. Gilles drops me by the newspaper stand at the edge of St. Peter's Square and after jockeying behind a man who takes an age to decide between *La Corriera della Sera* and *Il Giornale*, eventually settling for both, I buy a copy of *Il Manifesto*. I fold it, tuck it under my arm and head for my rendez-vous across the Via della Conciliazone. An oncoming Cinquecento forces me to sprint the last few metres of the wide, sunlit street that has already become a gauntlet for the unsuspecting. Just as I reach the safety of the pavement I hear my name called out behind me. I look round but see no-one I recognise, then from behind a passing bus Kristine appears on the opposite side of the street, now transformed into an angelic figure in a white dress. She looks left and right, and I notice that her hair is tied up in a ponytail with a black scrunchie. She crosses and gives me a kiss thick with the scent of morning moisturisers.

To my relief, she suggests we sit outside the Cafe San Pietro so we can watch the tourist buses passing, "to see who else is in town." As we seat ourselves she relates that she's just seen a beautiful dog with gorgeous eyes, "a cross breed. Probably shepherd dog and labrador but adorable in any case." Aquiline, I would say her nose was. "Oh, I must make a phone call to my mother." When she sees I have no comment to make she leans back and tilts her face to the sun. It is as if she wants to forget everything about last night. Or perhaps she's playing at keeping me guessing. In either case, it makes no difference to me: my thoughts are on the contact. A broad-brimmed priest shuffles past, bible-black, giving me a disapproving look. Does he think I'm a fallen man of the cloth, cavorting with a woman so immodest as to have one button too many on her dress undone? He is a despiser of life, I tell myself, an atrophying and self-poisoned man of whom the earth should be weary. Be gone, or at least lighten up and give yer face a joyride.

Without prompting, Kristine begins to tell me how her mother is the most important person in her life. By now she'll already have taken the dogs on their morning walk around the eighth district of Paris. Her mother was annoyed when Kristine decided to start writing her name with a K instead of the C she had been baptised with but she's got used to the idea now. She is the complete creation of her mother, she says, and it's not such a bad thing because her mother's a strong woman who's had to put up with a lot, like a drunken husband who wasted the fortune he married her with. Her father is nothing but a selfish rogue who knows no sense of moderation. There is bitterness in her words. A corner of her mouth has filled with white spittle. Her father is without feeling, as cold as an iceberg, and he doesn't care who he hurts.

I wonder why she's telling me all this. She reminds me of the Californian I met, who after five minutes' conversation felt obliged to mention that he was seeing a therapist and proceeded to pour his heart out to me, a complete stranger. It occurs to me that what she wants in me is not a lover but a sounding-board for the hatred and bitterness she occasionally gives glimpses of. It isn't me she wants to prise out of the shell, it is herself, or perhaps she just wants to expose the shell to see what the contents look like in another's eyes. Perhaps she does this with everyone, or anyone she gets reasonably close to.

"What," I venture tamely, "about your husband? Isn't he the most important person in your life?" Her eyes fire a volley of silence at me and then take aim at the heavens. Dear God, methinks, don't tell me I've got a complete frother on me hands. And what if the contact is already inside?

"Hasn't it occured to you, Owen, that I might have been lying about having a husband?"

"No."

"Do you realise just how much trouble you get from people – passengers, guides, anyone – if you tell them you're a single woman?"

"Well, I. . ."

"They take one look at your blond hair, another at your arse, and immediately decide you're available. Look at that cretin at Gino's last night."

"Aye, well. At least you're honest about having lied. C'mon, Kristine, what can I get you to drink?"

"I bet you thought the same when you first set eyes on me."

"Oh, I see. You're saying I took advantage of you last night."

"Are you any different from the rest?"

"I like to think so."

"Pfff! Tu parles! . . . An orange juice."

My heart misses two beats as soon as I set foot inside the bar. I calmly ask the barman for an orange juice and a cappuccio, all the while pretending not to have recognised the man over my shoulder, reading the *Repubblica* at a formica table jutting out from the wall.

-There's someone here thinks your tourist work could be useful to us . . . A Kerryman.

-So where do I get in touch with him?

-Not in Dublin. You'll have to go to San Sebastian, in the Basque country. Donósti, they call it in Basque. You shouldn't have any trouble blending in there what with your dark looks.

At another table, a petite woman sits with her back to him. I light up a Gitane and sit down opposite her to keep the man in my sights. "Na, wie geht's, Aaron?" she says to me.

"Fine. I didn't expect to see you here, Effi."

"First of all, I know I told you in Luzern that I didn't know this city. I wasn't lying. I don't, but because of the situation they decided to use someone who hasn't been seen here before."

"It's alright: I believe you."

"We need to meet with another colleague of ours, today."

"How about the piazza Argentina, around midday? I'll have a break there while the group's in the Pantheon."

"Good. You can give the thing to him there."

"The piazza Argentina, you mean, not the Pantheon."

"Is there a problem?"

"No. I just wanted to get everything straight. Bad place for whispers, the Pantheon. You know, the acoustics."

"No, I wouldn't know about the Pantheon. As I said. . ."

"I'm not trying to catch you out, Effi."

"Good. You know, Aaron, I still don't know any more than you do about what's going on."

"Ah, don't worry about it. As you can see, I haven't been caught yet. You remember what you said in Lucerne?"

"I'm glad my intuition was wrong," she answers with a smile.

"There is one thing I have to ask, though, Effi. Who is this other person at the piazza Argentina, this colleague of ours?"

"I cannot tell you his name."

"Then tell me who authorises the hand-over. I can't go giving it to just any Hinz or Kunz who happens to show up with you."

"Il Codino: he authorises it. Does that mean anything to you?"

"It does. Thanks."

The barman calls out that he has an orange juice and a cappuccio ready for me at the counter. "Vengo subito," I tell him, confident that a Roman subito will gain me some time. The man with the *Repubblica* stirs his coffee and turns a page with an air of complete detachment.

"So," Effi says, rising, "piazza Argentina at midday. I will know how to find it." As we kiss each other goodbye Kristine walks in and stops dead in her tracks. She quickly recovers, producing an actor's smile. "I don't want to interrupt, Owen," she says with a sideways glance at Effi, "but . . . I've decided to go for a walk while there's still time. Besides, I've got to find a phone that takes cards to call my mother, so I'll see you later." Silently I curse her for having mentioned my name in front of Effi. Cicero, Aaron, now that's fine, but Owen is not something Effi needs to know. Kristine leaves and through the window I see her pass by in the direction of Hadrian's Mausoleum, away from St. Peter's. Whatever her reasons, I am glad she has gone. There is only Effi to deal with now, and the man with the *Repubblica*. "The situation is very urgent, Aaron," says Effi, "we have to act very fast." "I understand," I reply, and she leaves in the same direction as Kristine. Now how the fuck can I hand on a parcel I don't have any more? Is that an ashtray I can smell?

Can't see one about. Definitely a smell of wet ashes, a doused bonfire, a kind of funeral pyre smell.

It is time to confront the man with the *Repubblica*. I go to the bar, dispatch Kristine's orange juice in one go and take my coffee, planting it down in front of him. He studies me closely as I sit down and puts his paper to one side, waiting to see what I have to say. "And what are you doing here, may I ask?"

"Ah Jaysus, he sez, would you believe me if I said I was playing the James Bond?"

"Thanks be to the gods you're here, Seoirse."

"Been having a hard time?"

"Y'ever been dancing with a blancmange? I got your message, by the way."

"Do you know what it is? Do you know what I'm going to tell ya?" He takes another drop of coffee before telling me what it is he's going to tell me. It is a welcome relief to see him here, sitting there in the yellow anorak that goes with him everywhere, a joy to see the rudder-shaped nose, the small warm eyes of brown, the lived-in face, the russet beard with ever more grey. Beneath the table – I don't need to look – there will be the feet pointing away from each other, the feet that made the ten-to-two footprints in the sand of Sandymount strand.

He leans forward and begins in hushed tones.

"Nolan's been pulled by the German police. The thinking is it was to do with springing that Volunteer out of the nick."

"Who told you this?"

"A certain party that you know and I know in Brussels."

"The ponytail?" I mouth.

"Himself. He of the limp handshake and cut-glass accent."

"And he sent you here?"

"He did, first flight out of Brussels this morning, with what ya might call a roving brief. I was told to render you every possible assistance, with the stress on the every. So who was the woman ya were talking to just there? I'll tell you one thing: I wouldn't trust her anny further than I could throw her. I have a nose for these things." He taps the starboard side of his rudder to emphasise the point and leans back with folded arms. "So give me the runnners and riders, Owen, and we'll see if two heads aren't better than one."

I begin a lengthy disgorgement of everything that has happened since Brussels. Seoirse blinks at every piece of information, committing it to memory. He scratches his beard and mmms ominously when I get to the episode with Gramsci and Luciano, dispenses an aporetic pursing of the lips when he finds out what I've done with the parcel. His silence is uncharacteristic, making the danger that seems to be creeping in on me even more sinister, more concrete and real because acknowledged now by him. He listens even more intently when I relate the missing fingernails of the Ulsterman killed in Heidelberg. Then he takes in a deep breath.

"Right then, seems yer woman there's the key to all this."

"But Effi must be in the clear, otherwise she'd have just taken the parcel in Lucerne and have done, right?"

"On the face of it, yeah, but as Wilde said, the truth is rarely pure and never simple."

"What worries me most about her is that she said this handover at midday was authorised by the ponytail, aka Il Codino. I mean, that's just the Italian for ponytail."

"But it means she does know of the ponytail. Something to bear in mind."

"And anyway, why would the ponytail want to send you here to help me and at the same time give her instructions to take the parcel off my hands? She didn't say anything about Diogenes. It was like, when I pressed her on the authorisation, she was using a fall-back position."

"Well, I was told MI5's involved. She could be working for them."

"Hold on. That knocks my sketchbook theory right on the head."

"Why?"

"Cos it wouldn't be anything to do with the Brits. Why would they stick their oar in?"

"But there is a British dimension to the Van Dyck, whether it's us who's got it or not. Jesus, d'ya not read the feckin papers, Owen? Look, join the dots up, right. Antwerp commemorates the three hundred and fiftieth anniversary of Van Dyck's death with an almighty exhibition. Yer man's Italian doodlings were on loan *to* the Fine Arts Museum in Antwerp *from* the British Museum. They're British property."

"But that wouldn't bring in MI5. That'd be Scotland Yard's ball game. They've got a special Art Squad for stuff that gets stolen."

"But it would bring in MI5 if it was known that we had it, wouldn't it? And how would they know that we had it *unless* some grassing gobshite's told them it's us. I mean, ya don't go broadcasting who you are in a ransom case, do you? You try to keep your own identity secret, restrict it to those who need to know. But y'know, Owen, maybe the ponytail did tell you."

"How?"

"Of all the sketches, which is the best known? The Diogenes one, right, that's the one been splashed all over the papers because–"

"Cos it's the only sketch taken from classical antiquity."

"Jesus! When did you suddenly become the art expert?"

"That's what they said on Swiss telly."

"Right, so if we're running with this theory, the ponytail would know that you'd hear the name of Diogenes sooner or later in the media once the story of the heist got out. And you did, you made the connection, which was what he was counting on. He sort of planted the name in your head for future reference, just in case you were the one left holding the baby."

"So where does that leave us, Seoirse?"

"Still up shit creek without a paddle. But it's not all bad news. I know Nolan's been pulled but there's no man better at holding out than him. At least he'll buy you some time. They won't get a peep out of him. He's been through that mill more times than anyone else. And there's more good news: I've brought the cavalry, me very own rapparees."

"Come again?"

"Rapparees, irregulars. Right pair of gougers, but hearts of gold the both of them. Irish speakers as well, which makes a bit of a change."

"And what do they do?"

"Strike while the iron's hot. Take out the opposition . . . if need be. Everyone's making a move bar you. Look, the Swiss woman's bringing along her own muscle, isn't she, or that's what it looks like to me. And if what happened to the guy in Heidelberg's anything to go by, they're not exactly dragging their feet, are they? And while I think of it, there's something you haven't told me."

"What?"

"The other woman, the looker, the one you had words with."

"Kristine." I fill Seoirse in on her, from our first meeting to last night.

"Holy Mother of God," he exclaims, "are you telling me a woman like that fell for an ugly sod like you?"

"I don't know. There's something not right about her either."

"Don't exclude anyone. Just because you and her have jumped into the scratcher together doesn't mean her hands are clean, if you see what I mean. Don't let yer prick get in the way. It's the oldest trick in the book."

"I spose I have been excluding her so far."

"Well don't. It's no good being wiser from six feet under. Has she been asking you about anything she didn't ought to be?"

"No."

"Ah, now, well, she wouldn't would she, if she's . . . digging with the wrong foot, y'know."

"She said she wanted to prise me out of my shell. But I don't know. She said maybe she'd tell me her reasons sometime, and then again, it's like she slept with me last night and today she's acting every bit as like she hadn't done so out of choice. But I could be way off the mark there, Seoirse."

"Still, I like not that, as yer man says. And her turning up right after the episode with those two clowns in Venice . . . The honey-trap, they call it."

"She'll be with her group at the piazza Argentina the same time as me. Both our groups are visiting the Pantheon."

"Ah, now that makes things easier, logistically I mean."

A gaggle of guides invades the place, tucking brollies under their arms and surveying the bar for familiar faces. I nod at Claudio, the city guide whose features resemble St. Francis in the frescos at Assisi, and shout over to Roswitha, my own city guide, that I'll be with her in a moment.

"I don't know," Seoirse continues, "first this Swiss woman no-one knows from Adam, then this other joxer she's with, it's like they're all acting as cover for someone who doesn't want to show his face."

"Wait a minute. You don't think it could be the ponytail, do you?"

"Mmm, playing for both sides, y'mean? Wouldn't have thought so, but like I say, exclude no-one. One thing's for sure: it can't be the Heidelberg guy."

"My hunch is still Effi, even though she didn't take the parcel when she had the chance."

"There is. . ." Seoirse pauses, surveying the contours of the idea has just pulled the features of his faces into a broad grin. "There is an alternative: you give them the parcel."

"When I don't have it?"

"Precisely. They're not to know the parcel you give them isn't *the* parcel, are they? Least, not till they open it. And once they do open it and find a load of junk, they won't know for definite it's you who made the switch. Someone else could have switched it before you, in Heidelberg, say, or even back in Brussels. Or somewhere else along the line. Only, it means you'll have to stay with your tour for the time being. That's what you were told to do anyway, so if you do break cover and go to ground someone's gonna think there's something up. Bit of an exposed position, like dancing round on the parapets with the bullets whistling round yer ears, but . . . What d'ya reckon, I mean, 'bout doing a switch?"

"No, I like it."

"But we've still got to be prepared to take them out, get our retaliation in first. I'll tell the boys, tell 'em to use knives so it looks like just another mugging in Rome. You up for it?"

"Aye, I'm up for it."

"I'll tell you one thing: if we do have to hit someone today, it's only going to be the monkey, not the organ grinder. I'm tellin ya, there's someone higher up at the bottom of all this."

In a neat little town they call Belfast
Apprentice at trade I was bound
And many an hour's sweet happiness
I spent in that neat little town

A sad misfortune came over me
That led me to stray from the land
Far away from me friends and relations
Betrayed by the black velvet band

Sweat trickles down the furrow of my spine. My passengers huddle at the top corner of the square. Lizzie asks me when the bank behind her opens. From two thirty-five to three thirty-five, I reply. Olive Oyle asks what the sunken ruins in the middle of the square are. The republican temples, I say, and urge her to stay close to the brolly-brandishing Roswitha. Diagonally across the square from us Seoirse comes into view, flanked by two men. I raise a discrete hand in acknowledgement. They merge into the shade of an awning. Roswitha gives the order to follow her off to the left in the direction of the Pantheon, telling her new-found charges to be careful of the traffic. Some hesitate and look at me. I smile and tell them to follow her: "She's the one in charge today." Now will yez feck off and go see the Pantheon. There is no sign of either Kristine or Effi yet. Kristine probably won't drop here where it's illegal but she'll be leading her passengers through the square, alongside Claudio. More sweat down my back. Calmness is what's called for, Owen.

In the street leading off from the bottom of the square, I see a blond head bobbing towards me next to a man with swarthy features. I raise a hand high, ostensibly to indicate my presence to her, but in fact to give the signal to Seoirse. I set off. Seoirse's men take their cue and move from the orning towards the same corner. Not too fast, boys. No, that's just right. Irish speakers, eh? The square is hot and noisy. A puff of smoke from a red-yellow bus. Loud blast of a car horn. Another blast back at the first. Obscenities shouted. Ti spacco la faccia! Ma va a cacare, stronzo! It's good there's plenty of noise. Good cover.

I'm just following instructions dutifully, just handing over the parcel like I was told to. The job's over and I can go back to being a humble tour guide. Washing my hands of it all, aye, that's the front. And if they catch on about the switch then I give the signal to Seoirse's boys in Irish: Lean libh, get on with it, avanti. End of story. Wergild, the Saxons called it, the price you pay for killing someone. Eriach, the Irish equivalent. What price will we pay, if it comes to it? Hope it doesn't. But it's she who's associated with all the anomalies. The thing is, I quite like her. Sounds daft but there.

Standing in front of me with a smile on her face. The strap of a bag slanting between her breasts. I shan't kiss her this time. Next to her stands the swarthy man holding a brown portfolio, already unzipped. Don't like the look of him. Watch his hands closely. Seoirse's men appearing behind, alongside the news stand, ready to move in.

"I don't suppose I'll be seeing you again, Effi," I say, reaching inside my jacket pocket.

"Not in these circumstances," she replies.

"I hope to God I'm doing the right thing here."

"You are." I hand her the parcel. She takes it, glances at it. "I think both our roles are over now," she says and hands the parcel to her associate, who slips it into his portfolio.

"Take good care of it and of yourself."

"Goodbye, Aaron."

"Bye, Effi."

I watch as they turn and leave the square by the same corner from which they entered. As planned, Seoirse follows them at a safe distance, shadowed, in turn by his two gougers some fifteen metres behind. So there goes Effi, who thinks it's all over, and there goes Seoirse, who knows it is not, Sniffer Seoirse, seeing who or what she might lead him to. For the first time on this ill-omened job things are looking up. No longer am I all alone, out on a limb. Now I have someone on whom I can count unreservedly, a friend I grappled unto my soul with hoops of steel ever since that afternoon when, looking down on the shimmering outlines of Florence from the loggia of the Badia, he told me he lived his life according to Polonius's maxim: This above all, to thine own self be true. And not for him, either, the bleeding heart of the whingeing, cringing liberals who wring their hands at the prospect of breaking the thou-shallt-not-kill commandment. No, he knows as well as I that this is not a moral beauty contest and anyone who pretends it is should go back to their short trousers and lollipops.

After the afternoon optional to the catacombs, evening eventually comes, and with it dinner, and a heavy lull in the conversation brought about by my disagreement with Koen. He started innocuously enough, complaining that there weren't enough passengers interested for him and Kristine to run the optional to the Tivoli Gardens and saying how little he'd earned compared to previous tours. Then, by means of a discursive hop, skip and a jump which left me for dead, there he was pontificating on the subject of Moroccans, maintaining that if they had to be in his beloved Belgium at all, the least that could be expected was that they should behave like Belgians. Gilles did the diplomatic thing and held his peace. Kristine obviously did not want to upset her driver with another seven days on the road still to go. Koen took our silence for assent, going on to say that Moroccans were arriérés, backward. I asked him if he'd ever seen the Alhambra in Granada or the Aljaferia in Zaragoza. No, he said gruffly, and gave me a look which clearly said, "What's that got to do with anything, you little arsehole?" I said no more.

Gilles gets up and says he'll go and fetch coffees for us all. Koen says he'll go without; coffee stops him sleeping and he wants to get an early night. Three coffees then, Gilles notes, making straight for the bar. "Alors, les valises à sept heures?" Koen asks. "C'est ça," Kristine confirms. Koen slides his belly out and slopes off in a sulk.

"You've just made yourself an enemy," Kristine tells me in a condescending tone that I'm beginning to find irritating.

"You think so?"

"I know so. And the Flemish don't forgive easily. They're as bad as gypsies."

"Ach, enemies like that I can handle."

"And what kind of enemy can't you handle?"

"The enemy within."

"Which is?"

"Ah, now that I haven't figured out yet."

"But you know there is one."

"I know there could be one, that's all."

"I wonder what your inner struggles are, Owen. Or is there just one: the struggle against yourself? Mmm? So many secrets!"

"Kristine, who is it that doesn't have secrets? Don't you?"

"Of course. Do you ever share your secrets?"

"Depends what the secret is."

"And what about this morning's secret?"

"Which one was that?"

"Your little friend in the Cafe San Pietro. If you don't want to tell me who she is. . ."

"Oh, just a friend. She lives in Rome. I arranged to meet her a few days ago."

"That's strange."

"What is?"

"Well, I saw her coming down the street and she seemed to be looking at a map of Rome. A Falk map, in fact. She looked lost so I offered to help her."

"Ah."

"She lives in Rome and she needs a map to find her way round?"

"Okay, so I lied. She doesn't live in Rome."

"And she's 'just a friend', is she, Owen?"

"Aye."

"Does this 'just a friend' have a name?"

"Look, Kristine, I've already told you I don't like people checking up on me."

"Tiens, I do believe you're being defensive."

"And I do believe you're being jealous."

"Oh no, Owen. I'm not jealous. She could be your wife for all I know, but I'm not jealous."

"Good."

"Is she your wife? I mean, I know I told you a little lie about having a husband but. . ."

"No, she's not my wife."

"I told her we were lovers," she laughs.

"Why on earth did you do that?"

"Because. Just because. I was feeling mischievous. You know, Owen, I think trust is the most important thing in any relationship."

"Excellent."

"Do you want to hear the good news?"

"What good news?"

"I forgive you."

"Excellent."

"And could I possibly. . .?"

"What?"

"Possibly. . ."

"Possibly what, Kristine?"

"Invite you to my room for a digestif?"

Gilles comes back balancing the coffees in his hands, setting them gingerly down in front of us. Unperturbed by his presence, Kristine unwraps a sugar lump and flashes me a benign smile as if to underline her offer. A mere nod from me would suffice, but I can't make up my mind. Does a digestif mean just a digestif? If I could be sure it was only that I'd be inclined to accept, down a quick grappa in Kristine's room and then retire to my own. But if it means more than a digestif, how likely am I not to wilt before temptation? Not very, most probably. "Live dangerously," Nietzsche whispers in my ear. "It's the oldest trick in the book," Seoirse answers back. The Irishman has it, I decide. I'll tell her something like it's too much too soon, or you're going too fast for me, something like that. Or tell her I've got a prior engagement in town. But then, if I do that, she'll assume it's with Effi.

"Vous avez des projets pour ce soir?" asks Gilles.

"I was just saying to Owen, why don't we all go up to my room for a digestif?" Hang on. Did she say that? She waves a hand at the surroundings. "You know, to get away from all this."

"Bon, ben, c'est pas le refus," he says with a look which assumes I've already accepted, and then, "just *one* digestif, and then I'll hit the sack." There's your opening, Owen. Off the hook.

"In that case," I jump in, "I think I'll plough my own

furrow down town. I want to get away from all this, too, but I fancy more than just one."

"But what if there's an emergency," Kristine objects, "with one of your passengers and you're not here to deal with it?"

"Oh, I'll take care of that. Siamo in Italia! Tutto è possibile!"

"Not everything, Owen," Kristine says, and before I can reply she's telling Gilles her room number.

I turn my back on them, and it feels good. It's as though I'm leaving all the events of today behind me, setting out for once on my own and with my own agenda, nobody else's. The world can keep all its intrigues and conspiracies and masks. If Kristine knows more about Effi than she's letting on, then so be it; I'll sort that out later. Even if she's doing no more than playing games with me, that's her crack. And she can keep her forgiveness. At least I'm well out of all that now. Tomorrow I'll be back on the ramparts, but right now my time feels properly my own and I will spend it as I choose, down at one of the Irish pubs near Santa Maria Maggiore, just me and my pint.

Sure there's a pome in every pint
At the Druid's Head in the dead of night
Doing in Rome what Romans do worst
Sinking a jar to get rid of de tirst

Smoke-filled air hangs all around
Dun rings dancing down and down
Brown turns to black just like in a dream
Crowned with a glorious millpond of cream

Aaaaah.

When things go wrong and will not come right
Though you do the best you can
When life looks black as the hour of night
A pint of plain is your only man

When Nietzsche's head is up his arse
And Kristine's also ran
When all I want is the time to pass
A pint of plain is your only man

Let Ulysses sleep and Kynddilig keep
My own bright winnowing fan
When it's all enough to make you weep
A pint of plain is your only man

Aaaaah.

9

I don't care what they say: there's nothing so overrated as sex and nothing so underrated as a good shit. It sets you up for the day, a good evacuation of the bowels. Straight away it puts you in a good mood. Take this croissant. This is, what, my fourth morning in Italy but only the first time I've really enjoyed my croissant, the first time I haven't longed for a proper French croissant instead of these Italian ones with the sticky coating that clings to your fingers. And it's all down to the boa-constrictor lovingly evicted from my bowels. There's another thing about croissants: why do they call them cornettos in Rome? Brioches, they call them in Florence. For that matter, where between Rome and Florence do they stop being cornettos and start being brioches? Orvieto? Siena? Hah, Declan that time asking the guy for a cornuto when he wanted a cornetto. Asking for a cuckold he was. Could maybe see him in Florence tonight, with Pepe. Foxrock man, Declan, pukka type. More at home in the Bargello than the Bar Fiasco.

Here she comes. Wonder what sort of mood she's in today. Impeccably groomed as usual. Stiff back, stiff hair. She must use them what you call thems, them gauffres. Waffles? Waffle-pressers? What the hell word is it in English? Irons, aye, crimping irons, that's it. Ooh dear, no, definitely not in a good mood. And what is it this time? Because I didn't take her up on her offer last night? That's right, no, of course: the receptionist. Dismisses him as a connard, a wanker. A connard who's not going to get a tip from her. Was it the same, yes, it was the same guy I bunged twenty thousand to last night. Dario, said he'd call me at the pub if there was an emergency.

Not going to tell me what he's done to be a connard? No, well, okay. At least she can't complain I took advantage of her last night. Biting into her croissant. Not even the hint of a dribble of coffee down her chin. Wish I could do that. There's me always dabbing myself with a serviette or using the back of my hand.

"So," she says, "did you have a nice drink last night?"

"I did. You do anything interesting?"

"I got an early night, and I feel so much the better for it."

"Good, good, good."

"Do you want to have lunch together in Florence? You used to live there, didn't you? You must know some good places."

"How do you know that?"

"Gilles told me. He's really nice. He even showed me his tattoo."

"Was that all?"

"You're not jealous, are you, Owen?"

"Don't be daft."

"So what about lunch together?"

"Okay. Do you know Sant' Ambrogio?"

The grey kilometres roll northwards now. The weather forecast predicted early morning rain in Rome, cloud over Umbria and sun in Tuscany. Fair stands the wind for Florence, then. Only road works, accidents and tolls can slow our progress. Breaking off the Gran Raccordo Annulare, the ring of tarmac that is our last link with Rome, we set our sights first for Orvieto, a city that thrives on lies and deceit; deceit because it claims to have an altar cloth that drips with the blood of Christ, and lies, barefaced lies, because it's the home of Pinocchio, or so a Presbyterian from Lossiemouth once told me. Foot I have never set in Orvieto. The closest I've ever come to Orvieto is quaffing its classico. Apart from that, I've only ever passed by it on the stretch from Rome to Florence.

Beyond us now lies hostile territory, Etruscan territory, where assassins and the memory of my father creep. Long before they subdued the Etruscans by sheer force of numbers at the battle of Lago Trasimeno, the Romans sent an assassin to kill Lars Porsena, the Etruscan king. He wasn't a very good assassin, old Caius Mucius, because he was captured, but my father nonetheless held him in high regard.

"What did they teach you in school today?" he once asked me in the days before half his stubbly face was paralysed. The Romans, I replied. "Did they teach you about Caius Mucius?" I asked him what one of them was. "Don't be stupid. Caius Mucius was a man, and a good man at that," and he went on to tell me how Caius Mucius was caught by the baddies and he put his hand in the fire to show how brave he was. At least, that was how my nine-year-old mind interpreted it. Only much later did I discover that the point of Caius Mucius thrusting his right hand into the fire was to show how little he valued his own life, and that, I think, was what my father had actually been trying to tell me.

There was another time when I found him on the sofa, swilling some kind of liquid in a glass, the way wine-tasters do. I said he'd catch all the germs in the glass doing that and then he'd die. "Yes," was all he said. I asked him if he wanted to die, and again he said, "Yes." I was ten by then. I don't think it was sadness I felt, hearing him say that so calmly and decisively. It was more like betrayal. And true to his wish, before the year was out he was dead. I cried when he told me I couldn't be a footballer because he'd decided I was going to be a barrister, whatever that was. But the day he died I didn't cry, because I was glad. He was out of the way. My sister and I would have Mum all to ourselves and I could now be a footballer and end up on the front page of *SHOOT!*

"What about making a stop in Perugia or Assisi?" says Gilles with that impish grin of his.

"Good idea, but I don't think Kristine'd approve of it."

"No. I don't think she would."

"And we must keep Kristine happy."

"Absolutely. I don't think she's a woman to be crossed."

"No?"

"No."

"I gather you showed her your tattoo last night."

"Oh, that," he laughs. "Somehow we got to talking about films and that one with Depardieu and whatsername. What's it called? *Green Card*. And that bit where he's showing her his tattoos, so I just showed her mine for a laugh."

"So you enjoyed your digestif?"

"Well, until I started talking about Carine and then I felt as though I was outstaying my welcome. So I finished my beer and went on my way."

Maybe that's one way I could find out about Kristine. Get her pissed. That's where you see the real person, with all their obsessions and fears and ambitions and disappointments. And secrets. Alcohol breaks down the walls they put up, strips away all the onion layers. Worth a shot.

A sign showing Florence thirty kilometres away sends me sliding back into nostalgia for the city that was home for three glorious years. Afternoons spent on balconies, looking out over the city with its strawberry dome. Nights that echoed the footsteps of the ghosts that once trod the same streets. Machiavelli, Donatello, Michelangelo . . . Heated arguments and friendly arguments with the Italian communists. Berlinguer and Gramsci and the conquest of civil society. Waking up in strange beds. Bacchanalian nights that turned to day, watching the sun rise over via Masaccio. Grappa, amaretto, amaro, multiple aperitivi. Pot-bellied wicker carafes of Chianti littering my room. Thomas waking up in the night after a heavy session. Drank fabric conditioner because he thought it was orange juice. Kenny the Scot on wine: never pay more than a thousand lire per litre. His joke about what have E. M. Forster and the test tube baby got in common. A womb with a view. Listening to real Catalans and Basques and Greeks and Danes. Iñakis and Tadhgs and Gerd-Jans and

Sørens and Despinas and Marie-Annics and Cinzias. Fleeting affairs of the heart, or of the loins more like. Seeing Deneuve in the flesh at the Alfieri Cinema. Saturday football at the Cascine with the Italians running for cover at the first drop of rain. Forty-year-old men turning up in their purple Fiorentina strips and me in my Man. City shirt. Learning the Florentine accent, hoha hola instead of coca cola, dugento instead of due cento, coll' ashentho. Reading Dante and Homer. People calling you dottore. Forty minutes to get a check cashed at the Cassa di Risparmio, shunted from pillar to post, from one sportello to another. Declan rushing into the bar to get me to look at the sunset from the loggia of the Badia. Tears wept for Mum. Mosquitos, the bastards. The Casa del Popolo at Pian di Mugnone, Beppe Napoli the communist brickie. A painter, too. Showed me some of his canvases. Him telling off that crass liberal of a Portuguese, the basenji dog: *qui* non si parla male del comunismo! Put him in his place. Ordinary workers discussing literature over their pizzas. First time I'd felt welcome anywhere as a student. Florence, my Florence.

A hungry feeling
Came o'er me stealing
And the mice were squealing
In my prison cell

Her tongue bends towards the twin-domed ice cream with desire. Who is she, this lone, lobster-fleshed woman whose frame is large enough to register on the radar, poddling across the square towards me? A tourist, clearly, by her backpack and the crumpled map in the other hand. One amongst hundreds drifting across the piazza or sitting in clusters on the stone benches. What has lured her to Santa Croce? The gold and silver shops herearound, or the leather shops where reign Messrs. Amex, Mastercard and Visa? She stops, frowning, open mouthed, sucking in the fierce white glare of the facade at my back. Is that her reason for coming to Santa Croce, to pay homage to the host of titan spirits lodged in this glittering pantheon of Florentine genius? The stern-faced poet at my shoulder glowers at her. She returns his look with indifference and, dipping her head, applies another coat of gelato to her broad, orange tongue, lapping like a dog at the bowl.

Not the debt of love I owed could quench deep in myself the burning wish to know the world and have experience of all men's vices, of all human worth. Is that not so? You should know, maestro poeta. To stay fixed, rooted, tied down in Rennes, or to see the world, to know places like Florence and the people Fortune washes onto her shores. Aye, that was the question is what's keeping Kristine? Standing me up because I stood her up in Rome. Or still with her punters in the leather shop, playing the honest broker in the hope

"Any news, Owen?" Dear God, where d'he spring from? "I'll tell you one thing, he sez: the parking doesn't get anny easier here."

"No, no news. How you keeping?"

"Ah, grand. Be an awful lot better for a few scoops of the black stuff, I can tell you."

"I'm just waiting on Kristine. She should be here any minute. I said I'd have dinner with her over in Sant' Ambrogio, y'know, the covered market. She's probably still in the leather shop with her punters."

"Just watch your back with her. Did ya bury the baldie fellah with her last night?"

"No, I went for a few pints by myself."

"You still on for the Fiddler's Elbow tonight?"

"Yeah, sure. Don't worry, I shan't be bringing her."

"I'll see who else I can round up, just so it looks all nice and normal, like ya haven't got a care in the world. But there's something I need to kick around with ya, a hypothesis."

"How d'it go following Effi? Turn up anything?"

"That's what I want to talk to ya about."

"Ah, you're doing a grand job, Seoirse."

"I must be. You didn't see me creeping up on you, did ya? Ah, the ould skills is still there y'know."

"There's Kristine now."

"Holy Mother of God, ya must have the eyes of a feckin lynx! Right, I'd better make meself scarce. I'll catch ya when I can."

He retreats behind the statue of Dante and disappears down the steps leading away from the square. Kristine is easily spotted among the crowds in her white tee-shirt and black jeans. But black and white! Dear God, Juventus colours in Florence! Has the woman no shame? Chi non salta è bianconero, heh! heh! I trot down the steps of the church to meet her but I've barely taken half a dozen strides across the piazza when a plastic football smacks into the side of my face. "Oh, scusa, eh," calls a guilty teenager, holding up his palm like a professional acknowledging a foul. "Niente," I say, rubbing the sting out of my cheek. Feckin eejit. "Salut, toi!" I call as soon as Kristine's close enough. "Hello," she replies. "So which way is Sant' Ambrogio?" I turn and point towards the Dante statue. "Sort of over there, about five minutes off." We walk on together. "Well," I add, to avoid future reproach, "five Italian minutes." She bursts into laughter. Come on, it wasn't that witty. Means she's in a good mood, though. "That was really funny," she says, "seeing you knocked sideways by the ball." I start to feel a spring in my step. I'm doubly glad: I've made her laugh and now I've got a topic for idle conversation. "Have you ever seen the calcio storico here?" She looks to the ground.

"You mean the calcio fiorentino."

"Calcio fiorentino, whatever."

"No," she answers with a tight-lipped smile, "never had time."

"Oh well. Still, at least the Blues won again this year. That's, well, sort of my team, the Santa Croce team."

"You know I don't like football."

"True, but it's not everywhere you get blokes dressing up in seventeenth-century costume to knock seven shades of shite out of each other." Ah, God loves a tryer. No, maybe it's my fault, talking too much about myself. Self-obsessed, Pepe, you were right, self-obsessed.

"Still," she says, brightening up, "perhaps one day."

The church of Santa Croce sucks people in one door and spits them out through another. The same fat woman rests on one of the stone benches. We step over a chain and leave the piazza behind, walking up a cobblestone street where already it is quieter. A few more streets and there won't be any tourists at all, just real Florentines. An injured pigeon lies helpless in the road. "Regard, Papa!" shouts a child and rushes out to its aid, unaware of the oncoming car. A sharp intake of breath from Kristine. The child's father dives in to pull the girl away in the nick of time. Kristine turns her face away as the wheels trundle over the pigeon. The father shouting his chastisement. Feathers and blood on the cobblestones.

Kristine follows me in silence as we turn left up Borgo Allegri. God, it was only a pigeon, Kristine. Don't go getting a gob on over a pigeon. Oops, mind that. You forget just how narrow these pavements are. Motorini and ASNU litter bins making it even narrower. The latteria up there where I used to go for breakfast, still going strong. The antiques shop where I never saw a customer. Have a peek in. No, still no customers. I love it. Thank-you for not having changed. Probably no-one remembers me round here any more. Can't be helped. Only to be expected, really. Never did find out exactly where Cimabue had his studio here. Everybody dancing in the street when he brought out his Madonna and Child. Allegria. Borgo Allegri. I think, yes, I'll have pasta e faggioli for dinner.

Crossing into the Piazza dei Ciompi, dominated by the robust Vasari loggia commemorating the weavers' uprising, I notice a transvestite relaxing with a spuma cedro at the Zoo Bar, his five o'clock shadow turned to the midday sun, only half listening to a lad perched on his motorino. Next shift tonight at the Cascine no doubt. Kristine following blindly, head down. We turn right into Borgo La Croce. Hang about, it would have been quicker to go down via dell' Agnello. Oh well, she'll be none the wiser. Maybe it was the near miss with the child that upset her.

"You must be very attached to your children," I venture, trying to break the ice. "How old are they?"

"I don't have any children," she mumbles back.

"But didn't you say on Burano you had two children?"

"Don't you listen to *anything* I say?" Steady on. That was a bit strong. What have I said now? "I only said," she continues, "that I have had two children. There is a difference."

"Sorry. I was blind to the nuance."

"Tu m'étonnes." That curious French way of saying that I do *not* surprise her. French through and through.

"Boh . . . Maybe we should change the subject."

There was the first abortion with Johnno the Irishman. "You *do* remember me talking about him, don't you?" I do. And then with a Spaniard, just because he refused to wear a condom. That makes two children she's had. No, I will not ask why she didn't insist on the Spaniard wearing a condom. And then more silence, silence as weapon. Offensive obtumescence.

"It's stupid," she says suddenly, "only having one night in Florence."

"Aye. I mean, I was here three years and would only have seen ten per cent of all the art. What chance do the passengers have of seeing anything?"

"I was talking about the job, Owen. If we had two nights we could fit in an extra optional and make some money. And with dinner included we can't even do the restaurant at La Certosa either." That's it.

"Kristine, why did you suggest having lunch together? Just so you can whinge about work?" She puts a hand on my shoulder.

"There's no need to be so confrontational, Owen." The melifluous veneer of conciliation. And how long will she keep that front up?

"I've had enough of this."

"Are you cancelling our lunch date?"

"Yes. Listen, there's a brick wall there you can bang your head against. At least it won't answer back." She slides her hand down my arm and squeezes my hand.

"I'm sorry. I want us to be friends. Can we still have lunch together?"

"Alright, as long as we don't have to play silly games."

"Agreed. I'm sorry."

The covered market is a cauldron ringing with exhortations, wailing lamentations, tempered obscenities and intemperate boasts, all cured in the hanging smell of cold meat. Bloodstained aprons vie for attention with the half-closed, death mask eyes of suspended chickens. Kristine declares it "génial!" Making bold and loud with my use of "permesso" and "mi dispiace", and deftly avoiding all manner of edges likely to pierce the ribs, I reach the far end of the market and the familiar sign of the Tavolo Caldo.

"Dottore!" exclaims the little man with the tash behind the counter. I give him a warm shake of the hand. "Pasta e faggioli with red wine!" he declares, denying any right of contradiction, "e per la signora?" Kristine asks him what's on the menu and reels under the machine-gun fire of the dishes he rattles off, settling rather meekly for a bistecca alla fiorentina. She looks a little dismayed at the two plastic cups he plonks down on the smeared formica top and peers inquisitorially at the label on the carafe of Gallo Nero.

"It's not Nuits St. Georges, Kristine. We're among the prolos here."

"No, I was just curious."

"We were lucky. You often have to wait hours for a table."

"Mmm, I think I like it here."

"Contenta tu, contenti tutti!" The glasses wobble at first when I pour. "Salute!"

"A la tienne, Etienne! It reminds me a bit of the market in Barcelona, the one just off the Ramblas."

"Aye, I can see what you mean. Didn't you say you used to live in Spain?"

"Yes, but not in Catalonia, in Granada."

"Really?"

"I shared a flat on the Sacromonte."

"Who with, if it's not indiscreet?"

"You'll only laugh at me if I tell you."

"No, go on."

"A young man training to be a bullfighter. I know, I know, it's just the sort of thing you imagine happening to an innocent young French girl in Spain, isn't it? Falling for the dashing young bullfighter. . ."

"Let me top that up for you . . . There. So what was his name?"

"Indalo."

"A fine Andalusian name."

"He had a nice bum. And nice hands."

"Ah, right."

"He was the one who, you know, it doesn't matter. . ."

"Ah."

"I used to work with horses in Granada. It wasn't exactly the work I wanted because it was with the old horses, the ones that come into the ring with the armour on. I used to walk them up and down outside the bullring, blindfold them, that sort of thing."

"Blindfold them?"

"Just one eye, the inside eye, so they can't see the bull charging at them."

"And Indalo? Did he make the grade as a bullfighter?"

"No, the last I heard of him he was an insurance salesman."

"Dear God! . . . Ah, grazie, capo."

"Bon appétit! No, start without me. I'll have some more wine."

"An insurance salesman! Bit of a come-down from bullfighting."

"Ecco la bistecca! Buon appetito, Signora! Tutto apposto, dottore?"

"Sì."

"It didn't surprise me of Indalo. It's in his character to take advantage of innocents . . . Enfin . . . Why does that man call you 'dottore', Owen?"

"He calls anyone with soft hands 'dottore'."

"Allow me."

"You're not trying to get me drunk, Kristine, are you?"

"The very thought!"

"So Andalucia's your favourite part of Spain, is it?"

"No. I much prefer the Basque country. Do you know it? You probably do."

"No, not really."

"You should go. It's so green, and it's got mountains and beaches and . . . everything."

"Will you have another drop?"

"We're not going to drink the whole bottle, Owen, are we?"

"No, and besides, we're not even half-way down yet."

"So how do they calculate how many glasses to charge for? Just by looking at the bottle?"

"No, it's a lot simpler. If he doesn't like you, he overcharges you. If he likes you, he undercharges."

"There's no middle ground?"

"No, which is how I like things . . . Sacromonte, did you say?"

"Yes, why?"

"Oh, it's nothing. Don't worry about it . . . Cheers! How's the steak?"

"A little overcooked."

"Ah, that'll be your French palate. In France they throw a

steak through a warm kitchen and call it cooked."

"Oh, come on. . ."

"I was only joking. Was he very macho, this Indalo?"

"Let's not talk about Indalo. What about you? Would you say you're macho, all this football and drinking?"

"Maybe I am. But then what would you say of the Catalan woman who has a season ticket at the Nou Camp and happens to be one hell of a fierce drinker? Is she macho, too?"

"But there can't be many women like that."

"It's not a question of numbers, is it?"

"I still think you're a bit macho."

"Fair play."

"And . . . no."

"No, Kristine, say what you were going to say."

"Well, since you don't like middle ground, I think you're a bit of a misogynist on the quiet."

"Not even in the deafening silence. But you don't have to believe me."

"You don't care if I don't believe you?"

"Nope."

"Because you don't care about me?"

"No, it's not that. It's because I could well convince you I'm not a misogynist while still being one. Assuming I were, of course, which I don't think I am."

"You have an elaborate way of avoiding the issue."

"Caring about you? No, I don't think I do . . . Oops, there I go again, talking honestly."

"Why not?"

"I think your head's fucked up."

"Oh, you do, do you? Well, you're enough to fuck anyone's head up!"

"Just because you slept with me doesn't mean you have a claim on me, let alone any claim of affection."

"I didn't know you could be such a bastard."

"But an honest bastard, at least. Unlike you."

"How have I been dishonest with you?"

"You really want to know what I think? You won't like it."

"I don't care what you think. You can keep your cheap wine and all your pally little Florentine chums. You can keep your smart comments and your plastic cups and . . . tiens!"

Kristine storming out. Not a tear spilled. A glassful of wine, though, all over my face. Just like being in one of those French films. If there had been a door to slam she would have slammed it. I expect to look up and see the legion hell-hath-no-furies in the upper balcony giving her a standing ovation, and among them Nadette, clapping furiously and nodding well done, Kristine. And Mum, muttering disconsolately as she always did, "You always think you're right. You're never wrong, are you?" Instead, there's Gigi handing me a serviette to wipe my face with. "I hope it wasn't because of the bistecca," he sighs with a wink. A bit of a sting in one eye. Wine in my beans. Sacrée Kristine. Sacromonte.

"Ah Jesus, he sez, now don't tell me: it was something you said. You're not going to leave that steak, are you?"

"That's twice you've caught me today."

"Sure wasn't I over there all the time having meself an aperithivo della hassa."

Seoirse starts tucking into the steak. Only now do I realise that not only is he without his glasses today – he must have his contact lenses in – but he's also shaved off his beard. No disguising the nose, though. Steer any ship safely round Cape Horn, that would. Nose in the trough. Should keep him quiet for a bit. Loves his food. Gigi sets down another cup for him and the wine flows once more. After the steak Seoirse orders a macedonia di frutta and proceeds noisily to scoop juice and segments of fruit into his mouth. Yes, this is the company I like, hedonism headlined on Seoirse's face, pure enjoyment of the moment. This above all things . . . Too bad about Kristine. "Ah, that was a gas feed, so," says Seoirse, folding his arms. "Well, d'ya want to hear about Rome?" We decide to go for a coffee elsewhere to mull over his hypothesis. Gigi's total comes to eight thousand. He must have knocked a couple of thousand off for injured pride.

I take out my packet of cigarettes and put one to my lips. Outside in the car park the sun gouges my eyes. "What about going to Gianni's bar there?" I suggest, groping for my lighter. "Sure," says Seoirse with a belch, "it has proximity going for it."

"Aye, nowt but a cock's stride." We enter the bar and order two espressi.

"Shame about yer shirt there," Seoirse remarks. "Still, it'll come out in the wash."

"Hmff. Well, I reckon we can rule Kristine out of any underhand dealings. If she was on the inside, a real pro with a job to do, she'd have stuck to the task. She wouldn't have risen to the bait and rushed off like she did."

"No, true."

"So what's the story with Effi?"

"Ah, ah now, wait till I tell ya. There I was, hot on the trail, and after only a couple of streets the joxer she brought with her hands the parcel back to her and buggers off down some darkened vicolo, ne'er to be seen again. He was just a decoy, and a feckin piss poor one at that. Annyway, guess what happens next."

"What?"

"She starts heading back north. I don't know if she's got herself lost or what but annyway she ends up by the piazza where there's the mausoleum of Augustus, just off the right bank of the Tiber?"

"Okay."

"And this is where she gets into a parked car. This is her rendez-vous, right."

"Don't tell me the car whisked her away and you lost her."

"Would y'ever get out o' town! Me, lose someone? Ya feckin unbeliever!"

"But you were on foot, right?"

"Ah, but the car stays parked. Course, I can't get close enough to see what's going on or who's in the car with her." He pauses, emitting a sound, unique to him, which is halfway between a chuckle and a gurgle. "You're gonna love the next bit, Owen."

"Fer fuck sake get on with it, Seoirse."

"Jesus, ya have no patience when a man's telling a story, do ya? Typical. So, there's me wanting to get in close and to make matters worse, don't I start getting hassled by a groupeen of gypsie kids trying to beg money off me. Y'know, the can-I-wash-yer-car-mister lot. That's when the two hundred lire drops. No, sez I, cos I haven't got a car, but if yez go and do that car over there and get the number plate and tell me what's going on, here's twenty thousand now and there's another twenty thousand when yez come back with the goods. Ah, ya should have seen their grubby little faces light up."

"Seoirse, I yield to no man in my admiration for your brilliant improvisation. However. . ."

"So after a while the car shoots off with all three in it and, okay, so now I've lost her but the kids come back and here's the picture: la signora piangeva, piangeva tantissimo, era molto sconvolta, i signori gli gridavano, tutti e due, erano stranieri."

"So Effi was upset."

"Distraught more like."

"Did they say what language the men were shouting at her in?"

"C'mon, Owen, they were street urchins, not linguists."

"And the car?"

"Aah, now here's the thing. Not Roman, right, and rented, with a targa beginning with BZ."

"So, we've got two foreign men shouting at Effi in a rented car with a Bolzano registration. Is that it?"

"And presumably shouting at her cos they realise she's taken the wrong parcel."

"Rented . . . Why rented and from Bolzano?"

"Aaaaah, y'are, aren't ya? You're thinking what I was thinking on the way up today."

"To disguise where they're coming from, to hide their tracks by changing cars at Bolzano . . . Aaand, Bolzano . . . right, I'm with you now, just happens to be one of the staging posts between Italy and Germany, if you choose to come through Austria via Innsbruck."

"And why wouldn't you if you was heading for Venice first? I checked it on the map."

"Mmm. You reckon it could be them two who crashed in on me in Venice again, operating out of Germany? Hold on, no, that doesn't make sense. The kids wouldn't call them stranieri."

"Exactly. Now, I'm paddling me own canoe here *but* who do we know in Germany, eh? Who might be coming out of Germany and changing cars to hide their tracks? There's the Swiss woman, who says she lives in Frankfurt. There's Nolan in Cologne and he's banged up. There's the Heidelberg fella, but dead men don't rent cars."

"So all three candidates are out of the frame."

"Ostensibly. But as they say, all that glitters. . ."

"Let's just think this one through. Let's assume for a moment it's Nolan, Nolan and some MI5 geezer. He knows my Aidan Flynn alias for a start. He does a disappearing act in Cologne. I don't know, he leaves some cryptic message on his answerphone for the ponytail saying the police are banging at the door and he's about to be lifted or something like that. Whatever. He's the hard man of the movement, his reputation precedes him everywhere, never been broken by the Brits under interrogation, the man who shot his own kid brother for informing. No-one would ever suspect him of having been turned."

"Yeah, but. I know it works in practice but will it work in theory?"

"How d'you mean?"

"The Volunteer he was instrumental in springing?"

"Fuck, yeah."

"Who got safe and sound to America. If Nolan had been turned, the guy wouldn't have made it past the check-in desk at the airport. He could have shopped him well before that even."

"So his arse is covered as far as that goes."

"It does look that way."

A troubled man, Seoirse studies the dregs of his coffee in silence. In moments like this he looks more his forty-something age, more the world-weary Mentor than the joker for all seasons and reasons, more the man I used to see in the upper cloister, bent for hours over the same text, certain that there was a gap in the argument and that, come hell or high water, he would find it. He sighs, puts his cup back on its saucer, and looks at me again.

"I still smell a rat, Owen. Bugger the ocular proof. And I'll tell you one thing: I'm not taking anny chances it's not Nolan. He's a nasty piece of work and when it comes to pulling strokes there's not many can match him. Nope, I'm gonna get meself tooled up. If I don't it could be very bad for me health so. You should think about it as well."

"I thought you were carrying already."

"Sure I had me rapparees in Rome to take care of that side of things. Different ball game now it's just you and me . . . Ah, don't ya just love Italy: the land where you can get annything you want if you know the right people."

"Okay. I'll see you tonight then."

"And in the meantime, rack yer brains. Try to find the missing details. They're there somewhere. And put on a fresh shirt, will ya?"

It's the same the whole world over
It's the poor that gets the blame

It's the rich that's getting richer
Ain't it all a fucking shame

It pains me to think that, come the morning, I shall have
to leave these people behind and take to the road again. Here
they all are in the serene twilight of Santa Maria Novella,
gathered at the Fiddler's Elbow like knights of the Round
Table. There's Rainer, Rachel's latest beau, a clinical chess-
player but decent enough skin to go for a pint with. There's
Rachel, whose rugged individualism can be seen in her orange
skirt and purple tights, ten denier sheer, apparently. Then
comes Seoirse, holding court, of course, and next to him the
heretical Declan, the Dublin Four man of law with the tennis
ball head. Lively blue eyes, never misses a trick. A blue-shirted
Fine Gaeler, but what the hell. And at my right hand sits Pepe,
my brave, noble, peerless Pepe. Altogether, an embarassment
of riches. Tourism has given me money. It is my friends that
make me wealthy. Pints of Guinness all round, except for
Declan and his accursed pear juice and tonic.

Seoirse is re-hashing the tale of how he once escaped from
Italian justice. Some of the others will have heard it before,
but that has never been a consideration to deter Seoirse. "So
in the end they overtake me on the Viale dei Mile and force
me to pull over. I get out the car, Owen gets out the car, the
two Scottish girls stay in the back. And d'ya know what this
Carabiniere has the impudence to allege? Drunken driving, he
sez. Well. . ."

"Are you sure it was impudence on his part?" asks Declan.

"Well, of course I denied it."

"You omit the fact that you had jumped three red lights in
succession," Declan adds.

"Alright, so there was that. But I was just trying to be like
anny other Italian driver. I was assimilating their culture."
Declan's eyes roll heavenward, despairing at the image of
Ireland Seoirse presents to the rest of Europe. "Then he wants

me to blow in his bag and, of course, I refuse. Then he wants to do a blood test on me, sticking some needle in me when I don't know where it's been. He even wanted to do a blood test on Owen, and he was only in the feckin passenger seat, y'know. I mean!"

"I believe it was at this stage that you claimed diplomatic immunity," says Declan.

"Alright, so it was a bad move. But then the girls get out and start flirting with the other Carabiniere, sitting on his bonnet, admiring his pistol, telling him how bello he is, all that stuff, and he actually pulls his gun out of the holster and gives it to one of them to play with. Can you believe that? Owen, am I lying?"

"Nope."

"And then what?" asks Rainer.

"Well, I'm telling the one who's giving me a hard time that these two girls, it's their first night in Florence and it's my solemn duty to make it . . . memorable for them, y'know. But he's not wearing anny of it. Then I look up and see – what was her name? Karen, yeah – I see Karen aiming this gun at me. At *me* of all people."

"Unfortunately," laughs Declan, "she was too drunk to pull the trigger."

"Right, and – what d'ya mean 'unfortunately'? – annyway, the other Carabiniere has the presence of mind to grab the gun off her in the nick of time. So I get slapped with a charge sheet telling me when and where to appear in court, the girls shag off to some club, and to cap it all they tow me car away. Feckin marvellous."

"So you had to go to court?" asks Rachel. Lovely warm red hair she has.

"Ah, no. It never got to court."

"How come?" she asks.

"I got on to Beppe Rao, this Sicilian fella doing the LL.M, and he got on to someone else and the case got sat on. Me file umm . . . got lost in the wash."

"Who was the someone else?"

"Ah now, my lips are sealed." Seoirse takes a long draught of Guinness, satisfied that a web of mystery has at last settled on the story.

"Come on," Pepe urges, "tell us who it was."

"I tried asking the Sicilian," I explain, "but he wouldn't give anything away either. All he said was he knew the right person in the right place. 'Conosco la persona nel posto giusto,' that's all he would ever say."

"So you won't tell us," says Pepe.

"Me lips . . . are sealed," Seoirse repeats and drains his pint to half-way. "So where you from, Rainer?"

"Bonn."

"Isn't he gorgeous?" Rachel whispers to me.

"Rainer?"

"Yeah."

"Is it true," Pepe interjects, "what they say about German engineering?"

"Honestly, Pepe, you're so obvious."

"Well?"

"It's not his body, it's his hazel eyes . . . And he says he prefers petite women. Shorties, in other words."

"Sure I know Nietzsche. Quare ould one he was so. Also Shhhprach Zaratewstra and all that."

"I didn't know you would bring Seoirse," Pepe says with a searching look.

"Neither did I."

Pepe wrestles with the puzzle that has just appeared on the horizon of his thoughts. Slumped back in his chair, he reaches perfunctorily for his pint, holds it up to his lips, delays, and then decisively drains his glass. "Hey!" he exclaims, slapping my thigh a little too hard, "it's my round."

"I'll give you a hand," I say and we rise amid the grating, rivet-rattling protest of our chairs. Pepe leads the way through tables and outlying chairs and into the bar. A babelish hum pervades the place, a riot of tongues thickly trowelled onto the familiar canvas of the Pogues coming from the loudspeakers. Lorca's Novena that is. My Goodness, my Guinness on the wall. Céad míle faílte in the mirror. A maroon and white Galway rosette pinned to a beam. Italians drinking halves of Kilkenny. A fiddle on the wall, but where's the elbow? That's Dutch they're speaking, them two. Jack's Emerald Army on the scarf. Framed photo of David O'Leary, signed.

"I understand everything now," says Pepe, turning away from the bar, his order secured. "Seoirse wasn't bullshitting me that time, was he, about being in the IRA. And if he's here now, that's because you're really fucked."

"He's just helping me out, like you did." I stand back to make room for a barman carrying a tray of drinks. "You haven't said yet if you did everything we talked about in Verona."

"I haven't had an opportunity, eh?"

"Is the parcel safe, then?"

"Yeah, I did everything you said."

"Excellent, Pepe. I've decided to leave it where it is. It's safest that way."

"So how big is the trouble you're in? I've been having bad dreams . . . pesadillas about that dead man and his fingernails."

"I think it's very big trouble, Pepe. Seoirse's already saying I should get myself a gun."

"Joder!" he cries, and then lowering his voice, "You're joking me. You must be joking me."

"No, I'm not."

"No vas a matar a alguien, tio?"

"If I have to, yes. I think the next couple of days are going to be decisive and if it's a question of matar or being matared then what choice do I have? The person we're dealing with, if we're right, would matar me at the drop of a hat."

"I knew it! I knew it! When I got off my bike and saw your face."

"What?"

"Like you were looking at me for the last time. Like you weren't going to see me again. God, I don't believe it! And when I saw Seoirse with you I knew something was bad. Hostia puta, this isn't happening."

"It'll be alright, Pepe."

"You don't know that."

"No . . . No, I don't."

"Aren't you afraid?"

"Afraid? No, well, yes. Have you heard of controlled fear?"

"No."

"Neither have I but I'm working on it."

"Thirty thousand, please!" shouts the barmaid.

"Just don't say anything to anyone, Pepe. That's the only thing you can still do for me. And don't let on in front of the others."

"Thirty thousand, Pepe!" she shouts again. I hold out a fifty thousand note but Pepe grabs my hand and tells me to put my money away. He pulls out three blue notes to pay for the six pints of Guinness lined up on the bar.

"Didn't you get a pear juice for Declan?"

"Oh, shit," he says, realising his mistake. "Fuck it, let him drink what we all drink." He picks up three pints, only to put them straight back down. He stares at the ground, shaking his head, thrusting down parallel hands. "It just doesn't make sense, Owen."

"What doesn't?"

"That you could be killed."

"Listen, Pepe, death is like wearing shellsuits and turning forty: it only happens to other people."

"Go on, then, joke about it."

"I'm sorry . . . Pepe, look, I've always been convinced I'll know when my time has come, and I just don't feel that now. You understand that, don't you?"

"Of course I do . . . Why did you say the next couple of days?"

"What?"

"The next couple of days are decisive."

"Because at the moment our adversary's off balance. He's going to have to re-group, re-think his strategy. So for the moment I'm safe."

"You sure?"

"Yeah. C'mon, Pepe, I want to see Declan's face when he sees you've got him a pint."

"Is there anything I can do?"

"You've done everything I could have asked you. Hey, viva Breogan! Eh?"

"Yeah, sure, viva Breogan."

We each lift three pints and, with shoulders hunched, tread gingerly out of the bar. The step down onto the pavement takes me by surprise and sends a white lava spilling over the fingers of one hand. I set pints down in front of Rainer and Rachel, transfer my pint to the other hand and shake off the foamy lumps. Seoirse looks agitated. "I mean," he protests to Rainer, "the guy ended up talking to a feckin horse in the middle of Milan. Some superman that!"

"Who are they talking about?" I ask, taking my seat.

"Nietzsche . . . still," says Rachel.

"And he was a feckin fascist so."

"No," Rainer replies with a studied firmness. "It was his sister who was the Nazi sympathiser. I still maintain that he was a valuable and original thinker." Declan remains aloof, until he sees the pint Pepe gives him, whereupon his face turns from surprise, to confusion, to indignation.

"And what's this supposed to be, Pepe?"

"Owen told me to get it for you."

"I did not!"

"Oh, well," Declan says, releasing a prolonged sigh in graceful acceptance of defeat. "If it makes you all happy." He takes a sip, wipes his upper lip. "Such a dreadful thing is peer pressure."

"Ah, don't be talkin, Declan," says Seoirse. "I could see you was just dying for one really. Like they say: you can take the man out the bog but you can never take the bog out the man!"

Uncomfortable hands quickly reach for glasses.

"And what do you think, Owen," asks Rainer, "you who have left the house of scholars and slammed the door behind you?"

"What about?"

"Nietzsche."

"I like his fluffy white moustache. Looks like a walrus."

"And his philosophy?"

"Ah, now, I seem to remember agreeing with Rachel on that one. The only thing he got right was the fourth error."

"Ah," he says, looking into the distance for reference, "the Gay Science?"

"Yep."

"Let me see now. In English it would be. . ."

"Man," Rachel cuts in, "continually invented new tables of values and for a time. . ."

"Joder! Is this a seminar," Pepe objects, "or are we going to have a good drink?"

". . .and for a time took each of them to be eternal and unconditional. That's why he said we should shatter the ancient law tables of morality, only he went and invented a whole set of new ones, thereby disappearing up his own bum. There now, let that be an end to all this intellectual willy-waggling."

"Hear, hear," chimes Declan.

"Salud! I'll drink to that," Pepe announces, and then leans over to ask Declan what willy-waggling is.

"Ooh, I haven't told you, have I?" says Rachel. "We're going to Aix-en-Provence, one of your old stamping grounds."

"What, you and Rainer?"

"Yeah, to get away from Florence. It's too hot here. You just can't sleep at night."

"It'll be hot in Aix too."

"Yes, but surely not as hot as here."

"No. But why Aix? Any particular reason?"

"Neither of us has ever been there."

"That's good enough reason."

"Do you know any cheap hotels?"

"Fraid not. I hardly know the place at all now. All the mates I had in Aix have moved on or moved out. But check out the Civette."

"The Civette."

"It's a drinking hole full of low life and shady characters. At least, it used to be. A sociologist's dream. It's in the centre but I don't remember where exactly. Sort of place you'd find Shane MacGowan."

"Oh yeah, did you hear he's leaving the Pogues?"

"Aye. If you ask me, he's better off without them."

"They say he's dying, from the drink."

"Ah, that's bollocks. Bit of harm the drink never did anyone. He'll outlive the lot of us."

Pepe gives out a laugh. "It's a little known yet curious fact," I hear Declan telling him.

"What is?" asks Rainer, avid collector of curious yet little known facts. "I missed what you said."

"That snakes have two penises."

"Two? Is that possible?"

"Absolutely, Rainer. Ask any snake."

"Any male snake," Rachel corrects.

"Jaysus," Seoirse bursts out, "that must be gas. Means you can have a piss and a wank at the same time!"

"Ah!" says Rainer, raising a finger. "But if you don't have any hands. . ."

"See," says Pepe, "that proves God does not exist."

If we drink
We shall die

186

And if we don't drink
We shall die
So we might as well
Say what the hell
And drink until we die

It can only be another couple of hundred metres to the hotel now but Pepe grows heavier by the step. I tighten his arm around my neck and urge him onward, glad, after all, and touched, that he insisted on accompanying me back to the hotel. He could have got a lift home with the others but no, he said, he'd come back to the hotel with me and have one for the road. A string of orange gems twinkles on the far side of a wonderfully oleaginous Arno and I look up at the benighted piazzale Michelangelo, wondering if I shall ever see Florence again. Pepe's arm tugs me to a halt. He takes in a deep breath and for a moment I think he's going to be sick. "*Astuuurias!*" he bellows out, and together we sing the next lines: "Patria querida, Astuuurias, de mis amores!" We walk on, each faltering step drawing us closer to a separation which, for all its inevitability, neither of us wants. "Hey, where's Seoirse?" he asks. I have to laugh. "I told you five minutes ago." He presses a finger into my chest. "Listen, you Welsh mariconazo, I've had two more Jamesons than you." I explain once more that Seoirse's gone on to the KGB Club to see someone. "Okay, okay," he says, and after another loud burp, "he'll need a tessera to get in there. He's a good man, Seoirse." Narrowing my eyelids, the twin lights in the distance merge into one, the small white lantern of the Plaza Lucchesi. Kristine will be fast asleep there by now. She probably hates me already. If she could see us now she'd probably call us a couple of pédés. As long as the people at reception don't object to taking Pepe up for a nightcap. No, they'll be alright. I haven't given them the voucher yet. If there are any eyebrows raised I shall say this is Jose-Maria Fernandez y Martin and he is my grappled friend, punto e basta. The Arno does look beautiful tonight. There is beauty in the world, there is. I will be back.

"Pepe, listen a moment."

"*Astuuurias!*"

"No, listen, even if you forget afterwards I said it."

"What?"

"Thanks, that's all."

"What for?"

"For all the good times."

10

My mind is made up: if this genial Pisan trader does not give me exactly what I want, I shall kill him. One shake of the head from him and he'll have my hands round his throat. But no. "Qui, c'è tutto," he beams back proudly, fetches a can from the fridge and pours it into a glass with a hand far steadier than I could muster. I take a seat and thank my lucky stars for having struck gold in Pisa. Aaaaah, magic. Misura Tonica, with tropical fruit juices: the isotonic drink of the sportivi, and essential hangover cure. Should steady us up a bit, take the wobble out of the gyroscope. God, my breath! Stale as a dead dog's dick. Alcohol seeping out of every pore. Have to get some chewing gum or something, aye, Cloralit, usually does the trick. Cut myself shaving, just . . . there.

Pepe all curled up on the floor when I left. Sheet wrapped round himself. Must have fallen out of bed. Didn't have the heart to wake him. Whole posse of woodcutters in me head. Face feels like it's on fire, hot molten skin. That vodka we got out of the frigobar. Left him a note reminding him where he left his vespa. Ah, cometh the hour, cometh the man.

"Jesus, he sez, they should call this place Kodak City. God, you look rough. Eyes like piss-holes in the snow."

"Some seagull must have shat in me mouth as well last night."

"Looks a nice little bar, this."

"It's not the one I normally come to."

"Good thinking. It's like Sam Beckett said: habit is the ballast that chains the dog to his vomit."

"Could we just stay off the subject of vomit?"

"Right, then, let's get down to it."

Seoirse presents me with a burgundy passport. I open it to find the picture of a bearded mole caught in the act of foraging, a man whose name is given as John Short, hailing from Mullingar. "Issued in 1989," I observe, "where d'you get this done? The guy in Cricklewood?"

"No," he grins, tapping his nose, "the guy in Genova." He chuckles to himself. "Sure there's no point going through official channels. So, where d'ya want to meet up?"

"Nice, tonight. Do you know a place called De Klomp, in the old part of town? It's a Dutch bar that does Guinness."

"Can't say as I've been there before."

"By the cathedral."

"It's alright," he says, imitating a bloodhound, "I'll just stick me nose up and follow the scent."

"Okay, I'll have to go in about five minutes but I've been racking my brains for the missing link."

"I'm delighted to hear it, Owen, delighted."

"We don't have a motive for Nolan, do we? So far we've been linking Effi with him, but what if the link's not with Nolan but with the Heidelberg fella? After all, Frankfurt and Heidelberg aren't a million miles apart, what, a hundred kays maximum? She's from Switzerland, he does tons of runs to Switzerland. Their paths could easily have crossed. She's a fair-looking woman, he's a fair-looking bloke. Now, consider this. He—"

"Don't tell me, he charms the knickers off her with his Ulster accent, the greatest aphrodisiac known to Man. You're not still pissed, are ya?"

"No, listen. He doesn't realise it's not love's sweet callings but a set-up. Like you said, the honey-trap. She's been set up to penetrate our network and when she's got what she wants out of him, news of this job, she does away with him."

"You reckon a woman like that could pull the fingernails out of a man? I mean, she may be cuter than we give her credit for but, y'know."

"Maybe not herself. . ."

"Owen, let me just ask ya something here: what was it that led you to this particular flight of fancy?"

"The ring."

"The ring."

"Yeah, I had a dream the other night about a salmon and a ring."

"Jesus, y'are pissed. Lord save us, a dream was it?"

"No, hold on. And remembering that set me thinking about when I met Effi in Lucerne. She was wearing a ring, a claddagh ring in fact, and where would she get that except from an Irishman?"

"Mmmmwell. . ."

"Now, I could be mistaken, but I'll swear blind that when I met our man in Heidelberg up at the castle he was wearing a ring too, a silver ring, maybe a claddagh ring. Now, I don't know if, when I asked her about her ring in the Lucerne restaurant, she thought I was making the connection, but the next thing you know she does a swift change of subject and starts banging on about holidays in the Caribbean, getting right away from the subject of Irish men as far as possible, leading me off the scent. And when I gave her the parcel in Rome, she didn't have any ring on, no incriminating evidence. And then–"

"Jesus, hold–"

"No, hear me out here. I know I'm a bit rough this–"

"No, Owen, just shut up. Just shut the fuck up a sec. You said the Caribbean?"

"Well, yeah, but it was just some old line she was spinning, the stars in the night sky, all that baloney."

"No it wasn't. We've got him. Ya might have gone about it all arse about face, but we've got him right by the short and curlies now."

"Whah?"

"Nolan. We've got him. A positive ID. And that . . . that could just give us his motive as well."

"How d'you work that out?"

"Look, Nolan's last bout with the Brits. He didn't break but it was one interrogation too far, right. He went a bit wobbly, so they pulled him out of Ireland, out of the direct line of fire and set him up in Germany. Not exactly a sinecure but not in the eye of the storm either. But before that, before plunging him straight back into active service, they send him off for some R and R, y'know, just to get over it all, take a break, get away from it all, enjoy some of the well-deserved luxuries of life."

"And you're saying they sent him to the Caribbean?"

"Yeah."

"Where exactly?"

"Where was it now? Fuck."

"Saint Kitts? Barbados? Trinidad?"

"No, it was a Saint something but not Saint Kitts."

"Saint Lucia?"

"Aye, that's it. That's the one."

"Christmas time?"

"Yeah, hold on . . . yeah, cos I remember him being over there in the sun and me being stuck up to me neck in snow."

"Then you're right. That's where Effi started out, Saint Lucia."

"So we've got a bullseye here. We must have. That's where your holiday romance is, not Heidelberg. That's where Nolan winds up with Effi and, knowing him, you can just picture it. He's the Othello, she the Desdemona. He woos her with tales of hair-breadth scapes i' th'imminent deadly breach. It's the first time she's met a real-life martyr to the Cause. She feels sorry for him. All his time spent in the nick, senza una donna. She admires him. Tortured by the perfidious Brits and all. All that be-Jaysus blarney works with her. I'll tell you one thing: you show me the Irishman who hasn't laid it on a bit thick trying to pull the foreign colleen and I'll show you a liar. And once he gets wind of the Sketchbook job, he starts seeing how he can make a new life for himself, and her. If I know Nolan at all, he won't have been happy about being pulled out of Ireland and having to take orders from some la-di-da ponytail with a limp handshake. He's taken enough punishment and he wants out. This is his chance."

"That'd mean he'd have to ransom the sketchbook himself."

"Or just sell it to some shady character, a private buyer of which there's never anny shortage, least not in Switzerland."

"So where does MI5 come into the equation?"

"Maybe they don't. Might just be a red herring. Like I say, there's not many to touch Nolan when it comes to pulling strokes. I'm tellin ya: he might have lost his bottle but he hasn't lost his marbles. Which is why he went along with the jailbreak job, clean as a whistle, to put himself beyond suspicion. I'm tellin ya: it's Nolan, Ned feckin Nolan for definite. It might not be the whole picture, we might not be exactly there, Owen, but we're thereabouts."

"Not looking good, eh?"

"Put it this way: I can think of nicer people to be up against. And he'll know it's us who's done the switch with the parcel."

"How?"

"He'll know. He'll just know. But maybe he doesn't know I'm with you, not yet."

We arrange to take different border crossings into France. Nolan is sure to strike soon. We must try to strike before he does. Neither of us is happy with the fact that we're only reacting to events. Somehow we have to wrest the initiative from Nolan. There are three hundred and fifty kilometres to figure out how.

I buy a packet of Cloralit and, leaving behind the Old Man of Mullingar, beat a path through tower-gazing tourists, past the Basilica, through the walls, and into the coach park. Searching the area, I come across the pitiful sight of Kristine, bent double, disgorging a splashing puddle of buff-coloured vomit onto the gravel. It's probably an ignoble thing, but my hangovers always start to lift when I see someone suffering more than myself. It makes me feel that things could be much worse, that I haven't hit rock bottom, that I've been making a meal of how bad I feel. "Food poisoning," the woman at her side pronounces, adding that she's a nurse. Kristine lifts her head, attempts a stoical, pale green smile, retches loudly, and vomits again. The nurse dabs and scrapes her pebbledash shoes with a tissue, folding it over and over. "Thank-you, May," Kristine groans, "oh la vache, ce putain de sandwich!" It was the prawn sandwich she ate yesterday to compensate for the Sant' Ambrogio bistecca she never got to finish. It must have been off. She accepts the stick of chewing gum I offer and looks at me with big, glistening eyes. "I wouldn't normally ask, Owen, but you couldn't possibly. . .?"

"Cover for you? Sure."

"She really is in a bad way," stresses the nurse anxiously, "and she's been doing such a good job."

"It's no bother. She'd do the same for me."

Gilles is typically relaxed about the new situation, indeed, more concerned with fixing his hair than anything else. He pulls the wing mirror round a notch to inspect his new look in profile. It's his feast day, he says, and he thought he'd mark the event with a new style. He looks just grand, I tell him, and happy feast day, Gilles. I explain things to Leahman: I'll have to split myself between the two groups, starting with Kristine's, but I'll be back after the lunch stop, so would he mind taking charge in the meantime? "No problem, Owen, relax. I'll soon have 'em whupped into shape."

I tell Koen, that Flemish mastodon behind the wheel, that I want to make the changeover at Varazze, the half-way marker along the Ligurian coast. "Okay," he grunts, adding for good measure a sarcastic "boss". I give Gilles and Leahman a wave as they pull out. Koen grunts again, and as soon as my door closes and the wheels start rolling I realise I've left my jacket with Gilles. I keep my peace, consoling myself with the thought that I don't much need it anyway. I have far greater worries than a jacket. For once, I welcome the extra workload. Throwing myself heart and soul into it will help keep fear on the back burner.

Kristine's group is, to say the least, frosty. I try to capture their imagination with an exposé of the Pisan Gioco del Ponte, the annual battle fought out over the Arno between the rival descendants of Etruscans and Trojans. There's no reaction. When we get to Carrara I point to the blocks of white marble, the same marble from which Michelangelo sculpted the "David". Nothing. When we get to La Spezia I tell them how Shelley drowned off the coast and how he was cremated on the beach. Still nothing. I tell them we're ploughing the same furrow as the ancient Via Aurelia, the Roman road stretching all the way to Arles. Lord save us! Genova, famed for its pesto? No. Genova, where Daniel O'Connell died, the huge-cloaked Liberator? No. Genova, birthplace of Columbus. No, no, and we won't tell you again. Perhaps they expected more. Perhaps they expected unbroken views over the Italian Riviera instead of this unending series of tunnels. Or perhaps the Cloralit hasn't worked. All the while Kristine lies curled up asleep on one of the spare seats. All the while Koen drives at the speed of global warming, seemingly intent on making my group wait around at Varazze. And all the while, whenever I look round, I am confronted with the homogeneous, frozen stare of sixty-year-old Midwich Cuckoos.

Well fuck the lot of yez. Dear God alive, it never rains but it pours. Twice the work today on one of the longest transfers going, and Nolan's out there somewhere. I think back to our first meeting in San Sebastian at the very beginning of my clandestine life. I was picked up at the airport in Bilbao and driven by a diminutive Basque calling himself Antxon to the place he insisted on calling Donósti. We stopped off on the way and ate squids in their own ink, an oil slick on a white plate. And then I was face-to-face with this thick-set Kerryman who had darting eyes that would only stop darting to look straight through you and see what few others would see. And what he saw was that we were the same people, he and I, cut from the same cloth. "Your heart is full of hatred," he said. "That's good." So was his heart but I couldn't tell for sure what it was he hated. I knew he'd been tortured with white noise and sensory deprivation in the H-Blocks. I knew, too, that he'd never cracked. He was tough, one of the toughest, the very backbone of the movement. But I couldn't help thinking that it was life itself he hated. Life, and weakness in those less tough than he.

> In eighteen hundred and forty-five
> When Danny O'Connell was still alive
> When Danny O'Connell was still alive
> I was working on the railway

I watch Kristine's passengers file towards the cafeteria and wish Koen good riddance. His molluscan driving appears to have paid its intended dividend: to arrive at the services so late after my own group that I'll have to miss lunch. Kristine looks considerably better than she did at Pisa, though her lips are dry and cracked. She smiles awkwardly.

"Thanks, Owen, and . . . I'm sorry for throwing the wine at you yesterday. It was weak of me."

"Ach, no, that was all my fault. Listen, I'd better catch up with my group. They're probably all on the bus waiting for me."

"Sure. I'll see you in Eze tonight, at the restaurant."

"I hope your appetite has returned by then."

Relieved that my ordeal is over and that Kristine seems to have buried the hatchet, I hurry towards the area where I caught sight of our coach, already preparing my excuses for the delay in the changeover. A small crowd is gathered in front of it and I note the ominous presence of a carabinieri van and a squad car of the Polizia Autostradale. Don't tell me Gilles has been done for speeding, not on his feast day. I push my way through to find Leahman and Chuck remonstrating with a carabiniere. Lizzie sits on the tarmac with splayed legs, resting against a wheel of the coach, her ashen face expressionless despite the tender ministrations of her mother. Someone shouts out my name but I can't take my eyes from the form lying on the ground, covered over with a bloodstained yellow blanket. "Owen! Come here and make this goddam cop understand." And so I become not death's instrument or onlooker, but death's translator, passively relaying the end of someone's life through the words of another.

I relate to the stone-faced carabiniere that, according to Leahman, while they were waiting for the latecomers to get back from lunch, Gilles was horsing around with the mike, sending me up in my absence, just for a laugh. He even had my jacket on for special effect, to really look the part. And where was he at the time, this man Leahman, the officer asks? He was in the driver's seat, pretending to be the driver, and the few that were on board were laughing and clapping and lapping it up because Gilles was so funny and then . . . and then – Leahman abandons the struggle against tears – this guy gets on board and shoots Gilles clean through the head. Leahman points to the bullet hole in the roof of the cab. The guy rifles through Gilles' pockets and – Leahman clicks his fingers – suddenly he's gone again, disappeared. Could he give a description of this man, the officer asks? Well no, not really, there wasn't time to take anything in, it all happening so fast, and, well, Lizzie there was one of the closest, but she's in a state of shock.

They talk about the gun laws in the States, Leahman's croaking voice continues, and Florida and all, and then you come to Europe and it happens here just the same. I put a hand on his shoulder. He was one hell of a guy, Gilles, he says. He blames himself: maybe if he hadn't started the horsing around none of this would have happened. Chuck steps in and tells Leahman not to reproach himself. Leahman stares up at him for a moment, then buries his face in Chuck's chest. Andy Capp comes on the scene, fresh from lunch, and I have to tell the story all over again.

More green and white vans arrive. "E morto?" I ask the carabiniere, indicating the blanket. "Sì," comes the dispassionate reply. So what do we do now? He closes his notebook and tucks it into a pocket: the coach will be impounded and we will all be taken to the police station. Once everyone is a little calmer, proper statements can be taken. Men in white coats carry Gilles away, on his feast day. And it is not Leahman's fault. It is mine. Seoirse in Rome, saying it'd be like dancing on the parapets with the bullets whistling round my ears. Only it was Gilles' head above the parapet. His head, my fault, mine. Kristine pushes her way through, having only just learned of what has happened, and says I'm not to worry: she'll make the necessary calls to Austerlitz for me.

The police station in Varazze turns out to be one of those enclosed spaces you'd rather not be in, much like a dental surgery or a hospital waiting room, but instead of disinfectant, the walls here ooze the nauseating smell of fresh paint. The latest word in local police chic, moreover, has ordained their colour be that of a cold caffè-latte. Uniforms come and go, avoiding your upturned eyes, or, when you do manage to hold their attention, nipping your half-formulated questions in the bud to attend to something they've decided is far more pressing. Bars on the only window and guns waggling in hip holsters lend an element of coercion to the whole, protracted, proceedings. I have asked, but it's still not clear whether we're under arrest or merely wanted for questioning. The only saving grace is that they've managed to produce a plod with a Union Jack and French tricolour on her arm, so at least I am relieved of translation duties. When I asked where the nearest phone was, she told me it was half a kilometre down the road and, in any case, I was not allowed to leave the station. She's taking statements and personal details from every passenger, whether they witnessed the incident or not. As things stand, she's barely halfway through yet even when that task is completed, she said, everything will have to be typed up on carta bollata, official police paper. When that is done, and assuming they don't run out of carta bollata, I feel sure they'll produce another bureaucratic nicety to prolong our stay. Thankfully, though, not every letter of the law is obeyed: a sign on the wall, its edges spattered with flecks of paint, reads VIETATO FUMARE, but I'm already on my fifth cigarette and no-one has said anything.

Occasionally I give someone a reassuring smile, only to find it has the same effect as the sight of a dentist's drill. People are cracking up all around me. They all expect me to do something, to perform a miracle, to whisk them away from the nightmare of Gilles' death and a ruined holiday. I can sense their mood turning ugly. The longer we stay here the more I will become the object of resentment for each and every one of them, from the nastiest right down to the likes of Leahman and poor Lizzie; and the more time Gilles' killers will have to realise they've shot the wrong man. We could pass for brothers, that punter said way back on Day One. I have to escape, from the passengers, the tour, the police, and whomever might already be waiting for me outside. My stomach chooses this moment to add its own rumbling complaint to the general discontent. I can't think, not in here, with everyone watching me. Stubbing out my cigarette, I pop in another Cloralit and tell the person nearest me I'm going to the toilet. I can always phone Carine later with the bad news. First, somehow, I've got to make it to De Klomp.

As soon as I'm through the door and in the corridor I find myself confronted with a carabiniere who asks me where I'm going. "Dov' è il bagno?" I enquire, looking over his shoulder to two colleagues of his down to the left, at the far end of the corridor we came in by. He points me to the right and a few paces along, walking away from the exit, I push open the door to the gent's. For a moment I think I've found a little corner of privacy in the toilet cubicle, until I discover the unflushed detritus of terminally unhealthy bowels, the sight and stench of which turn my stomach. Opting for the relative salubrity of the porcelain urinal, I unbutton my fly and read over the graffiti scored into the flaking paint: FORZA DORIA, GENOA MERDA, MANDALI IN B. Through an open, though barred window I can see the pound and a police car parking under a bamboo shelter. Its driver gets out and exchanges casual expletives with someone hidden from view before saying something about "una bella siestina". Genovese dialect. He must feel like a god in that Alfa of his. Left the window open to let the heat out. Possibilities there, but walking straight up to the car and getting in, no, someone would be bound to see me. Only Indiana Jones does things like that. And how would I get past the guys at the exit anyway? Can't just walk out of jail, like Casanova did in Venice, straight past the watchman without a word. Impossible. No, tutto è possibile, everything is possible in Italy. Problem with dictums is they're never true when you want them to be. God, stuck with the Carabinieri! Common wisdom is they're all thick as pig shit and here's me can't even out-wit them. Got to get out. Anything's better than going back in that room. Like *Huis Clos* in there.

The door is thumped open behind me and in comes the same carabiniere I saw in the pound. Surely there must be a staff toilet. Or perhaps it's way down the corridor and he's desperate. He assumes the position at the adjacent urinal. I look straight ahead at the graffiti but out of the corner of my eye I can see he's looking at my business. Standing here with my cock in my hand and nothing coming out. Nothing coming out of his either. Maybe that's why he comes here, just to ogle at other men's parts, like that pervert in the toilet at Frankfurt airport, standing there with a hard-on, salivating at every new dick unfurled. Hate these situations. Longer you stand here with nothing happening, more you look like one of the dirty mac crowd yourself. Pretend I've just finished. Don't want him getting the wrong idea.

I button up my fly and go to wash my hands. The carabiniere grunts as I turn on the tap and, inspired by the sound of running water, forces out his own steady trickle. I give the dryer a smack and wring my hands under it. The carabiniere turns round. I instantly cast my eyes upwards to avoid his and feign uncommon interest in the smoke detector on the ceiling. Between a rock and a hard place here, between a pervert in uniform and the room of hell, between Scylla and wait a minute. We have the technology. I've got cigarettes. I've got chewing gum. I've got the hump with that guy and he's got what I want, my passport out of here. Desperate times call for desperate measures. Go for it, Owen bach. Make a name for yourself. Aut Cesare aut nihil.

My mind made up and my heart racing, I creep up behind him and deliver two knuckles into the base of his skull. His forehead thuds into the wall and, as if that weren't enough, his chin hits the edge of the urinal on the way down. A yellow fountain spurts up and falls onto his chest. Grabbing his armpits, I drag him into the cubicle, lock the door and listen. Nothing. Have I killed him? Don't think so. Just stunned him. No time to be thinking about him anyway. I put another tablet of Cloralit into my mouth and chew frantically. On with his cap and undo his shirt. Ach y fi! Soaked in piss. But it could work to my advantage. Who's going to hang around a man who stinks to high heaven? First wine now piss. I put his shirt on over mine, do up two or three buttons and light a cigarette. Chewing and puffing in alternating stints, and trying to keep the smoke out of my eyes, I unbuckle his gun belt and strap it round my waist. Nearly there. The car I can hotwire, piece of cake. Thank God for Moss Side days. Live dangerously. This is what it's all about. Still no noise from anywhere.

I unlock the door, go over to the washbasin and jump up. Old gymnast, fair play. Stretching hard, I reach up, stick the lump of chewing gum to the side of the smoke alarm and press the cigarette into it. Jumping down, I hide in the cubicle and wait in the rancid smell of piss and shit for a trumpet blast of Jericho proportions. Of course, there is one minor flaw in the plan. Hadn't thought of that. What if the smoke alarm's out of order? What if it doesn't go off? Guy still out cold. Oh, come on, it should have gone off by now. What if the cigarette's petered out, burnt down to the chewing gum and fizzled out in the saliva? Great plan, Owen. Nice one. Should maybe have rustled up some toast to set it off. Or what if the cigarette's fallen down, smouldering uselessly on the floor? Think, think, think, contingency, think.

WAAAAAAAAAA! Screwdrivers in the ears. It is pain most divine, better than Jericho, more like the Harrowing of Hell. I step briskly outside into scenes of delightful confusion and panic. Faces grimace tightly. Hands cover ears. People flap around like a distraught goldfish. Uniforms rush about, each looking to someone else to take charge. Imitating their panic, and looking for all the world like a copper caught with his pants down, I run the length of the corridor and out into the sun. Slowing to a walk and straightening my cap, I turn into the deserted car park. Just as I'm about to put an arm through the window of the Alfa Romeo I notice the keys have been left in the ignition. Very thoughtful of him. I pull up the door catch, get in and switch on.

An obtrusive blue Mazda loiters with intent outside the station as I swing through the gates and onto the main road. That's them there. What else would a car with Bolzano plates be doing in downtown Varazze? Check in the mirror. Doesn't look like they've spotted me. Wing mirror, no, nothing coming. Excellent! Wait till I tell Seoirse this one. Twenty-five kays to Genoa and they won't be expecting me to go there either. Twenty-five kays at, what, an average of sixty kays an hour, that makes half an hour to Genoa. Get up on the motorway and it won't even be that long. Dump the car in Genoa, burn it out, stop them getting me abdabs. Then get a train into France, but not all the way to Nice. Jesus, this shirt's humming. Need to find a Standa or something to get a new shirt, and some smellies. Got the other passport, got the money. Autostrada on the left, sea on the right, Seville and Ceüta. Things can only get better. Free at last, free at last! To the Finland Station! Things can only get better, yes. Bumbaclaatraas!

> In eighteen hundred and forty-four
> I landed on the Liverpool shore
> Me belly was empty, me hands were raw
> To work upon the railway
> I'm sick and tired of the railway
> Poor Paddy works on the railway

Subterraneous to the square of the mercenary Masséna, the untimely aged Paul Chevrette, now thirty-six, born in Port-de-Bouc near Marseille, having liquidated both former self and cheques of the helvetian order in Monte Carlo, marks for future reference the location of his Monégasque vehicle – de location, of course. Regaining Masséna's superfice, his back firmly turned against the promenade of the roast beefs, he orients himself to appropinquate the old quarter of the italo-gallic, celto-ligurian metropolis to which its hellenic founders accorded the name of Nikaia. Protean city, protean man. Through the Daedalian ruelles in which Chevrette loses himself with the joy of a returning son he strews the ephemeral aroma of distillate of musk, imperceptible to any but his shadow, least of all to the extramural gourmands restoring themselves on fruits de mer, espadon, coquillages, saumon fumé. Espying the low-lying object of his nocturnal peregrination, to wit, de Klomp, he breaches its threshold eagerly to salute the hibernian friend and comrade-in-arms, whose first duty is to enquire whether it is at all himself that he is. "It is," says re-born Chevrette, accepting the proffered crock of anthracite servoice.

"What kept y'Owen? I've been here ages."

"They've shot Gilles dead, Gilles, my driver."

"Shit," he says. "You okay?"

"No, I'm fucking not." I want to scream and shout that killing Gilles wasn't fair, that it was unnecessary, gratuitous, stupid, vindictive, especially when he was so happy after Carine told him she wanted to have a child. I want to stand on the highest moral soapbox and protest his innocence, his entitlement to life and happiness, but the soapbox would only shatter at the very sound of such words coming from my lips and sink me up to my neck in the stinking mire of hypocrisy. Who am I to say thou shallt not kill? All I can say is thou art a vile bastard for killing someone I'm fond of and I'm already mad and I'm going to get even.

As I apprise Seoirse of the facts surrounding Gilles' death, the escape, and my passage into France, a bony-faced, guitar-toting youth with a mop of curly hair and designer stubble steps up onto the tiny stage, adjusts the microphone, fiddles with the harmonica hanging round his neck and breathes a sultry "Hi". Undeterred by the lukewarm reaction of his audience, he pulls his face into an anguished contortion and launches into a Bob Dylan song. I suggest we go and play a game of pool in the back room, if only to escape from the unerringly accurate imitation of that adenoidal whine which has always driven me to distraction. Armed with fresh pints and a handful of tokens, but sadly not before having to endure the aural assault of "Knocking on Heaven's Door" from the wannabe Dylan, we penetrate to the inner sanctum of red baize.

"Lord save us," exclaims Seoirse, sealing off the music with a firm push of the door, "d'you know how long it's been since I played pool?"

"It'll relax us, help us think."

"Jesus, he sez: I don't even know which end of the cue to chalk any more."

We stand our pints on a small table. A cascade of balls answers the thrust of my token in the chrome slot. Seoirse selects a cue from the rack and rolls it over the baize, checking it for straightness. Satisfied, he searches for the chalk, finds it dangling from the table by a length of string and applies it to the tip. He blows off the chaff, sending a cloud of blue particles through the wedge of light over the table. I rack the balls and gesture at him to break.

"So it was the same car I saw in Rome," he says, the tip of his cue jabbing behind the white ball, "hanging around outside the police station. Ah, bollocks, I'm just going to whack the fuckers." He draws back his elbow and lets rip. The cue ball blasts into the pack and flies off the table, whistling at alarming proximity past our glasses and ricocheting off a pillar. Seoirse roars with laughter at the plastic kerplunk of pocketed balls. "Jesus, Mary and Joseph! Two stripes and a spot was that? Don't tell me you're going to claim a foul shot?"

"Rules is rules."

"Ah, y'uncharitable Welsh heathen, ya. Two shots, then."

"I want to get back at these bastards right away, Seoirse." I retrieve the cue ball and place it in the semi-circle. Chalking another cue, I eye up the plump, juicy red lying just to one side of the middle pocket, a stripe which would leave me with three balls down. "I'm sick of chasing shadows. Aren't you?"

"Sure, and I spose you've got yerself a shooter at last, courtesy of the Italian federali."

I roll the cue ball gently down the table, trying to get the angle for the orange into the opposite middle, but play it too straight; the red bounces off the near jaw and comes to rest the wrong side of the pocket. "Ah, fuck. What was that?"

"I think we should give the ponytail a bell on his mobile."

I try a fine cut on the orange and miss that too. "No, Seoirse, not yet. God's teeth, I don't believe that shot."

"Y'know, Owen, the thing with two shots is to use them wisely. But there – now tell me if I'm wrong – you was already thinking of the clearance. And you're thinking the same about Nolan."

"I might be."

Seoirse sinks a long purple stripe. The cue ball rolls up behind a green into the bottom pocket. "Listen," he cautions, lining up the green, "don't just go charging in because of Gilles and all that. We have to think this through carefully." With a stun on the green, he sinks it and turns to the red I missed, tapping it deftly into the middle. "We've got to stay professional, Owen, not let it get personal. That's what Nolan wants. He's making you play the game by his rules and that way you're only gonna run out the loser."

"Kristine'll be eating at the Cheval Blanc in Eze right now."

"What's she got to do with annything? She's out of the frame." He moves round the table like a panther on the prowl.

"No she isn't, Seoirse."

"You trying to put me off me shot?" He chalks his cue and sizes up the orange.

"After Eze, she'll be going to Monte Carlo and the Casino, then back to the hotel."

"So?"

"The Hotel Univers, on the rue de la Liberté, just up from the place Masséna. Two entrances, two exits. With a bit of blagging I could get into her room while she's out. I know the staff well enough."

"Bit of right-hand side on this one and you're in serious trouble. I'll tell you one thing, he sez: I just love sinking orange balls so I do . . . And why would ya want to get into her room?" He bends towards the orange and doubles it into the middle, sending the cue ball down the table and snookering himself behind one of my numerous spots. "Ah fer fuck sake! See, that's where rushing yer shot gets ya. As yer man said: say beau may say pas la guerre."

"Kristine told Effi in Rome that we were lovers. Bit of amorous mischief, she said it was."

"So?" He attempts an escape shot off two cushions which only just misses his one remaining stripe. "Two shots to you. Ya realise there's only one of your balls gone down, and I fucking potted that!"

"I'm painfully aware of the fact, Seoirse, painfully aware."

"You were saying, about Kristine."

"Hold on." My first two spots are straightforward and I fluke the next one into a pocket I hadn't even dreamt of. The black is lying safe against the top cushion. I line up a long red. "So Effi will have passed the information on that me and Kristine are an item. Nolan might think I've run to her or will run to her because I need a place to hide. Or because, naïve, romantic thing I am, I'm doing the knight in shining armour thing and whisking her away from the danger she's in by mere association with me."

"He could use her as bait, y'mean?"

"Precisely. As it stands, she can either lead them to me or she can lead us to them, if you see what I mean." I pot the red and cannon the yellow onto the blue, sending it into the corner pocket and fortuitously disturbing the black with the cue ball. I miss the next ball, an easy yellow, but manage to dispatch it with the shot in hand. The black, I feel sure, will go.

"I see what ya mean alright. Trouble is with this kind of game, you never know who's chasing who."

"No, bit like the dog chasing his own tail. What it comes down to is who's left pointing the guns once the dust has settled."

"It's a high-risk strategy," Seoirse pronounces. "Jesus, will ya feckin play the shot? This is where we see if you've got the bottle. When's Kristine likely to be back from Monte Carlo?"

"Around . . . eleven, eleven thirty." The important thing here, I tell myself, is not to leave the black waggling in the jaws and over the pocket. I hit it hard. It waggles. Over the pocket. Right on the brink. Seoirse points his cue at me.

"Don't whatever you do kick the table!" I sit with my pint and watch him fluke his last ball. At least he has the good grace to admit it was a fluke. He turns to ogle lasciviously at the easiest black that ever was and chuckles to himself. "Is that the fat lady I can hear warming up?"

"Best of three?"

11

Half-eleven. Thirty-five minutes I've been here now, my darkened vigil still unbroken by the plastic rattle of Kristine's zingcard in the door. The discomfort of feet swollen through waiting is compounded by the vile smell crawling out of the shower, nowhere near as bad as the toilet in Varazze but I could well do without it. It wouldn't be so bad if I could smoke, but I can't, not if I want to remain hidden. The bathroom door stands ajar, letting in a faint glimmer of light, enough to tell the time by. Penumbra of silence. I've not done this kind of thing before. My first time. Still, I'm steeled in the combat now, the Houdini of Varazze. Seoirse outside, in case they try to snatch her in the street. Surely she must get here soon. Unless she's won a fortune at roulette and done a runner, like me. No, she wouldn't do a thing like that.

She's a quare one alright. The complete creation of her mother, she said. But then, can the patient know what ails them? Could be the father she's obsessed with. She turned all gloomy when the pigeon got run over in Florence. But was it because of the pigeon or the child, and the father rushing in to save the child? A display of fatherly affection, devotion even. Would her father have done that for her? She said he was cold, unfeeling, said I was too. Vicariously reclaiming the father figure by conquering me, could that be it? Hell, what do I know? A psychologist I am not. And spelling her name with a K, like two horns drawn out, posturing invulnerability. Giant with feet of clay more like. Still can't figure out all that stuff about babies and abortions.

Groans of pleasure come from another room, someone's

tender night. Coming up through the plughole or something. Water a better conductor of sound. Reminds me of swans, the sound I used to hear when they flew low over the footbridge. Used to watch them on the river, standing outside the kitchen at the top of the steps in my short trousers. Mum inside singing Myfanwy or Calon Lân, making the dinner. Dad of the generation ashamed to speak Welsh. Forbade it, forbade her. But she could still sing in Welsh, and tell me bedtime stories in Welsh, without telling him. It was our secret. Only he must have known about it. Used to stoop to words of Welsh to lure me out of my hiding places. It's funny. Here I am, still hiding in cupboards. But that last dream, Kynddilig didn't say anything about my father coming. Maybe I've exorcised him at last.

Can't believe Seoirse beat me two-one. Not enough Guinness, that was the trouble. Need three pints at least to get into me stride. Always play better after that. Ah, but what a swerve shot to get out of that snooker. Touch of flamboyance. Can't play any other

Clickety clack, a key going in. A turn of the handle. Clackety click, key going out. Door closing to. "Je peux au moins aller faire pipi?" Kristine's voice. "Tu permets?" "Don't take me for an idiot." His voice. Excellent, Kristine, if only you knew it. Using the "tu" in her condescending, mock informal way. So there's only one of them, just him and her. "Just sit there. We'll wait here nice and quiet. See if loverboy shows up." So I was right, they have moved in on Kristine. Forward, Owen, and aim low. Mustn't kill him. We want him to talk. Now's the moment, nice and easy. Come on, Seoirse. An abyss of silence. "Tu veux bien me laisser. . ." Silenced in mid-sentence, poor woman. Dash, dot, dot, dash, Seoirse's knock. Will she go to the door or will he? Either way they'll both have their eyes on the door. The element of surprise. Now!

I clench my gun in both hands and burst into the room. Kristine stands petrified between the door and her abductor with a silencer held at the nape of her neck. For a split-second his face mirrors hers in a shared terror. I aim at his abdomen and pull the trigger. Nothing happens. I squeeze again. Fucking fire, fire. Nothing. His expression turns to a sneer when he realises my gun has jammed. Now he aims his gun at me. "Just the man we're looking for," he says. He's not at all the man I expected to see. I expected someone in a balaclava and combat jacket but this one looks more like Timothy Dalton, a little rough round the edges perhaps but he could pass for Bond on a good day, were it not for the Cockney accent. "I'm sorry, Kristine," I say, throwing the useless lump of metal in my hand onto the bed. God, I've really ballsed this up. Outgunned, outclassed, humiliated. Fucking stupid idea in the first place. He jerks his head at the door: "Who was that?" he demands. Kristine blurts, "I don't know," thinking he's talking to her. "Room service?" I say. "Shut the fuck up, smart arse," he barks, and fires a single, muffled round through the door at chest height. Pushing Kristine aside, he snatches up my gun and stows it in the pocket of his expensive-looking jacket. Surgeon's gloves he's wearing.

He tells me to stand in front of Kristine, facing the door. "Nice and cosy like this, isn't it," he snarls, "all pressed together like sardines." I feel Kristine's body start at something he did to her. Definitely not the gallant Bond. "Just remember, Flynn, you do anything funny and she gets it." More like a bouncer on the Old Kent Road with a penchant for B-movie cliché. On his orders I open the door and we walk some dozen paces down the empty corridor to the lift. I press the APPEL button. Things can only get better, eh? And where's Seoirse? Hope he wasn't hit by that bullet. A couple with the fruity reek of alcohol spills out of the lift, too drunk to care and too incapable besides. We shuffle inside at the Cockney's discreet prodding and descend to the ground floor. Habib greets me with a gold-toothed twinkle behind the reception desk: "Allez, bonne fin de soirée." I make no reply, hoping he'll suspect that we're anything but a happy threesome about to hit the town.

We're bundled into the back of a Citroën waiting on the Avenue Jean Médecin. The thick-necked driver is wearing a balaclava rolled up on his head to look like a docker's cap and has angled the rear-view mirror away from his face so I can't see it. "You don't need her," I tell them, "she doesn't know anything." "Shut it," says the bouncer, shoving the warm silencer into my neck. The driver throws him a Galeries Lafayette bag over his shoulder. He takes out a couple of black hoods and tells us to put them on but Kristine hesitates and looks at me as though it's going to be for the last time. She jumps when the bouncer barks at her and pulls the hood down. Is that the last thing I'm going to see, genuine terror on her uncomprehending face? When I pull down my hood the deep smell of leather upholstery instantly gives way to stifling, fusty felt. A surge in my back as we pull away. Where the fuck was Seoirse? No, I shan't curse him. I shall cherish him, make him into a warm feeling to comfort me in the moments that lie ahead. Aïe! My wrists. Not rope, something sharper biting into them. Must be those plastic twists. The weight of his body against mine, leaning across, binding Kristine's wrists. Christ knows where they're taking us.

Poor, poor Kristine. The dread hand of death planted firmly on her shoulder and she without even the dubious comfort of knowing why. Connelly's last words spring to mind, the letter he wrote to his wife: hasn't it been a full life and isn't this a good way to go? But bound and hooded, comrade, call this a good way to go? Brave it out, Owen bach, brave it out. Easier said than done. Controlled fear. Death, hah, anyone can do it. Moira did it. What's so terrible about the void beyond? No different from the void before birth and no-one finds that terrifying. If I don't fear one void why should I fear the other? Right then, right then, keep that thought. Yes, I shall go into death laughing, the only appropriate response, laughing and dancing like the skeletons on the bridge at Lucerne. All is lost now, and I shall go where no-one knows, down where the dead men go.

Cheering thoughts, anybody? Comforting thoughts for a man about to die? All offers gratefully accepted. C'mon, Owen, think of something. Yes, it has been a full life and I'm happy with what I've done. At least I've never taken the path of the mortgage and the kids, the wife and the Sunday lawn, the pension plan and the crushing mediocrity of days spent waiting for the weekend to come. This above all, to thine own self be true. Strange, though. This doesn't feel like the end, even though it must be. Perhaps that's what the condemned always do, always see a chink of life beyond the impossible situation, like the bull who refused to die. But I shall die, because they will torture me to get me to talk and once I've talked I'll be of no further use to them. I'll have signed my own death warrant. What torture will they contrive, I wonder? No end to human imagination in that department. Will they string me up by the legs and beat seven shades of shite out of me? No, far too tame, that. Lighted cigarettes in the eyeballs more like. Repeated drownings in an icy bath. Electrodes on the testicles. Razors splaying the tongue. Forcing your elbow the wrong way till it snaps like a wishbone. Needles, God I hate needles. Or pulling out the fingernails, is it, like the guy in Heidelberg? How can anyone withstand torture? Not to go like Lorca, snivelling and cringing and begging for mercy, that's the thing. As long as I don't shit my pants. I don't want to shit my pants. Better not to think about it.

And the old triangle
Went jingle-jangle
All along the banks
Of the Royal Canal

A hand grabs my arm and pulls me along the back seat. I hear the crunching of gravel beneath my unsteady feet and through the stale, sweaty, stifling oppression of the hood I detect something reminiscent of my mosquito machine, the faint odour of lavender. Ridiculously, I begin to picture plump little bags of hessian tied up with slivers of red ribbon until, shoved in the back, I stumble forwards, my fettered hands instinctively groping out into the darkness and my shins cringing at every step, certain of imminent bruising. My testicles seize at the thought of a nearby precipice and with quickening breath and heartbeat I imagine being pushed over the edge and falling, blindly, having no sense of when the moment of death will come. But no, they wouldn't do that, not yet at least. Blackness inside the hood and the dead of night outside. Car doors are slammed to and unintelligible words mumbled. The gravel becomes louder. I trip against something hard and feel a steadying hand on my shoulder. I tap the obstacle with the tip of my foot and decide it is either a rock or a doorstep, yes, a doorstep because that sounded like a latch being lifted. A door whines on its hinges. I feel another prod in the back. "Inside." The unmistakable voice of the bouncer. I tread forward. Stone gives way to bare floorboard. Footsteps creak behind and in front. The door rattles behind me and a dry click which seems to come from outside tells me it is locked. Wood scrapes on wood. "Sit." I bend my legs gingerly, seeking solidity, and lower myself onto a chair.

"Well, then," comes a different, more distant voice, "let us have a good look at you both." The hood is whipped off. Darts of light fire into my eyes. Recoiling, I shut them tight. The air seems fresh and good to breathe until a rotten fustiness makes itself known. When I open my eyes again I see a single dim lightbulb suspended in mid-air and, below it, a bare wooden table some seven metres away, encumbered only by a pair of black-gloved hands. To my left, Kristine leans forward in an effort to make sense of the surroundings. She glances at me and leans back. Her right knee begins to bounce nervously. Hers is the only face I can see. The others have either disappeared or been swallowed up by the all-encompassing blackness.

"Mr. Parry," says the voice behind the gloves, "allow me to

begin by apologising for the most unfortunate death of your driver. Believe me, I find it a most regrettable affair but," he pauses, "there really was no other way of stopping you in your tracks, quite literally." The cavernous resonance of his words hints at the spaciousness of, say, a hall or a farmhouse, but if so, where are the windows, or the walls for that matter? Surely the light would reflect from some imperfection or other. But no, there is just this dank blackness, the lightbulb, and the unmoving hands on the table. One thing I do know, though: it is not Nolan's voice. "The fact nonetheless remains that you have caused us no end of bother with this tiresome chase around Europe. Consider, I beg you, the damage you have done. This young lady, for instance: now why involve her? The poor creature looks positively and understandably distraught at the ordeal to which you have subjected her."

"She is not involved."

"It is very simple, Mr. Parry. All I ask is your co-operation in the matter of the item with which you were entrusted."

"I don't even know what's in it."

"Oh, but I think you do. I think you know only too well. Let me say that we were not deceived by the substitution you effected in Rome. No, we know, as do you, what the parcel contains and we know to whom it rightly belongs. What we do not know is where it is."

"Mais de quoi il s'agit, Owen?"

"You see, Mr. Parry, your young lady is as concerned as I am to ascertain the truth. And such a charming young thing too, I might add."

"She is not my young lady."

"No? Be that as it may, I feel sure you would not want to see her come to any harm. She must be dreadfully tired already."

"Yes, yes, I'm very tired."

"There, now: why cause her further discomfort with your taciturnity? It does not redound to your credit, Mr. Parry."

"It wasn't me who abducted her."

"Oh dear, this really is inexcusable. I had rather hoped you would spare us such prevarication. You know, Mr. Parry, whenever I read a book I dwell on neither preface nor foreword but turn straight to the first page. So let us hasten things on. Mademoiselle, you will have heard no doubt of the Salyans?"

"I'm sorry, I don't know what. . ."

"No, no, Mademoiselle, there really is no need to be sorry. Who is it, tell me, who can know everything? I myself sometimes shudder at the paucity of my share of the wisdom mankind has been able to gather unto himself. If I may continue. . .?"

"Yes, continue, please continue."

"Utterly charming . . . The Salyans were an ancient race of people who used to inhabit these parts. I often think it a sad fact of history that a race – in much the same manner as a person – is seldom remembered for more than one thing. But there it is. And the Salyans, for all their not inconsiderable achievements, are chiefly remembered for one particular habit of theirs, something the delicate palate of modern Man finds distasteful in the extreme. Perhaps Mr. Parry could enlighten us?"

"I'm afraid I'm not. . ."

"Then let me fill the gap. They are remembered above all for the cult of decapitation."

"Mais ils vont pas nous. . ."

"I am so sorry, Mr. Parry. Do forgive me. How discourteous of me not to offer you one of my Gitanes." Click. "I regret not having any other kind to offer you but, you see, I am an ardent partisan of respecting local custom and they are . . . so very French."

I watch in bemusement as, without any movement of his hands, a cigarette appears out of the darkness, suspended in nothingness. A yellow flame springs up at its end, turning it red and then disappearing in a metallic clunk. The cigarette burns brighter. One of the gloves reaches up and takes it from the invisible mouth. A wisp of blue smoke curls up to the light. I hear footsteps coming towards me but the gloves stay where they are, resting on the table, waiting. The floor creaks a foot away. Another cigarette appears in front of me and is pushed between my lips. Click. I pull back at the sudden flame held close to my face and in its hissing glow see a pair of demonic, piggy little eyes, darting back and forth over my features. I inhale on the cigarette and hold it in my lap. Clunk. The last cigarette for the condemned man, is it? I listen as the lackey's footsteps retire to a position that seems to be behind my shadowy interlocutor.

"Mr. Parry," he says, sending up another plume of smoke, "do not force my unwilling hand." A glint of silver flashes from a different corner of the room. "Do not make a Salyan of me. Simply acquaint me with the whereabouts of your item."

"Tell him, Owen, for God's sake tell him!"

"I fancy there is nothing quite so heart-rending as the plea of a fair damsel, moreover, one who you maintain to be completely innocent in our affairs. Your answer, if you please, Mr. Parry."

"How do I know that if I do tell you you'll let her go?"

"Owen!"

"I am not a man to be trifled with, Mr. Parry." He snaps his leathery fingers and in an instant we are swamped in total darkness. "Have it your way," comes the voice from the void, cold and menacing, final.

Footsteps approach again, but there is something different, something irregular about them this time. They seem to be making not for me but for Kristine. I take another drag on my cigarette, wondering what will follow. Are they going to rough her up in front of me to get me to talk? What if I tell them I buried the parcel myself, somewhere other than Florence? Or put it in a safe deposit box, a locker in a station, Termini?

The footsteps stop and I hear a gasp come from Kristine. In vain I try to prise open the blackness with my eyes but every last detail, every contour, every surface has been effaced in the click of the magician's fingers. The only thing I can see is the tip of my cigarette. Until the light comes on.

Pressing down on Kristine's blond head are the splayed fingers of another black glove. Hovering above her exposed neck is the sword of Damocles, a broad, still machete. "Your last chance to save her," shouts the Svengali, the éminence noire, the unwilling Salyan. I could leap at the henchman and grapple with him after a fashion, but I know it would be nothing more than a hollow gesture. I cannot save her. I cannot save her any more than I can save myself and the only chance of saving either of us is my silence.

"I have nothing to say."

Darkness returns. Seconds pass and then a sharp swish cuts through the air, followed by the sound of a head falling on the floor. I don't want the light to come on again. I don't want to see Kristine's eyes looking at me from the floor, the eyes that once smiled at me in a moment of beauty. Do the face muscles relax once all the nerves are severed? Is that what gives the expression of peacefulness you always see on the face of the beheaded? Danton's words trip across my thoughts: show my head to the crowd, it's worth seeing. Gilles saying something about Danton the other day. Yes, think about Gilles. Is it my turn now? Where was it he was talking about Danton? De l'audace! De l'audace. Germany was it? Mario und der Zauberer. Her blood seeping into the floorboards. Nausea in the pit of my stomach. Kristine! Kristine.

"Is it the Cause," asks Svengali, "that sustains your stubbornness, Mr. Parry? Is it? You have the choice," he shouts, ranting now in the pitch black, "the Cause or your life. You have five seconds before you meet with the same fate." One for sorrow, two for joy, three for a girl, four for a boy, five and the light is on and Kristine's still there, alive. A black hand releases a sob from her mouth, like a cork from a bottle. "Forgive the deception, Mr. Parry," he says, now calm again. His apology sounds almost sincere. Was that why he was ranting, to drown out any noises that would make his sadistic sleight-of-hand less convincing? "Remarkable, is it not," he continues, as the footsteps and the machete return to the table, "how a melon can sound like a human head, with just a mite of imagination? On reflection, I, too, find it in bad taste. Cheap theatricality. And perhaps you think, as I do, that the swift death of decapitation is in many ways a preferable option. You see, our Salyan friends were not as barbaric as they are made out to be. I read some time ago about the case of one recently departed from this mortal coil. Recently departed, but not swiftly. Seventeen minutes it took him to die in the electric chair. Can any of us imagine how long those seventeen minutes were for him? Fortunately for you, electric chairs are not as abundant in these parts as melons."

"You sick bastard."

"Sickness? Yes, I agree that it is a sickness, an insanity to prolong your torment."

"Tough."

"Oh yes, and it will get tougher, let me assure you. We have, however, established that it is not your feelings towards Mademoiselle – or rather, the regrettable lack of them – which will unlock your secret. Curious . . . But there we are."

"Effi told you about me and this woman, but she was wrong. You can let her go."

"Effi? Ah yes, 'Effi'. That is, of course, the name by which she was known to you."

"Was?"

"Enlighten me on one point, Mr. Parry, for my own peace of mind, would you? I am a perfectionist. Were you instructed by your Heidelberg contact that on no account were you to surrender the sketches to anyone in Switzerland, that anyone who approached you for them was to be regarded as hostile?"

"I'll swap my answer for one of yours."

"Very well. That seems equitable to me. I'm so glad we understand each other and can treat on honourable terms like gentlemen."

"The answer to your question is that at no stage did I ever receive such instructions. What made you think I had?"

"Is that your question?"

"It is."

"Then I shall answer it. Let me see, we were on his third, or was it his fourth fingernail? No matter. He had already yielded the password you were using, Patrick Henry, but even when it came to the most painful nail of all, the thumbnail, he remained adamant about your instructions on not surrendering the parcel in Switzerland. And so it was a risk we could not run. The password proved to be genuine, why should not the other element have?"

"Ah, my heart bleeds for you. You must have been really gutted, I mean really gutted when you found out I actually offered to hand it over to Effi. Hah! You stupid bastards."

"The Germanic peoples do have a rather touching faith in the sanctity of the orders given them, do you not find? The letter of the law rather than the spirit. All that was required of her was a modicum of initiative, a capacity for independent action such as her Heidelberg counterpart exercised. Perhaps pain enhances the imaginative powers. Ah me, it really wasn't his week for extractions, was it? What with his wisdom teeth and then his fingernails."

"I see why Effi told me not to break my cover, so you could pick me off as and when it suited you, further down the line. Only you ballsed that up too, in Venice. A perfectionist, did you say? P-lease!"

"I rather fear we are drifting from the point. There you sit before us now, a ripe lemon simply waiting to be squeezed until the pips squeak. And they will squeak. It is only a matter of when. Incidentally, the same practitioners who attended your associate in Heidelberg attend you now."

"Delighted."

"No, Mr. Parry, you are afraid. Believe me, I can tell."

"Grand."

"Or should I call you Aidan? Or Aaron? Or Owen? Alpha and omega, the beginning and the end. You have a most Christ-like image of yourself, which is entirely appropriate, given the discomfort you are about to endure. And for what, Mr. Parry?" He bangs his hand down on the table. There is the roar of a blue flame, lighting up another corner like one of Rembrandt's candles in the dark. The machete shines again. Could that be a blow torch? "You know, Mr. Parry, one only had to show Galileo the instruments of torture. The mere sight of them was sufficient for him to acquiesce."

The heat from the torch has already reddened the machete's blade. It's going to be the eyes, isn't it? I couldn't handle that. Where was it I was going to say I buried it? Shit, I can't remember. I can't remember. "Galileo," he continues, "was a man of sensitivity, an algophobic, not one whose pain threshold lies somewhere in the stratosphere. I have witnessed a good many who come into the latter category but you, I am convinced, are not one of their number."

"No?"

"You might be interested to learn that I recently availed myself of the opportunity of visiting your flat in London. You must forgive the intrusion. You have an interesting collection of books. What is yet more interesting are the passages you mark for special attention in the margin. All those exclamation marks and ticks and question marks. A few declamatory expletives of a genital nature, but that is your manner, is it not, Mr. Parry? Are not books the eyes of the soul? I have long thought that. And what was it, that passage of Rosa Luxemburg's on the subject of not until every tear is staunched, etcetera, etcetera? Very moving. Or that little gem of Marcuse's which etched itself on the tablets of my memory: Even the ultimate advent of freedom cannot redeem those who died in pain."

"I trust the experience was edifying."

"Oh indeed, most edifying. You see, reading between the lines, it told me that you have an aversion to pain."

"I wouldn't mind seeing you or any of your superiors in pain."

"Ah, but that is simply abstract speculation, is it not, Mr. Parry? Whereas here and now, your own, real pain, you are bound to allow, is not. You are a novice at this sort of thing, Mr. Parry, not the hardened veteran that perhaps you like to think yourself. If I might venture a simple observation: you are out of your depth."

"Really?" I look at Kristine but she only turns away, like kids who try to make themselves invisible by hiding their eyes. It's as though any attention I pay her will draw the attention of those who seem for the moment content to ignore her. "Really," he replies.

"Well fuck you."

My reply seems to be the signal for the torch to be extinguished and the machete to start towards me. I flick my cigarette to the floor in a gesture of defiance. What else can I do? Run? No, I will not run away and cringe in the corner and shit my pants in fear. It is time to put an end to those days for good. For once in my life I will meet fear head-on, face it down. I take a couple of deep breaths and, as the henchman tears at the sleeve of my right arm, summon the myriad demons that dwell in my soul, the demons of anger. Again, his piggy eyes look deep into mine as he holds the blade close to my arm, smouldering, smelling of metalwork classes. Something in his eyes suggests that under his mask he is smiling, positively salivating at the prospect of burning flesh in his nostrils. He presses the fizzing blade hard against my arm.

Aiiie ya bastard, hurts, it hurts like fuck and, no, I will not flinch. I will just get angrier and angrier and my anger will externalise the pain. The pain is outside. It is part of me, but outside. It is where it belongs, outside, in its right place, where it is just pain, no more, no less, just pain and unimportant. I will blink, and stare straight ahead, but flinch I will not. See this, ya bastard, my anger is enough to match your pain, you gobshite cock-sucker, you. Oh, don't you worry about that. I know who you are. I know your kind. Fuckers just like you who tortured Rosa. You are a poodle, a spineless poodle doing the bidding of the ones you call your betters. This is the moment of glory you live for, seeing others writhe in the pain you inflict. Gives you a hard-on, does it? Well, you won't get one out of me.

"Mr. Parry, a simple location will suffice. You need not divulge any names."

"Go fuck yourself, you public school twat." The poodle turns the machete over, taking with it a swathe of skin, and applies the other side of the blade to the same place.

Jeeeeesuh. White-hot, searing pain, cutting my arm in two. Externalise it, by force of will, externalise it. Ecce homo. And he calls me a novice, that one. He doesn't know shit from pudding. Fucking arsehole, fucking rapist, raping my books. Well, he is not my better. Angry? I'll show you angry. I have an inexhaustible supply of anger to call on. Go fuck yourself with your Old Boy network and your old school tie and passing the port the right way. I wouldn't give you the steam off my piss. Go fuck yourself with your privilege and your silver spoon and your ignorance and your condescension, born with opinions already coming out your arse. And you dare ask me about the cause. The cause is in my will. Recognise that one, you shit-for-brains book rapist, you Gilles-killer? Anger, that's my privilege, coursing through my veins like sweet morphine. No end of bother, is it? Oh, how very unsporting of me. Simply not cricket. Well, I shit on you from a great height. I will not bow to the likes of you. You want to know what my anger is? It's anger, pure anger that your kind exists at all, that we haven't eradicated every last trace of you from the face of the earth. Uuh.

The pain remains but the blade is taken away and the henchman slinks back to his master. "A most stubborn and futile performance, Mr. Parry," he sighs contemptuously. "Do you ever stop to consider that your efforts, as indeed mine, are only modest walk-on parts in what some call the Great Irish Tragedy? Yet there is nothing tragic or heroic in any of it. It has all the romance of trench warfare, Mr. Parry. Do you think any will remember either you or me when it is all over? And it will soon all be over, in another decade perhaps, at most. It is all futile, futile. Indeed, have we not already stated that we no longer have any selfish strategic *or economic* interest in Ireland?"

"So get the fuck out, then."

"Mr. Parry, let me remind you that you have not even begun to understand what pain is. It would be a grave error on your part to think that. For the present, however, I think it best to leave you and your companion time to reflect. By the way, I should be on your guard against scorpions if I were you. They really do seem to be everywhere in these parts."

With that the light goes out and the curtain of the hell-black night falls again. Footsteps. Another door is opened, closed, and bolted.

"Are you okay, Kristine?" I ask once I'm sure they've left. She does not answer. She could be too shocked to speak or too frightened. It occurs to me that she is probably too angry, with me, and cannot yet find the precise words with which to vent her spleen. I begin exploring the room, shuffling about with outstretched arms like a blind mendicant. My hip bangs against a sharp edge. With tentative, crab-like steps I feel along four sides and decide it must be the table Svengali was sitting at. I discover a small bench lodged in the angle of two bare, smooth walls, blackwashed probably. This must be where the blow torch was standing.

"What *are* you playing at?" comes Kristine's dismissive voice.

"Just trying to get some bearings," I reply, bumping into an object whose cold, dusty contours suggest an old stove.

"He said there were scorpions."

"Scorpions, my arse. He's just playing mind games with us, trying to wear us down, letting us make ghosts of our own out of the dark."

"Of course! You would know better, wouldn't you?"

"That's just what I reckon, that's all."

"How's your arm?"

"Sore, but there's no point worrying about that now."

"How very stoical of you!" Instead of responding to her sarcasm I resume my explorations. At the far end of the room I find the door through which our captors left, opposite the one we were brought in by. I press an ear to its fusty wood but can hear nothing in the adjacent room. They must be somewhere else, in another room perhaps, or outside. Someone, at least, must be on watch outside, guarding the exits. I come across some rough wooden planks nailed to the wall at chest height, a window, it would appear, boarded up to keep the light out and us in. Aïe, fuck, a splinter. I pace out the room while Kristine remains resolutely silent. It is rectangular, fifteen paces long and eight broad, almost certainly part of a farmhouse. I sit on the floor with my back to a wall and try to convince myself that with some lateral thinking I might yet devise some means of escape. To escape, though, it helps if you know where you are. Where could we be? In a farmhouse in the country. The smell of lavender when we came in: something to do with the perfume business? But no, I've never smelled lavender in Grasse or Eze. At least I can eliminate them. It's a start of sorts, I tell myself, shortly before Kristine erupts.

"Don't you think you owe me an explanation? *Why* am I here? *Who* are those men? *What* do they want with us, with me, and why won't they let us go? They could let me go, couldn't they? I don't know anything. But that's what he said, he said it was your fault. I wouldn't be here if it weren't for you."

"There's no need to shout."

"Shout? I'll shout as much as I like till I get an answer out of you!"

"It seems everyone wants answers out of me."

"They could at least have left the light on."

"Yes, that would have been nice and considerate of them."

"He was right. He said you were stubborn and you are, as stubborn as a mule. Just tell me what they want with you, Owen."

"It's political, in case you hadn't guessed. They're on one side and I'm on the other."

"But you're a guide!"

"An ex-guide now, with something they need to know."

"So tell them and then we can go."

"Don't be naïve."

"Or if you can't tell them, tell me."

"If I didn't tell them, Kristine, do you think I'd tell you?"

"What you don't understand, Owen, mon coco, is that I have a right to know what's going on, a right to know what's happening to me!"

"Rights do not exist any more than the Man in the Moon."

"Putain de merde, tell me!"

"Just who do you think we're up against, Kristine? We're not dealing with Mother Teresa here, you know."

"We? We? You can leave *me* out of it."

"Fine."

"You would have let me die, wouldn't you?"

"Do you seriously think there was anything I could have done?"

"Did they really kill Gilles?"

"Yes."

"How long are they going to keep us here?"

"How the fuck should I know?"

"There was no need to kill Gilles . . . Do you think we're going to die as well, Owen?"

"Yes."

12

It was a stupid idea of mine to climb up here, a half-baked idea born of mounting desperation. The chances of finding a rope or ladder hanging from the ceiling were always going to be zero. At the very least, I thought I might find something, anything, by which to gauge the height of the roof but the pitch blackness of the upper dimension is as mean and begrudging as any other. I clamber down from the bench onto the table and from the table onto the floor, berating myself for having conceived such folly in the first place. Rather than undermining the sense of hopelessness that assails us from every quarter, it has added to it.

At least our attempt to untie each other had some sense to it. It seemed a logical thing to try but the plastic twists proved worse than the Gordian knot and our grunting efforts succeeded only in breaking our fingernails and making our wrists swell. We found ourselves worse off than before, with our hope severely dented and our discomfort all the greater.

"Ça va, Kristine?" I ask, rejoining her at the foot of the wall but not encroaching on the space she has marked out as her personal domain in this blackest of cells. There is no reply. I did not expect one. Only once has she moved from this spot and that was to go and crouch in another corner to relieve herself. It must have been difficult for her. It must still be, since every now and then the odour returns as a persistent reminder of her humiliating loss of dignity. After all the other trials that have beset her, it was the last straw.

I haven't helped. At first we talked about anything, to fill the emptiness, to put darker thoughts to the back of the mind.

When you're desperate for conversation, for the mere sound of another's voice, you'll grab at anything. It was as though every piece of conversation, no matter how trivial, was another piece in the fragile dyke we both trying to build to stave off sleep.

Because sleep for one meant solitude for the other. Not that I think either of us, for all our fatigue, was actually capable of sleeping. When you hear death knocking at the door you don't feel inclined to waste your remaining hours and minutes in so wanton an activity. I suppose that's what our captors want. They want us to weaken ourselves and we have done, not only by staying awake all this time but by fighting each other, wearing each other down.

We started discussing where we were. Kristine had smelled the lavender, too, and thought we might be somewhere near Riez or Allemagne-en-Provence because of their lavender distilleries.

I'll laugh if it actually turns out to be Riez. We'll probably never know. It did us good, though, talking about where we were and for a while fear seemed to start thinking about retreat, so much so that we progressed from where we were to thinking of places we'd most like to be. Dubrovnik, said Kristine, on top of the city walls, looking far out to sea. Verona, I said, without really knowing why but then I fell to thinking about Petrarch and how it was there that he received the news of Laura's death. No, better still, I said, but was lost for an alternative. In the end I settled on Thiaki.

Gradually and cleverly she started sniping again at the secret I was witholding, seasoning her remarks with humour to make them sound less obvious and intrusive. She soon relented, however, and each new conversation became more strained and stilted than the last. I think it was more to put an end to an incipient lull than out of any real interest that Kristine asked me if I had meant what I said about rights not existing. That was the moment we entered the spiralling nose-dive. Yes,

I replied, I'd meant it. Rights are like values, I went on: they have their origin in nothing. Because they are not founded on Reason it is impossible to argue conclusively for, or against, any value. I was building up a head of steam by then. Any standard against which you seek to judge a value or set of values is just as arbitrary a construction as the value itself. No value is logically more compelling than its opposite. Values are nothing more than a personal preference. You can no more have a standard of morals than you can a yellow logarithm. These arguments were hardly earth-breaking, I said, no more revolutionary than the recognition that the earth is round. Kristine thought for a while before countering. How come, she asked, her voice already a semi-tone higher, millions of people shared the same, age-old values, and were even prepared to die for them, if there was nothing in them? How come, I retorted, millions of people prefer Guinness to lager? The only difference is that there are few people willing to die for Guinness.

"That's all hot air," she said.

"Aye, that's what it usually becomes."

Then she said, more or less, that I was a real shit for believing all that. She said the world was built on values and standards and morals: "c'est ça qui fait tourner le monde, après tout." Without those things the world would have no order and nobody would be able to make sense of anything and besides, if nothing was more valid than anything else, what was I doing here, now? She was shouting again. If our captors were on one side and I was on the other and neither was more valid than the other, why didn't I just change sides, easy as that? Why didn't I change causes? "Hah!" snarled the woman of positives and negatives, "you haven't got an answer for that one, have you?" I was tempted to say no for the sake of peace and quiet but, hell, there was little else to do but talk, even though I felt like someone trying to explain colours to the blind. So I said she might just as well ask me to switch from

Guinness to rum, a drink I have never been able to stomach.

"And you have the cheek to say *my* head's fucked up! You're pathetic, Owen."

"Rachel understands these things," I lamented to myself.

"Who's Rachel?"

"A woman of towering intellectual integrity who doesn't deny things just because she finds them distasteful."

"Oh, and I suppose you'd rather be with her now instead of me."

"No, I'm glad she isn't here." She seemed to brood for a while but soon hit back.

"Hah! Got you! How can you use a word like 'integrity'? Isn't that the kind of word moralists use?"

"The limits of my language are your world," I said, hoping the stock answer would put an end to this pointless slanging match. I think she wanted an end to it, too. Her parting shot was to say I was talking bullshit, but it was the way she said it, in a kind of taunting, playground, baby-talk:

"Tu parles que du caca, mon coco."

"Will you stop calling me 'mon coco'?"

"Que du caca, mon coco."

"Fine."

"Caca, coco. Coco, caca." She carried on like that for ages until she fell into a long silence. She hasn't uttered a word since. I think she has broken, cracked, snapped like a brittle fingernail.

Since then I have been alone in a dank desert of permanent night, prey to all the savage imaginings that solitude can bring. One of the low points was seeing the darting little eyes of the torturer as Declan's eyes, even though I'm pretty sure they're Nolan's. But the lowest point, when I really plummed the depths of depravity, was the absurd suspicion of Seoirse's complicity in my capture. There have been other moments, though, uplifting moments, such as when I imagined the whole room filling with the suffusive glow of Rhonabwy's emerald ring and I heard Kynddilig's avuncular voice inviting me to walk free through the walls like one of the knights of Annwfyn. But the vision was usurped by another voice, telling me that Kynddilig would not deliver me and that there was only more pain to look forward to. If there were to be any deliverance at all it would be the final deliverance from pain.

If you try hard enough you can see all sorts of colours in the dark. Purples and mauves, colours like that. What I crave to see most, though, is some real colours. Night's candles are burnt out and jocund day stands tiptoe on the misty mountain tops. Could it be dawn yet? No way of telling. A shaft of crisp, morning sunlight, the kind I used to wake up to in Aix, that'd be nice. I'll think of Rachel and Rainer basking in Provençal sunlight when the moment comes, their pleasure to come, they can have my light. Provence will have a special place in my heart for as long as I live, which won't be long. Tarnished, though, blemished by, what's a nice phrase, aye, the syphilitic excrescence of recent years. Hail the French disease! Hail the FN! Aïe, my fucking arm. Sharp sting raking through it. Can't manage to feel it though. Impossible with these bastard twists on. Just can't get at it. Probably busy forming a scab already, fighting infection. Amazing, the regenerative capacity of the body. Futile labours now, in my case. Futile, obstinate labours. Wouldn't be in this shit-hole if that fucking pervert slob's gun hadn't jammed. Oh fuck it, what's the point mulling over that now? Oh ye mighty gods, this world I do re

A petrifying, neck-shortening thunderbolt crashes in from outside, followed by another which rings clean through the padlock and springs the door ajar. I grab Kristine and pull her to the wall by the door, poking it open a further couple of inches. Fresh air at last.

"Owen!"

"In here!"

"I know you're feckin in there, Jesus! Just run straight, ten yards. Covering you on five."

With both hands I tug on Kristine's arm but she resists. "Allez, viens, Kristine! C'est le moment ou jamais!" Three seconds. Again she hesitates. Four seconds. Five. A storm of bullets breaks. Head down, I sprint out into a brighter darkness across the gravel and hurtle into a barrage of thorny bushes. A hand seizes the scruff of my neck. "Now roll, Owen, just roll. Down the bank." He pushes me and I fall, bumping and scraping through the undergrowth while glass shatters and thunderclaps pierce the moon, tumbling with fettered hands down the bank till the earth knocks the wind out of me.

'Tis the rising of the moon
'Tis the rising of the moon
And harrah, me boys, for freedom!
'Tis the rising of the moon

"God, it's good to be out of them handcuffs."

"D'ya not want to hear the rest of the story?"

"Sure."

"So, I thought he was coming over to the bushes to unfurl a reef, y'know."

"The bouncer fella?"

"Yeah. I could just see meself getting covered head to toe in piss, only, sure haven't you got the copyright on that?"

"Hmff."

"But he doesn't. He puts his shooter away and starts lighting up a cigarette. So up I leap and give him the Jaysus of a swipe round the teeth with the wheelbrace. I'll tell ya one thing: smoking can seriously damage your health. You should have seen him go down, though, like he'd just run into a right hook from Mike Tyson."

"Why d'he come over to the bushes in the first place?"

"I d'know. Looked like he was staring out over the view. Pretty boring work being on watch. I've done it meself."

"Jesus, a wheelbrace."

"So annyway, fools rush in where angels fear to tread, so I

sez to meself, hang on, I'll see what else I can find out. So I creep around to me right, still in the bushes, to the bit sticking out, y'know, at right-angles. So I take a step forward out the bushes and take a peek inside the windy. And do you know what I'm going to tell ya?"

"What?"

"Do you know who it is I see?"

"Who?"

"Jawin away over a bottle of Jemma, wielding a huge lump of a cutlass or something."

"The gobshite Nolan?"

"Yeah. How d'you know?"

"Just a stab in the dark. No, it was him who worked on me arm."

"Better put the ponytail in the picture quick, d'ya not think?"

"Yeah. This time, yes. Set up a rendez-vous."

He changes down into third gear and races through a bend illuminated by white reflectors on tree trunks. The pitch of the engine dips as he changes back into fourth. Scorched earth driving. A straight stretch of road opens up. Our cushion of light presses on through the night, uncovering the grey bark of roadside sentinels whose gnarled branches twist up into arthritic fingers reaching out at nothingness. Van Gogh's trees. Seoirse picking a pine needle from his hair.

"I still can't figure out why herself didn't make a run for it with ya."

"Me neither."

"Lord save us, ya should have heard yerselves, giving out yards like that. What was that all about?"

"Ach, nothing much. Still, she was right about one thing. She said we might be near Riez."

"Fair play to her."

"Fair play to you, Seoirse, following us all the way from Nice like that. You're a star, the brightest star in all the firmament."

"Aaaaah."

"What?"

"There's something I haven't told ya."

"Well?"

"Didn't the eejit have a broken tail-light. Stood out a mile in the dark, like a wee white sign saying 'this way to the gold'. Sure anny tosser could have followed him."

"So where we heading for now?"

"Fuck knows. I'm just keeping me foot down."

"Don't go to Aix. Nolan'll know I used to be there."

"Just leave it to me, Owen, and get some sleep. You look shattered."

Becalmed. Still. Standstill. Stopped. My eyes open on a pristine morning awash with colours I thought I would never see again. So this is what freedom looks like. It is beautiful.

"Where are we?" I ask.

"Arles," Seoirse replies. "Place dew Forum."

"Why Arles?"

"Would you think of looking for yerself in Arles?"

"No."

"There y'are, then." He looks at his watch and lets out a yawn the size of Galway Bay. "Oaaaaaaaaaaaahwah. Sheven . . . o'clock. Let's get some breakfast, eh?"

"Grand."

"Better keep an eye on the car. Don't want it getting towed away by the jondarms."

We get out and I let Seoirse stride off on his own while I take stock of my new surroundings. On one side of the square stands a Hotel du Forum, a building which looks like it wished the century had never turned. On another corner, with a section of Roman columns grafted into its facade, is the Hotel Nord Pinus, whose shapely wrought-iron balconies hint at a grandeur now lost amid the flaking paintwork. Leafless plane trees rise all around the square, dwarfing the statue of some dignitary whose bearing and ruffles make me think of

D'Artagnan. Scanning further round I come upon a gaudy yellow establishment calling itself both the Café de Nuit and the Café Van Gogh and, a few steps beyond, the Bistrot Arlésien, where Seoirse has already installed himself at an outside table. Coffee, yes, lots of hot coffee.

"Messieurs?" asks a world-weary man in whose languid smile lurks the sympathy of one who knows what it is to feel as rough as a badger's arse.

"Deux grand-crèmes et deux croissants au beurre."

"D'accord," he says, leaving a puff of starch in his wake.

"I know this guy from Newry," says Seoirse, "who says the colleens in Arles are something else."

"What, they're men?"

"No, y'know, they're supposed to be stunning. Trouble is, I know for a fact he's never been further than Dundalk." A sudden wind brings a roar from the trees and a swirl of dust around the square. "Would that be the mistral getting up?"

"Could be," I say, inspecting my wound, wondering whether it will turn septic, picturing all manner of puss beneath the rice pudding skin of a still delicate scab. Seoirse rubs his reddened eyes and stretches, pushing pillars of air apart with his fists.

"That's a nasty arm ya've got there. You'll need to get a dressing put on it."

"Listen, Seoirse, thanks a million for getting me out of that place."

"Ah, bollocks. Sides, it's not me you should be thanking, it's the hero of Heidelberg. You'd probably be brown bread already if he hadn't thought up a way of saving your bacon and keeping the ball alive."

"I know. The pity is I can't thank him . . . Shit, two dead men already and possibly Effi. And Christ only knows what's become of Kristine."

"Holy Mother of God, I could sleep for daaays. Jesus, these contact lenses are killing me . . . And will ya stop looking at every man jack that goes past like he's out to get ya? You're making me nervous so. I'm telling ya: we're well shot of them here."

"Aye, sorry."

"So where d'ya want to meet the big white chief?"

"That rather depends on him. I don't care where but as soon as possible. We can hole up here in the meantime."

"Grand," he says, leaning back and crossing his fingers behind his head. "Nice little square, this. The sort of place you could just sit and watch the world go by."

"Voilà," comes the voice of the waiter, sounding like Tom Waites after sixty fags. He sniffs, coughs and beneath arched eyebrows watches as the receipt he presses onto the table curls and falls to the ground. He shrugs his shoulders. "Eh ben, merde alors," he mumbles, and ambles back into the bar.

"I think yer man must be on something," says Seoirse as he rips the horn off a croissant and soaks it in his coffee. Left-handed, I lift a spoon and stir, staring into space, thinking of Kristine. Tu parles que du caca, mon coco. We could be breakfasting together now if only she hadn't held back. Why didn't she come with me? Why did she choose to stay in that hell-hole rather than make a break for it? Was it the bullets that frightened her or had she just given up the ghost, on everything?

Golden mmmm butter melting on the tongue, she could have been enjoying this too. And buckets of coffee, ah qahwah, hot elixir lashing your brain, each, uuh, mouthful slaying the beast of numbness. Why?

"D'you reckon Kristine'll be alright?"

"Ah they probably high-tailed it and just left her there."

"Yeah."

Yes, in all likelihood that's what they'll have done. They'll have had to strike camp, and why? Because we know their hideout and we know about Nolan. And what use is Kristine to them, without me? None. But that doesn't mean they won't have . . . After all, she's seen the bouncer's face. She could identify him. Hell, they might even have shot the bouncer themselves as a punishment. Ach, she'll be safe enough. Battered and bruised and walking an unknown road. Tattered and torn and traumatised. Find a kindly voice somewhere along the way, and safety. She had the chance, she had the choice. She could have legged it with me. But she didn't.

"Je vous dérange pas?" asks a young woman, pulling out a chair and turning it to face us. Now why's she doing that, sitting with her back to the square? Don't want to make Seoirse nervous.

"Non, non, ça va."

So lucky to be here at all. Wouldn't be here if it wasn't for Seoirse. And the Heidelberg guy, holding out like that, just to protect me, give me some precious latitude. Not drawing us, is she? Some kind of artist. Don't even know his name. Greater love hath no man. And God so loved the world that he gave his only begotten son. Didn't give himself, though. Someone had to mind the shop. But the Ulsterman did give himself, for someone he didn't even know. That is love. I'm not sure I like her drawing me.

"What is it," Seoirse asks, wiping his hands on his trousers, "about breakfast in France that makes you feel like a million dollars?"

"You mean you wouldn't prefer porridge and rashers?"

"Will y'ever get out o' town!"

"Are you hEnglish?" asks the young woman, looking up from her pad with the arresting gaze of a bird of prey.

"*No!*" we say.

"American?"

"Ah fer fuck sake! Pardon me French. Sorry, he's from Wales and I'm from Ireland, God's own country."

"Have you been to the amphithéâtre, Walesman?"

"No. Why?"

"You look like you were thrown to the lions."

"Eh ben, non, c'est pas ça."

"Or peuraps you have a fight with the Tarrasque?"

"Wi' de whah?"

"It's a big, nasty beast, très méchant." Her green eyes smile and dimples form in her cheeks. Mid-twenties would she be? Thick eyebrows, not one for plucking. Very striking, the green eyes with jet-black hair. High cheekbones. The Newry guy was right.

"Ehm," Seoirse begins, "you're not going to want fifty francs or something for doing our picture?"

"No," she chirps, unoffended, and turns her falcon eyes back to the pad. Little finger looping hair over her ear. Pout of concentration.

"Jesus, he sez, I didn't know I was so photogenital."

"Would you know where there's a pharmacy?" I ask.

"For you harm?" she says without looking up.

"Yes. It's just a flesh wound."

"Un quoi?"

"Une blessure superficielle."

"Place Lamartine. You know Arles?"

"I always get it confused with Nîmes."

"Then I accompany you. You have been a good subject for me so now I return the service."

"That alright with you, a chara?"

"Ah sure. I'll get us checked in over there at the Northern Penis. I need a good long kip in the scratcher and I'm past arguing about it." He gets up and holds out his hand to her. "I'll see ya so, ehm. . ."

"Claire."

He forgets to give her his name and plods off, ten-to-two in grass-stained shoes. There goes a man of worth, Paddy Polonius. Who needs Kynddilig when I have him? God's own country indeed.

By the time we reach the banks of the Rhône, where gusts of wind blow rippling patterns on the broad grey sweep of its surface, I feel completely at ease in the company of my new-found Samaritan. I find her unsolicited kindness touching, her insouciance refreshing, her smile alluring, and her story charming. An artist and fervent admirer of Van Gogh, she worked for a year as a cashier at Monoprix to save the money for this holiday. She would have come last year for the centenary of Vincent's death but fell in love with a friend's Deux Chevaux which unexpectedly came up for sale. She just had to buy it. So she worked for another year in the same job and here she is now, a year late, but what does that matter? This way she can mark Theo's demise as well as Vincent's. She takes life as it comes, she says, and though many say such things, I feel instinctively inclined to believe her. Perhaps one day she'll become an artist of renown but she doesn't much care if she doesn't. The important thing is to try. She quotes Vincent himself: what would life be like if we never had the courage to attempt anything? She doesn't mind working at Monoprix in the slightest. Bon d'accord, she has to live, so she has to work, but if she has to work she'd rather be a cashier than have a job which people would expect her to take seriously.

"Voilà!" she announces as she trots down the quayside steps. "Place Lamartine. Y'a une pharmacie là-bas." Welcome droplets of water blow into my unkempt face from the fountain in the square. And there's another thing about Claire. She doesn't mind being seen out with a scruff whose face feels like it's been dipped in swarfega, pores all blocked up and prickly, eyelids heavy with gunge. She's not one of the ugly-by-association crowd. Straight back to the hotel with me for a shower after this. No, not a shower, not with this arm. A wash, a good all-over scrub with a basinful of boiling-hot water. "You aren't surprised?" she asks.

"Errr. . ."

"The railway is still there, you see, behind, but not the Maison Jaune. I thought it would still be here."

"I'm afraid you've lost me, Claire."

"Van Gogh's Yellow House. I came here and expected to see it. I wanted to paint it."

"Did they demolish it or what?"

"No. It was destroyed the Luftwaffe. And now everything is too modern, too hugly."

"And there's even a Monoprix."

"That's where the house was."

"Well, thanks for everything, Claire. You've been really. . ."

"You want to get rid of me?"

"No, far from it."

She comes with me into the pharmacy, waits around while I'm being served, even helps me choose a new shirt in Monoprix. We stroll back along the river, she with her yellow canvas bag, I with my Monoprix bag, and just when the absurd hope begins to form in my mind of an address or a telephone number, a hotel, anything which might hold out the promise of seeing her again, she stops and looks up at a lone cloud drifting across the sun. "I have to leave you now," she says. "I must go to the Alyscamps before the light changes too much."

"Where's that?"

"The other side of the town," she says, her lips tightening into another pout. A momentary sadness seems to steal across her face as her fingers slide from mine and, spellbound, I watch her walk out of my life as suddenly as she entered it. Run after her, says a voice in my head, her voice perhaps, saying run after me. What would life be like if we hadn't the courage to attempt anything? I call out her name and catch up with her. She turns to face me, this breath of fresh air, this vision of youth with the falcon eyes that could light the darkest dungeon.

"Will I see you again?" I ask.

"It is possible. The world is small, you know."

"You couldn't, err, make it just a bit smaller for me, could you?" She laughs.

"I go back to Paris tomorrow."

"I mean, I won't ask your address or anything. I could be some raving psychopath for all you know."

"You really want to see me?"

"Yes, I do."

She hesitates, sizes me up, the artist looking for the essence. She's seen chancers like me before. Is that what she sees, a chancer? Or does she see me without all the grime? "Okay," she says at last. "Look for a bar called Chez Obélix, comme Obélix le Gaulois." She kisses her first two fingers, puts them to my stubbly cheek and leaves once more. I stand there dumbstruck and joyous. Yes! God knows where the bar is but I will find it. Yes! Things can only get no don't say that.

Seoirse wakes when I enter the room and after a wash which proves more painful than pleasurable he bandages my arm and goes back to bed, clad only in boxer shorts exhorting Jack to give it a lash. I try to sleep but can't. I don't want confinement. I want to be out in the open, in the colours and the sunlight and the warm swirling air and the accents of the Midi. Besides, what if Claire changes her mind and doesn't go to the other side of town after all? I leave Seoirse a note and sneak out to the Bistrot Arlésien. The same waiter appears. I order an exprès. He brings me a pastis. Oh well, when in Arles, I suppose. Water splashes from the jug's overhanging lip onto the brown-tinted rocks below and, hey presto, a pale yellow emulsion stands high and handsome before me, ambrosia à l'arlésienne. If only it were that easy to conjure up Claire. How long shall I give it, this waiting? The answer lies close at hand: fifty-one, says Monsieur Ricard. But fifty-one what? Minutes? The square is devoid of clocks and, without my watch, that will mean constantly asking the time. I decide to count people coming into the square. After I've counted fifty-one newcomers I shall conclude my waiting is forlorn and I shall up and leave.

After the first ten people I order another pastis, cheering myself with the reflection that this isn't such a bad way to spend one's morning after all. Yep, it's a sad and beautiful world. To kill the time, I cast myself in the role of diviner and find a certain entertainment in trying to guess the profession of passers-by. A black man in red overalls trailing a broom of twigs after him: ooh, that's a tricky one. A young man with low forehead, bull neck, briefcase and sharp suit: clearly, a lawyer. A bald man with bull neck, briefcase and sharp suit: an accountant. A bespectacled twat in corduroys: literary critic. A woman scurrying past like a hunted beast, blowing a pink nose one-handed: a doctor. Physician, heal thyself. A young chap in a faded Chairman Mao jacket with delicate hands: a student who wants to be close to the workers. The novelty of the game wears off with the coming of the twenty-mark. The thirty-mark is notched up, and the forty-mark too. At forty-five my heart leaps, but it turns out not to be Claire. She could be at the Alyscamps all day for all I know. But I'll wait some more, and have another pastis. The fifty-one-mark comes not in the form of an artist or Monoprix cashier but of a wino who asks, "T'as pas cent balles?" I oblige him with ten francs and cast around the square. There must be some mistake. Fifty-one, said Monsieur Ricard, and there is still no Claire. At least I tried. I will see her again. I will. But not today, not here. It will have to wait till Paris. I know! I must have miscounted. Even if I didn't, out of the fifty-one there were two coppers for sure and, statistically, ooh, at least five Lepénistes, and seeing as the brain-dead and sub-human don't count I'll wait for another seven people.

Plunged into the Slough of Despond by the passage of the fifty-eighth person, a vile curate who looked like a child-molester, I drag my anis-addled body back toward the hotel, stopping to prolong the agony by taking a look at the inscription at the base of the statue of d'Artagnan. The words seem at first more Catalan than French, until I recognise them for what they are: lines of poetry first read long ago in the library in Aix, lines which now fire me with a defiance of which Capaneus himself would be proud. Yes, I will follow her.

Cante uno chato de Provènço
Dins lis amour de sa jouvènço
A travès de la Crau, vers la mar, dins li bla
Umble escoulan dóu grand Oumèro
Iéu la vole segui

I sing of a young girl of Provence,
In the loves of her youth,
Across the Crau, towards the sea, in the wheat,
Humble scholar of the great Homer,
I want to follow her.

—Mistral, "Mirèio"

13

The bells toll eleven o'clock on the Place de l'Horlorge. The leftovers of Avignon's Theatre Festival sit at tables outside, sipping menthe à l'eau, wondering what to do, where next to go now that the party's over. Inside the Venaissin, a feeling of unreality hangs heavy in the air, an atmosphere defined by the very moment I saw him standing in the doorway, a slender, well-preserved man in a white jacket, looking just like the Man from Delmonte. He removed his straw hat, exposing a shining head on which not a single hair grew. The ponytail had lost his ponytail but none of his presence. Behind him stood Effi. Our eyes met and they came over to seat themselves at our table. Ever since then, I have been unable to expel the memory of being hauled in front of the headmaster, called upon to account for why I was caught fighting in the classroom during playtime. And Effi's presence is like that of the sinister Latin teacher who sits in attendance, saying nothing, noting everything. At times her dark eyebrows knit in contemplation of a particular point in Seoirse's report. There are bags under her eyes. She seems altered, wearied, altogether older than the fresh young woman I met in Lucerne.

"So it's Nolan," says Seoirse, concluding his debrief. "Owen's got the scars to prove it and I've seen him supping with the Devil with me own two eyes. I'd say the ball's in your court now."

"Nolan will be taken care of," says the ponytail, "as soon as we find him. He is, in a manner of speaking, past his sell-by date." He smiles at me, his face transformed into a riot of crow's feet. "And I believe I know who your interrogator was.

From your description, it could only be a man by the name of Harrington, formerly of the Coldstream Guards. It fits his modus operandi like a glove. It shouldn't be too difficult to track Nolan down now. Mmm, so that's who's been pulling his strings all along."

Nolan had of late been acting erratically, he goes on, but there was never any clear evidence of outright treachery. As soon as the sketchbook was stolen, the ponytail put Nolan on stand-by for its transferral to Switzerland via Germany. Nolan therefore knew of the operation from the outset and knew that the Ulsterman was to be the courier. But shortly before the operation got underway, a hitch developed. The ponytail turns to Effi, inviting her to pick up the thread.

"It was Ned," she says, her sunken eyes moistening. She twists the silver ring on her finger that bears two hands clasping a crowned heart. She should never have let her relationship with Nolan drag on and on, she says, but she did. When she finally told him there was someone else, someone she was genuinely in love with, someone who made her laugh, Nolan went apeshit. She didn't tell him the other man was Ciaran, the Ulsterman. She just told him there was someone else. But Nolan believed in his own god-like powers. He frightened her. "He kept saying, 'Oh, I'll find out who it is alright. You think I can't? Just try me! See if I don't mean it.' He was like Habakkuk, capable of anything." Effi was afraid. Ciaran was afraid. Ciaran contacted the ponytail to say that he was in danger, but he couldn't say from whom. To do so would mean admitting to his entanglement in an all too incestuous triangle of love which he thought it every Volunteer's duty to avoid. Ciaran even gave Effi a number which she was to phone should anything happen to him. He said it was the number of someone who'd be able to get in touch with his parents. He didn't talk much about his parents, but he thought they had a right to know. It was the ponytail's number in Brussels. So Nolan didn't have to show his hand, didn't have to make the moves. He had Effi make the moves for him. Effi pulls a balled tissue from the arm of her indigo tee-shirt and holds it to her nose.

"He said, 'Do this one thing for me and I'll make no more claim on you. I'll forget all about loverboy.' I still don't know whether he meant it. But what choice did I have?"

"So you decided it was safer to stay with me," I ask the ponytail, "once you had word from Ciaran that he was under threat?" I ask.

"Yes," the ponytail confirms. "And when I got the message that Nolan had been arrested for the previous operation, I sent help. I was worried. There was every chance it was a ruse."

"When did you find out about Ciaran, Effi?" I ask.

"In Rome, when Ned discovered the parcel you gave me was false. 'Why don't you just fuck off back to Frankfurt, you useless, stupid bitch.' That's what he said. 'And by the way, don't bother looking for loverboy.' Then he told me what he'd done. It's barbaric."

"I'm so sorry, Effi."

"It isn't your fault."

"I'll make arrangements to recover the parcel," says the ponytail. "Neither of you need involve yourself any further."

"That's it, then?" Seoirse objects.

"As far as you two are concerned."

"What about Owen here? This Coldstream Guards bastard knows all about him."

"Yes, indeed. We'll . . . correction, I'll have to take care of that as well."

"So the killing goes on?" I ask.

"The killing has to go on. In the meantime, lie low. I'll get word to you."

"What will you do now, Effi?"

"I don't know, Owen. I really don't know." The ponytail looks at his watch.

"I'll see you later, then, at the Hotel Ibis," he says to Effi.

"I've just got a couple more things to discuss with these two."

"Okay," she meekly replies, rising. She kisses us goodbye and walks out into a loveless world which is not her friend.

"Gentlemen," says the ponytail, "we have an appointment to meet."

"Who with?" I ask.

"Nolan. We have already picked him up. I had to tell a little white lie just then, about Harrington. I wanted to spare the young lady any further trauma. She's been through enough." He stares into space. His face is blank and drained. "Ciaran was my godson, you know. I never wanted him to join."

Some say the Devil is dead
The Devil is dead
The Devil is dead
Some say the Devil is dead
And buried in Killarney

More say he rose again
He rose again
He rose again
More say he rose again
And joined the British Army

Beneath a vast blue sky, the four of us stand in a cornfield that could have been painted by Van Gogh. There are no black crows circling overhead, no sunflowers, no windmills in the distance, just the constant, crackling electricity of the cigales in the stubble. The landscape could not be further removed from the damp, dark Tolka Valley and yet it has all come down to this: another informer about to die. The ponytail takes the gun by the barrel and presses it into my hand, a Glock 19, nine millimetre, and once again Camus' words go through my head: all intellectuals dream of being a gangster. Nolan's eyes dart across my face. His breathing is regular. He seems to look at me with contempt.

"Anything to say?" I ask. He remains silent, his gaze unflinching.

"Or would ya rather go like yer handler, Harrington, eh, soon as you're cornered?" says Seoirse. "Blow yer own brains out rather than be taken alive. Trouble is, Ned, that'd mean giving you a gun, and we can't really do that."

"Were you going to double-cross him," asks the ponytail, "and take all the pickings for yourself? Was that the plan?" Nolan only laughs.

"You just don't get it, do you? Any of you?" he says.

"You're not going to tell us it was love," says Seoirse. Nolan laughs again.

"You mindless, stupid, weakling fuckers. You think the Movement's made out of people like you? You? Don't make me laugh." His chest swells out and he bellows, "Fuair siad bás ar son saoirse na hÉireann!"

"What?" Seoirse barks back at him. "You have the nerve to say that? You? You who's taken the soup? Others have died for . . . yeah, but it's not *you* who's going to die for Irish freedom, you warped feckin whure." Nolan rounds on me.

"You'd have broken, Parry. You'd have broken. You haven't got what it takes. We'd only just started on you. You're one of the ones who needs weeding out. You haven't even got the bottle to shoot me now, have you?"

"You're sick," I say. He draws down the corners of his mouth.

"'You're sick.' 'You're sick.' That's all you can say. 'You're sick.' Hah! You're just like that mad bitch back at the barn."

"Why kill someone who's done you no harm?" I ask. "Why? She was just a tour guide. Just a fucking tour guide, Nolan. No, you just like killing. You killed my friend who did nothing more than drive a fucking bus, because you like killing. Like shelling peas, isn't it? And Ciaran, because you like killing, you like punishing others."

"I was putting the mad bitch out of her misery."

"No, you were putting her out of your misery, you sad, twisted fuck." Nolan just shrugs.

I squeeze the trigger. A thunderclap silences the cigales and a cartridge falls mutely on the parched grey earth which will slowly turn as dark as wine. I hand the gun back to the ponytail and walk away.

Two hours and a short drive later, I place a bunch of red roses on the grave of the man with whom, for one too brief year, I shared the same world, breathed the same air, bathed in the light of the same sun. I stand and read the words engraved on the porcelain book lying, page open, at the edge of his immortal remains. Depuis que tes yeux sont fermés, les nôtres n'ont cessé de pleurer: since your eyes were closed, ours have not stopped crying. It is time to leave the hamlet of Lourmarin and its most celebrated deceased. I will not brood over death any longer, not Gilles', not Ciaran's, not Nadette's, not Kristine's, not even the death of Camus here. I have had my fill of graves and deaths and coffins and tears. I am sick of the sight of them. It is time to go towards not death but life and laughter, to find the breath of fresh air who is so full of life, who sees in art not money or posturing but simply art, whose name is sunlight and clarity itself. Iéu la vole segui.

"Seoirse, I can see there's something weighing on the gilded fabric of your mind."

"There is."

"What is it, pray?"

"Just wondering what to do with meself. Feel at a bit of a loss now, y'know."

"Back to Brussels, is it?"

"Might as well. Aye, rue Melpomène number four. Jesus, I hope I didn't leave the shaggin gas on when I left . . . What about you?"

"Paris."

"To try and find Claire?"

"To find a fucking Obélix first."

"Yeah, well, good luck so. And remember: this above all. . ."
"Aye, this above all."

We stand in the Place de la Concorde. Red and yellow snakes swirl around the square, headlights, tail-lights. Palais Bourbon to the right. I look to the left. A hundred ragged and bloodstained Communards wave at me from the steps of the Madeleine. "On n'est pas mort!" shouts one of them. "Non, je sais," I shout back and raise a clenched fist high and proud in the coppery night air. Petrarch's horses prance atop the Arche du Carrousel and low in the warm night sky hangs a pure white moon. I lower my eyes. On the other side of the square sits a woman in robes. Seeing me, she steps down from her seat of stone and dips a foot in the lake of snakes. She approaches, gliding through the kaleidoscope water with graceful steps. I know her, I know her, I do. Last time I saw her was Heidelberg. Face to face. "Remember me?" she asks. "Of course I do," I reply, "but isn't your name different now?" Her eyes flit towards the stars. "The woman of Roazon," she says, puffing out her cheeks in exasperation, "tu t'imagines?!" I put my hands on my hips. Take the mickey. "Roazon, is it now? Allez, Nadette, you never could speak Breton." "Bon, d'accord," she confesses, "the woman of Rennes alors. They put me on a pedestal already, at my age!" "It's better than la pucelle de Rennes," I console her. Her soft hand insinuates itself between my legs. "No," she laughs, "I was never much of a maiden, was I?" Her eyes grow wide. "Mais putain," she says, "qu'est-ce tu bandes dur!" Embarrassed, Madeleine, Palais Bourbon. She tosses her head at my companion. "C'est qui, ton copain, là? L'Irlandais?" "No," I tell her, "Seoirse's gone already, back to Brussels, rue Melpomène, number four." "C'est qui, alors?" she presses. "Never mind who this is. Écoute, mon amour, there's something I have to tell you." There is sadness in her face. A silvery tear starts down her cheek. Oh no, I knew this would happen. "I know," she says, wiping the tear away, sniffing. "I know, Owen. Ciaran says you found her on the Minitel." She tries to force a smile through trembling lips. She points a warning finger at me. "Just remember, though: elle c'est elle et moi c'est moi et puis c'est tout." A tear rolls down the other cheek. I hold her face between my hands and kiss her lips. They are warm and taste of the sweetest salt. "Do you still have my love spoon?" I ask her. "It is like the day you gave me it," she replies, "and it shines in my heart." Tears begin to fill my eyes and I will not hold them back but these words I must speak. "You will always shine in my heart too, Nadette."

"It is time," says Kynddilig. Nadette kisses me one last time and runs away. I look resolutely straight ahead. She is gone.

"Is it your time too?" I ask.

"Annwfyn waits for me."

"May you fare well in Annwfyn."

"Dyna doethineb."

"What wisdom?"

"That which she said was wisdom."

"Yes, it was."

"Fare well, Owein."

He takes Rhonabwy's ring from his finger. Powerful emerald light envelops us both until it is snuffed out by the closing of his fist. He steadies himself for a moment on his elder staff, summoning the strength of his youth. His right arm draws back and he launches the ring at the moon. Silently it flies towards the jet-black waterfalls of the ever darkening moon and bursts into two viridescent jewels. I want to wake. I don't want to see him go, not even in dream. I close my eyes tight. The ground beneath my feet bounces like the first trembling of an earthquake but still I will not open my eyes. An invisible hand strokes my cheek. Hoel fawr, Kynddilig, farewell, Kynddilig, Kynddilig, Kynddilig.

The ground bounces again but this time I am on my back and there's something tickling my face. I open my eyes and realise it was the bed bouncing. Claire frowns over me, her jet-black hair dangling in my face. There is suspicion in her deep green eyes. "Tiens, tiens. And who is she, this Kynddilig?"